THE SHAKESPEARE MANUSCRIPT

Stewart Buettner

PERFOR
MANCE
ARTS
PRESS

DEDICATION

For Kara

London
March 29, 1729

Your Most Esteemed Lordship,

I know you requested that I not write you unless utterly necessary because you fear compromise. In keeping with those wishes, I have not used your name or mine, nor will I in future correspondence certain to result from the great news which this letter brings. I well recognize that any indication of your identity could jeopardize you in ways I cannot bear to contemplate, as I value your sweet friendship above all others in this unjust world.

I write you for a singular purpose. I have made the most marvelous discovery, one we both had hoped for. I know that Shakespeare's Double Falsehood, *which we jointly mounted at the Drury Lane Theater with your generous support, was not the success we might have wished. As you intimated at the time, however, it did have the desired effect. A friend, that distant relative of the Bard's sister who supplied the script for our previous venture, has again stepped forward, this time with a second play. Most certainly, it is another of Shakespeare's lost dramas, a prelude of sorts to his masterwork,* The Tragedie of Hamlet, *but in manuscript form.*

 This new drama is full of marvelous invention of almost every sort. A noble king who must go off to war. A brother who would assume the throne and who plots the lawful ruler's death. That same brother so in love with the queen that he cannot contain his lusty desires. A son, our Prince Hamlet, so enamored of that same woman, his own beautiful mother, that he must mask that love and so he woos another, the young Ophelia, whom he seduces with tragical consequences. All this wrapped with a bow of sweetest language and depths of thought not equaled by this country's greatest playwrights in over a century.

I would send this treasured manuscript to your Lordship, but it is far too valuable to entrust to the unreliable carriers of the General Post. So I will bring it with me personally at your Lordship's bidding. You may keep it however long it pleases you and see for yourself that it possesses all those qualities of which I have boasted, and many more.

I do believe that, with your kind patronage once again, we could present this discovery at the Drury Lane to much greater acclaim and financial success than that which greeted Double Falsehood. Do, please, inform me of your interest in this project. If you are willing to favor me with a sum of, say, a hundred-thirty guineas, that should be more than sufficient to purchase the Royal License and prove the sincerity of our intentions to theater management. After that, I will bring this new Hamlet to your Lordship forthwith for your inspection and enjoyment. If we are cautious, I am certain we can do this thing with no harm coming to either of us, especially to you.

Your most adoring friend,

L.

1 THE ONCE AND FUTURE *KING*

When the doorbell rang, April was closing up for the evening. She glanced at the security monitor to see the shadowy figure of a UPS deliveryman in typical mud-brown, summer uniform. The headband of his cap, the underarms of his shirt were soaked with sweat from near-record August heat outside. Beside him, a wooden crate rested on a handcart. She was all but certain the man had never made deliveries to Oliphant's before, and that alarmed her.

The doorbell rang again. As it did, her chest tightened. Her mouth grew dry, her palms clammier. For strength, she looked up at the poster of Vanessa Redgrave in *Julia* that hung on the dark brick wall beside her desk. If only April could be as wide-eyed and courageous in the face of the world! From the time she was nine, she had wanted to be just like the great actor, but those hopes had long since faded. All she had left of a flourishing stage career was the theater of memories that occupied the walls and shelves around her.

Once again, the doorbell jarred her out of her meditation on acting and why she could never go on stage again. Then the UPS driver shouted "Is April Oliphant there?" in a voice so loud it carried all the way to the back office. His summons drowned the growl of passing trucks, even the horns of impatient cabbies outside Oliphant's Rare Books. He must have found her name on the invoice. Near panic, she realized she had no choice but to accept the shipment even though it was after five.

"Hail Mary, Mother of God," she chanted as she started up the aisle of theater books toward the front of the store. "Pray for us sinners now and in the hour of our death."

Through the front window, she saw a slender, sun-starved face. The friendly, brown eyes that looked out at her from behind black-rimmed glasses didn't seem so threatening after all. Quite the opposite, in fact. Their genuine warmth told her she had nothing at all to fear from the man.

What was wrong with her? Why had an ordinary UPS driver frightened her so? Even if she knew the answer to those questions, she wasn't going to admit it. Not to herself. Certainly not to anyone else. Any insight she gained from that exercise would only send her scurrying back down the hole she had recently dug for herself. The hole where she felt safe.

Gradually, she relaxed her guard. What else could she do when looking out at the kindest face she'd seen in days?

"Just leave the crate there," she raised her voice, moving her lips slowly so he could read them through the window.

"Don't you want help? It's heavy."

"Thanks, I've got a handcart in back."

"I'll need you to sign this then," he said and held up an invoice.

"Just slide it under the door."

He did as instructed while she retrieved a pen from the front counter, signed the top sheet and returned it under the door. The deliveryman picked it up and started back toward his truck, double-parked in front of the store.

Getting the handcart from the office, April opened the front door just enough to look in both directions. None of the passersby seemed threatening, so she quickly jostled the cart's scarred front edge under the wooden box. Scooping it up in a single, practiced motion she hauled it inside, all in seconds. Then triple locked the door to close up for the evening and steered the crate back to the office.

With the claws of the shop hammer, she pried off the lid. Inside she found a set of journals, the foxed brittle edges of which filled over half the box, plus a thick sheaf of letters. She emptied the crate and carefully set the contents in piles on her desk. She was annoyed when she found no receipt. Without one, she had no idea from whom her father had purchased the lot, or how much he had paid for it. She hoped he hadn't forgotten it, as he had other things lately.

Sorting through the shipment, she spotted a thin, ancient portfolio buried among the letters. Bound with fraying ribbon, it didn't appear to have been opened in decades, perhaps centuries. Carefully, she placed the tattered brown case flat on her desk and untied it. Inside she found a manuscript, slightly darker at the edges, but otherwise in excellent condition. Each sheet of precious foolscap had been written in cramped script, words crammed from top to bottom. Her eyes locked on the title atop the first page

HAMLET, KING OF DENMARKE

and refused to move further.

At first she took the manuscript to be a handwritten copy of Shakespeare's famous tragedy. Then she realized something was wrong with the title. The original Hamlet was the *Prince* of Denmark. He had never lived to be king. Perhaps some copyist had mistaken the title or willfully changed it, she thought. Surely Shakespeare would have never made that mistake himself.

April sensed she might be looking at the greatest discovery of her father's career. For a moment, she thought he did not even know, or remember to tell her, about the *King Hamlet*. After all, it had been sandwiched in the letters, and painfully large gaps were developing in his memory. If he *had* known about it, he certainly wouldn't have sent it in an ordinary packing crate. He'd have hand-carried it back to New York, just as he had the Ainsley First Folio.

Leaning forward, elbows on her desk, she read the first page of the manuscript. It took only a few lines to realize the text was even more questionable than the title. None of the characters she remembered from the first scene took a part, large or small, in the *Hamlet* in front of her.

April had appeared in the play only once, and that was in college. Now, almost six years later, she had gained so much insight into Ophelia's character, but she'd never get a chance to use it. Maybe she'd write down her thoughts, share them with some eager ingénue, far more capable of taking on the role than she.

Since it was well after closing, she carried the manuscript upstairs to the apartment she shared with her father. This particular evening, she paid little attention to the all-white interior. After months on Shelly's sofa, weeks on the streets of New York, she had no right to complain about the loft's bland walls.

By the time she had read less than an act of the new *Hamlet*, she had many more questions than she'd had to start with. There was only one way to answer them, and that was to call her father. She had to find out who he thought had authored the manuscript, and why Hamlet was King, not Prince of Denmark. Phone already in hand, she realized her father was in transit, due to spend the night at some airport hotel. She had no idea how to contact him before he took off, bound for JFK in the morning.

She knew only one other person who might be able to answer her questions, and that was Avery LeMaster. While a guest professor at Stony Brook, he had taught a class on the comedies, which she had taken. Then he'd cast her as Rosalind in *As You Like It*, which the great man himself had directed. In three short months she had learned more from him than from all her other professors combined.

In February, Professor LeMaster had stumbled into Oliphant's in search of Murphy's *Life of David Garrick*. On that visit, April had permitted herself to get within a couple feet of him. No more than that, though, no matter how strong the attraction. Nothing had happened, of course. How could it with twenty-four impossible inches separating them? Since then, Professor LeMaster had stopped by sporadically, usually in search of some obscure title or other. Much as she wanted to think he had other reasons for visiting the shop, he spent far more time looking at books than talking with her.

He hadn't come by in months, but now it seemed she had something he'd surely want to see. It took two false starts before she realized why she was having so much trouble with the telephone keypad. Teddy's picture was propped to one side of her father's nightstand. Tears had started to form before she set it face-down where she wouldn't have to look at it. With ease this time, she punched in the number they had on file for her former professor from orders he'd placed in the past. Her efforts were greeted by a recorded message on the other end.

"You've reached Avery LeMaster. Sorry, I'm out of town for rehearsals, but I'll be checking in for messages. Please leave yours after the beep."

She didn't have time to think, just told his machine the reason she'd called in her usual clipped, succinct manner.

"Professor LeMaster, this is April at Oliphant's Rare Books. I have a manuscript of something you might be interested in. A very unusual *Hamlet* actually. The number here is 212-623-7741. Hope your rehearsals go well."

Only one thing remained, and that was to sit back and wait for the call that would never come. Professor LeMaster's message had made it clear. He was conducting rehearsals, probably somewhere far from Manhattan. At best, she would get a polite return call.

"Got your message, Miss Oliphant. Sorry, but I won't be back in the city for two months." Yada...yada...yada.

She hung up and sat there on the edge of her father's bed, eyes fixed on the back of Teddy's photo. She turned it toward her again and stared at it the longest time, unable to hold back the heartbreak. When she couldn't take looking at it any longer, she hid it away in the drawer of her father's nightstand.

Then she glanced at her watch, amazed that it was already quarter-to-seven. Hard to believe, but less than two hours had passed since that unwitting UPS driver had first appeared outside Oliphant's. Two hours she would not soon forget. Two hours that would end up seeing her Little Engine That Couldn't pushed off the siding where it had been stuck for ages. She wouldn't exactly say that engine got put back on the fast track. Still, it was much faster than any track she'd been on since her meltdown two years earlier.

By now, surely, her father was tucked safely in bed in some hotel near Heathrow. She would see him again in less than twenty-four hours. Then he'd answer all her questions about the baffling *Hamlet* he'd sent from England, but what if he couldn't?

What then?

2 HOMEWARD BOUND

Sullen Miles Oliphant couldn't get over the change in the weather. After almost three impossibly muggy, overcast weeks in England, the sky had cleared, and it was almost brisk out. According to the geographically challenged taxi driver in the front seat–a Pakistani or Bangladeshi or some other hapless emigrant from the Indian sub-continent–it was going to be that way all next week, too.

"Where are you flying to, sir?"

"What business is that of yours?" Miles snapped, more ill-humored than usual because, for the moment, he had no answer for that question. The simplest things sometimes eluded him now when he had long prided himself on his powers of memory. For this particular trip, Nick had been forced to write out a detailed itinerary, which Miles carried with him everywhere he went in case of lapses like the present one. It was just so embarrassing, and in front of a taxi driver of all people. Life couldn't get much worse.

"Just inquiring. It helps pass the time, that's all."

"I'm paying you to take me to my hotel, not to pass the time."

"What's the name of that hotel again, sir?"

"It's the...the...? It's on the piece of paper I gave you."

Why did the driver have to put him on the spot again like that? It just wasn't fair, but what could Miles do about it when his mind was so dodgy. He did remember that Nick had booked him into some hotel or other for the night before his scheduled return. According to him, it was just a stone and a halfs throw from the airport. It was the added half throw that caused the cabbie real problems as he attempted to navigate the seedy streets of that lower-middle-class suburb of London.

Nick had been planning to come with him on this trip to England, in part to celebrate Miles' sixty-first, but his dear mother had fallen and broken a hip four days before their scheduled departure and, of course, he had flown home to Grand Rapids to be with her.

Miles had wanted April to take Nick's place, just to have someone there with him, but, of course, she'd turned him down. He'd tried everything he could think of to get her to change her mind, but he'd had fallen so far short of the mark he wondered why he'd made the effort. The answer was simple. He needed her far more than she needed him, especially when his bearings occasionally went adrift. April was so clever when it came to learning the trade, so challenged when it came to learning to live life again. He'd have given anything, traded places with her even, to get her beyond all that.

This trip it seemed to him he'd covered half the island in his quest for new items for the store. Books had been his passion all his life, yet the early days and some of his greatest finds pretty much eluded him now. He did remember discovering some valuable old book in the attic of an abandoned house as a young boy. He'd sold it to a local dealer for ninety dollars, a handsome sum then, but couldn't remember its title or author. And what fun was the hunt if the hunter forgot about the fox at the end?

He could vaguely recall buying and selling books during college, then afterwards at a very big store. Schulte's, that was its name, near a big park where he got off the subway. Learning the ins and outs of the trade at Schulte's, he finally went into business for himself, first in a rented store, then in an unoccupied building he'd purchased for almost nothing during the recession of the early eighties.

The rundown shops passing by the taxi window were ominous indeed compared to the neatly trimmed, painted ones to be found on his favorite street in London where Reg Sloane, an old friend, owned a bookstore. In fact, it was on Reg's advice that Miles had driven to an ancient house in the west of the country where he had found a collection of some antiquarian interest sealed off in an attic room. His friend had no idea the value of his find, the details of which would come back to Miles eventually.

In the end, he had come away with a crate of items, which he'd sent back to New York. Once he returned home, he intended to sort through the entire collection item by item, which the hurried circumstances of the sale had not permitted. It had been a matter of taking the entire lot or allowing it to go to a competitor scheduled to arrive not much later that same day.

Peering through the window, Miles thought the buildings looked strange indeed.

"Are you sure you're not lost?"

"Oh, yes sir. Very sure. Very sure."

"Then why have we gone down the same street three times?"

"Not the same street at all, sir. Different streets."

Miles was confused. He was certain they had passed that way before. Something was wrong, or was it all in his mind? He felt so terribly vulnerable that time of night in a part of town he was certain he had never visited before, especially since he had no one else along, Nick or April or anyone really, to fall back on in case he lost his way. Or the cab driver lost it for him.

A glance at the antique, gold Rolex Nick had given him for his birthday a year ago told him it was just minutes after midnight.

"Then why aren't we there yet? I have a plane to catch early tomorrow. That's in the morning, not the evening!"

"Just another minute or two, sir. No more."

After turning in his rental car at the airport, Miles had called April, but got only a recorded message, which was strange because April never left the shop. He hoped nothing had happened, not after what she'd suffered through recently. He'd call again the moment he got to his room.

He was at the limits of his patience when the driver turned, guided the taxi to the curb and pointed to a sign in the bay window down the narrow street that read "Heathrow Guest House."

"This is it, sir."

"A guest house?" Miles couldn't help saying. "You've brought me to the wrong address. I'm going to a hotel."

"Not according to the sheet of paper you gave me. You're staying at the Heathrow Guest House, this address precisely," the driver said, groveling for the tip he would never get. "I'll help you with your things, sir."

That offer presented Miles with a choice, a dicey one. Let the dysfunctional driver help him on this poorly lighted excuse for a street. Or travel the few steps alone to the seedy guest house Nick's travel agent had booked for him. In fact, it turned out to be no real choice at all. He'd rather brave the short distance to the front door himself than be guided by some fool who couldn't find his way up a set of stairs without a topographical map, which undoubtedly he couldn't read.

"That won't be necessary."

"This part of town, I don't know?"

"I can do it quicker myself."

"Pick you up for your flight in the morning?"

"Are you joking, man? I don't want to miss it completely. I'll arrange something with the owners of the hotel, thank you all the same."

Miles looked at the meter, pulled out his billfold and counted out eighteen pounds, forty pence more than his total fare.

"Keep the change."

"Thank you very much, sir," the bungling driver said as he retrieved Miles' bag from the boot. He was too thick-headed to count the bills he'd been handed, just stuffed them in his pocket as if he'd been given his biggest tip of the day. Miles felt cheated somehow.

"Pleasant flight, sir."

"I doubt it very much."

He stood there, staring in simmering disbelief at the cab as it pulled away. When he finally cooled down enough to turn in the opposite direction, he saw that his hotel was indeed a guest house, located on a dead-end street.

For the moment he felt abandoned. Blinded by false self-pride, he had dismissed the cab driver. What's more, he would have to spend the night alone in a guest house that looked as welcoming at that hour as a burned-out tenement in the Blitz.

The moon, shrouded by a lone ominous cloud, hovered just above the abutment wall at the far end of the street. He had no desire to take in the eerie beauty of it all, just picked up his bags and struggled with them toward the lone brick building with the guest-house sign in the window.

In the darkened glow of the moon there on that dead-end street, Miles had almost reached his goal when he heard the rush of footfalls on the pavement behind him. He turned to glimpse two young men coming up rapidly from behind. One grabbed at the suitcase in his left hand.

"Le'go a'th'loogage, you bloody faggot," he snarled.

"I will not," Miles said, tightening his grip.

"I said, le'go. And giv'us the effing wally while yr a'it."

"Why should I give you something that doesn't belong to you? If it's a late-night thrill you're looking for, why not just go home, turn on the telly and watch *London's Burning*. This business of snatching strangers' luggage is going to get you in...."

Miles' voice fell off, and his free arm came up to defend himself as the stockier of the two balled his right hand into a fist and brought it around, delivering a blow to the jaw that sent Miles sprawling forward while the boxer's pal finally wrenched the suitcase from his left hand.

The last thing Miles remembered seeing was the bottom step of the entry speeding toward him. And nothing after that.

Nothing except pure and utter darkness.

3 THE GROANING BOARD

"Would you like a second helping, Rob?" Joanna asked, softening her voice a little as she gazed over at her husband, whose high cheek bones, jutting jaw and full head of sandy hair, faithfully dyed every two weeks, never failed to remind her just how much she had once loved him, and still would if only that love were returned.

"No thanks."

"You don't like the stew?"

"I didn't say that. I just don't have time, that's all."

Joanna repressed a look of displeasure. There was no reason, she knew, to appear unhappy at his response. She fed her husband, son, and the others stew or soup half the week, it seemed, only because it satisfied their different schedules and needs.

That evening's Brunswick stew hadn't turned out so badly, she thought. It was plentiful, nutritious, and, if not exactly tasty, at least it had passed the gag test. If Rob Junior didn't fake throwing up after his first mouthful—an antic he'd learned in this, his first year in college—at least the dish was palatable.

Joanna didn't exactly hate to cook. She tolerated it the same way she tolerated the occasional unwanted stares of men as they passed on the street. Others' looks weren't going to kill her, and she had far more important things to worry about. The same with cooking. It was something to do to get on with the rest of life. Only now she was feeding the three of them, plus the actors of the East Village Players, who had much higher standards than her husband and son, though none had ever adopted RJ's occasional display of displeasure, at least not in her presence. Usually they were so busy gulping wine and bitching about the profession they loved to hate, they didn't have time, or the lack of tact, to do the same with the food. She worked as long and hard as both sets of diners, family and actors, and enjoyed the rewards of neither.

"Where are you off to tonight?"

Rob had told her before, but it was a different town almost every night, sometimes two, and after a while they all seemed to blend together.

"A town-hall in Arlington."

"Do you ever end up in the wrong place, you know with all your different speaking engagements?"

"That's why Dad has me along," RJ spoke up. "We always get where we're supposed to be going. We've been late maybe a couple times, never by more than ten minutes. And Dad's getting more brilliant every day. You should come hear him."

"Don't know what I'd do without RJ," her husband said. "Thank god he doesn't go back to school 'till after the election."

"Then I get to come to Washington with you."

"Remember, you've got three years of college to finish."

"After that?"

"There are nepotism laws. You can help your mother and her theater types. No laws against that."

"Yeah, but the pay sucks."

"Not if you're Samuel Pilgrim."

"But I'd need a skin transplant. And besides, he's just big and brawny. I'd want to...."

"Enough, RJ," Joanna said, looking longingly at the drawer next to the sink where she once kept her cigarettes. She'd have given anything for a Virginia Slim just then. The thirty-seven days she'd gone without had almost killed her, but she just couldn't fall back on the one vice that dependably gave her solace. Then have to go through the process of quitting all over again because she had to get off. And stay off!

In fact, Rob Junior, who turned his wrist toward his father and tapped his watch, did have talent, lots of it. He'd won a small part in *Antigone* his freshman year at college. Despite his long, white face and wisp of a beard, he might fill out and become something of a leading man eventually.

Not in Hollywood, lord forbid, but in regional theater. Maybe even in New York. Forget film. That corrupted even veteran stage actors.

Joanna had hoped the summer would go a little differently for RJ when she'd invited the company to their country place outside Oakville to rehearse *Othello*, the play that had originally catapulted their non-profit into the forefront of classical-theater ranks in New York. After many successful years, the Players were still fighting for their collective lives in the financial crisis that afflicted all New York theater in the wake of the Savings and Loan Crisis.

Less than a month before company members were scheduled to arrive, Rob had decided to run in a special election for Congress from the Twentieth District. He'd won the Republican primary in a squeaker. Now his opponent was campaigning as an independent, and siphoning off enough votes to make a real contest in a district that had gone Republican since the time of the Big Bang. RJ had volunteered to help his father when his mother had wanted him to fall completely under the thrall of theater taking place at The Gables night and day.

The only part of the company that seemed to have engaged him was Hope Wrightsman, who still looked RJ's age, though she was a good ten years older. A little summertime crush was alright as long as it remained just that. At least he'd been reading *Hamlet*, almost certainly at Hope's urging. If Joanna had suggested it herself, he wouldn't have picked up the *Classics Illustrated* version. He'd even said something about wanting to play the title role while he was still young enough. So a little Hope was a good thing. As long as it was just a little, and Joanna was there to pry him out of the arms of someone who might derive just a little too much pleasure from taking the young and still very impressionable boy to her milky white breast.

"What kind of stew tomorrow?"

"Don't get that way, Rob. It's not easy cooking for two sets of people, both with very different tastes."

"Yeah, one set has taste alright, the others are liberals."

"Let's not go there, please. You've been great about this so far."

"Time to go," RJ intervened, true diplomat that he was. "We're late already."

"I have been decent, haven't I?" Rob said. "I may not stay that way, though, if my intestinal track gets blocked with all the gooey stuff in your stews."

"Then maybe you should schedule a checkup with your gastroenterologist?"

"Gastronenter...?" Rob cut himself short. "This is an election, Joanna. I don't have time to indulge in that kind of foolishness. Just remember what we agreed last month?"

"I know...I know. Not a cent more of your mother's generous donations to shore up the Players' finances. That's why I brought the company out here this summer. And have been working myself to death on the end-of-summer subscription campaign."

"Just so we understand one another."

By this time RJ was standing. Rob patted his thin lips with a paper napkin, rose from the table and kissed Joanna briefly on the forehead. It had been so long since her perpetually youthful husband had given her anything more than a perfunctory kiss that Joanna felt neglected, though, fortunately, she hadn't had much time to think about it with fourteen others now living more or less under the same roof with her.

What would happen when they all left as they inevitably would? She knew the answer to that, of course. She'd move back into the city with Rob. If he won the election, which seemed unlikely, he'd be off to Washington. If he lost, she'd still be living alone in the same monstrous apartment with him, hoping he'd turn just a little attention toward her, but knowing that was as likely as a sudden snowfall in the middle of the heat wave they'd been suffering through since the day the first of the company's actors had arrived at The Gables.

She waved good-bye to her two departing campaign warriors and looked up at the kitchen clock. Thirty-five minutes, give or take an hour, before the theater crew rolled in for their evening meal. Joanna poured a half bottle of cheap chardonnay into the stew, added a little corn starch to thicken the gruel, then cleared the kitchen table. In no time, she had the dishes rinsed and in the dishwasher.

When the dining-room table was set for the second seating of the evening she retreated to the study that served as her summertime office, and sat down in front of her grandfather's old roll-top. That room was her favorite in the entire house, with windows looking out almost 180 degrees through the porch and over the surrounding grounds.

The furnishings were quite simple really. Besides the desk and chair, there was an old, cut-down library table, and a reupholstered, antique wingback. She stared half longingly at the framed photo of Rob as CEO of the Garnet Corporation, and then remembered the way he'd treated her in the time since that formal portrait had been taken, and turned away.

She began jabbing the desk calculator so hard she was surprised the little white buttons didn't come sprocketing up and put out an eye in revenge. The machine was lying. It had to be. No matter how badly she abused it, the numbers didn't change. The Players would have to sell ninety-eight percent of their seats that season and double charitable contributions just to break even.

She had debated raising prices last spring, but with the economy still in a nose dive she couldn't justify the increase, either in subscription or in individual ticket prices. She'd hit up every member of her board, and they in turn their friends, until even the most generous were skipping meetings when any discussion of finances was on the agenda. They'd lost almost four-hundred thousand the year before, and needed a minor miracle or the limited 1991 season might well be the last for the company.

Then there was the matter of the theater itself. Their landlord, Lars Carlsson, was threatening to pull their lease unless they paid back rent and offered guarantees for the coming year, something Joanna was not prepared to do.

Carlsson was just establishing a bargaining position. He had to be.

She had written grants, attracted sponsorships, hired every last intern she could find, cut operating expenses so much she winced at the loss in production values for which the Players had been so noted in their thirteen-year run in the East Village. That summer she had even sublet the theater to a group of Flamenco dancers, which, in turn, necessitated rehearsing their *Othello* at The Gables, the country place she and Rob had bought and remodeled six years earlier, and from which Rob had launched his political career.

Why, she wondered as she stared at the numbers in front of her, had she ever gone along with the Players' resident director, Avery LeMaster, when he had proposed to set *Othello* in Kuwait during the Gulf War, with all males in the cast of military age wearing desert cammies.

Joanna didn't know just what she had been thinking when she had agreed with Avery that the so-called relevance of that production concept would appeal to a younger audience. If they truly wanted to be so relevant, why not take their *Othello* on tour with the USO? Or set it in Crown Heights? Hell, why waste money on sets and costumes? Instead do Nude Shakespeare! Even though the latter would undoubtedly pare costume expenses to nothing, it was almost as bad as the idea of the Gulf War as the point of departure for events in *Othello* that took place in the Eastern Mediterranean at the end of the sixteenth century.

What had led her to take on everything Avery proposed, take on the entire world in fact? Had she inherited a defective gene from her father, who had been a workaholic all his life? Had Rob made her feel especially neglected? Or had life become so empty she needed to fill it with a collection of impostors—a dozen actors, a son whom she was guiding down that same career path, a politician husband? This last notion came so frighteningly close to the truth, Joanna had actually scheduled an appointment with a therapist, but then cancelled it at the last moment because she couldn't imagine telling anyone things she would barely admit to herself. An empty life was one thing, being made to feel good about it by a psychologist something else entirely.

She had just begun thumbing her top-heavy rolodex in search of that one, magical name that might be willing to bail the East Village Players out when the phone rang. And it kept ringing until she was well into the Bs. Sensing the caller would not give up, she lifted the receiver to her ear. Who knew? Maybe it was some wealthy donor, wanting to offer her a large sum, and without any thought of naming rights. What had become of good old-fashioned generosity in the Age of Celebrity?

"Priestly residence," Joanna offered in weary voice.

"May I please speak with Avery LeMaster?"

She thought she recognized the thin, slightly tremulous voice on the other end.

"I'm sorry, he's in rehearsal now."

"Is...is that you, Joanna?"

"Yes. Who is this?"

"Ap...April Oliphant."

That's why the voice had sounded familiar. April had gone on to bigger things when she left the Players. Too big as it turned out, proving Joanna right when she had initially advised the ingénue against diving into the small Broadway pool from an eighteen-meter board.

"How are you, April?"

"Not so bad. And you?"

"You know things at the Players. Still looking for Daddy Deep-Pockets. You're not calling because you're thinking of rejoining us?"

Joanna could hear a deep, very audible gulp on the other end.

"I'm not really up to it at the moment, I'm afraid. I wanted to speak with Avery. Could you give him a message? It's important."

"Of course. What is it?"

"We've been playing phone tag for a day now. Just have him call me at Oliphant's Books as soon as he can. The number here is 212-623-7741."

"Got it. I'll put it on our message board and remind Avery when he comes in for dinner. He'll be delighted you called, I know. And if you ever change your mind...you know, about coming back, you've always got a home at the East Village Players."

April thanked her and hung up.

Joanna sat there, momentarily stunned. For two seasons, the mere mention of April's name would sell out shows months in advance. She was one of those rare talents a person would have felt thankful to have seen just once on any stage. And Joanna had worked with her in four different productions. Her Emily Gibbs in *Our Town* was so down-to-earth and moving it had brought Joanna to tears, and that happened so rarely it wasn't worth the trouble of holding up fingers to count.

The reviews they got while April was with them— especially from Shawn Kirby, the *Chronicle's* critic–were praiseworthy enough Joanna felt as if she could have written them herself. After the ingénue's sudden departure from the company, however, Kirby had savaged their groundbreaking *Emperor Jones*. Joanna suspected a connection between April's desertion and that review. Since then, she had seen the city's most important drama critic at one, only one of the Players' productions.

About to return to searching for the name of that big donor, she peered out through the window in the direction of the big red barn behind the house. There, coming in her direction, were three-fourths of cast of *Othello*. Charles Cassidy was in the lead, his arm around the waist of their Desdemona, Hope Wrightsman, who was attempting to fend off his advances. Avery had promised her Charles' recovery was real. Otherwise, the veteran actor would perhaps have been performing in Akron, and misbehaving just as badly there.

As Joanna hurried to the kitchen, she resolved to ask Avery, who brought up the rear, what, on God's green earth, April Oliphant was doing working in a bookstore?

"I smell stew," Charles exclaimed as he burst in from the patio. "I hope its laced with something strong enough to overcome the taste of those abominable vegetables." He paused here theatrically for effect. "Just joking, Joanna."

She had no intention of telling him that he was going to have to be satisfied with a six-dollar bottle of chardonnay, the alcohol in which had boiled off by now. But then someone had to look after Charles, and by default that task had fallen to Joanna, den mother to the world.

"Of all people, guess who called?" she said to Avery when he finally walked in.

"I don't have time for guessing games, Joanna. Who?"

"April Oliphant. Here's her number. She said it's important. I guess you told me she's working in a bookstore now. How did that ever happen?"

4 COFFEE AND SHAKESPEARE

Recently, the telephone had seemed the only modern invention worth its weight in plastic. Ever since moving back in with her father, April had used it as her lifeline to the world. It was the only real way she had of reaching out and almost touching someone. Yet, in spite of AT&T's advice, she never seemed to get in touch with anyone who really cared.

The first person she tried calling was Shelly, her former college roommate and one true friend, but got no answer. Probably because Shelly had moved in with her new boyfriend. Next was her father, who hadn't arrived at JFK when he was supposed to, and that worried her. In his growing forgetfulness, she hoped he hadn't got lost in transit somehow.

She'd found out he was late when Art Kass, whose limo service he used, called from the airport to ask if he'd changed flights. Perhaps, but he certainly hadn't told April, who immediately dialed the last number she had for him. According to the desk clerk, Miles Oliphant had left the hotel on schedule. Finally, she phoned Miles' lawyer boyfriend, Nick Reed, who hadn't heard of any change in her father's plans either. According to Nick, Miles could have found another West-End play he wanted to see. Taken a long weekend in Paris. Gone off to the Lake District. He'd call, or show up at JFK sometime. Until he did, April had to put on hold the questions she had about the manuscript he'd sent from England.

She was cataloging her father's new finds when the doorbell brought her head up from her computer. There, on the security monitor, stood Avery LeMaster, long blond hair sticking out from under his black, no-logo cap. Even though months had passed since he'd last visited Oliphant's, there could be no mistaking him. He was dressed in the same black jacket, tee-shirt and jeans he always wore. They had talked briefly two nights before. When he'd asked why she had called, she told him about the strange manuscript her father had sent from England, but nothing more.

She buzzed him in, then reached up and touched the poster of Vanessa as Julia for courage and more than a little good luck.

"Professor LeMaster, I didn't know you'd come by so soon," she said when she greeted him in the front of the store.

How many times since his call had she gone over her opening lines? "Thank you for coming by." "How nice to see you." Usually, the clipped way of speaking she'd recently developed put people off, which was fine ninety-nine percent of the time. What about the one percent of people she didn't want to alienate? She couldn't get things right with them no matter how much she rehearsed. If practice truly did make perfect, then it had made her a perfect fool.

"Sorry. We're rehearsing at Joanna Priestly's place outside Oakville, and I have to get back. We open in just over three weeks. Still, after your phone call I drove in as soon as I could."

"What are you doing?"

"*Othello*. It's a disaster."

"*Othello*? Isn't that the play...I mean, you started your career with that brilliant *Othello* how many years ago?"

"Thirteen. I should know. I just wrote the director's note for the program. This new production is to be a chance to show how the company's vision has grown in that time."

"I know it's grown. I saw that much in *As You Like It* at Stony Brook. It was as if you were wearing Shakespeare's skin, inhabiting his body."

April couldn't stop the words that came gushing from her mouth as she recalled working with Avery in that production. She had been playing Rosalind as little more than a lovestruck teenager. Then, one evening after rehearsal, her car wouldn't start. She'd had to take the LIRR back to Hicksville where she lived with her boyfriend, and who sat down beside her on the train? Professor Avery LeMaster on his way back to Manhattan.

For the entire ride they talked about the one thing they had in common then. The play. Toward the end, Avery had asked one simple question that made her completely rethink the character of Rosalind. Could she, April, ever remember a time when she'd worn boy's clothes? All she had to do was think back to the sun-bleached Led-Zeppelin tee-shirt Teddy had given her, and that was it. She was Teddy-in-Arden for the next six glorious weeks, all because of that casual question. Avery LeMaster simply brought out the best in her.

"Why, thanks. But this production's got me in more knots than a sailor knows how to tie."

"I'm certain it will be a success."

"I wish I had your confidence. Much as I can use the strokes, I'm in a bit of a rush. Need to be back by one. This manuscript...if it really is that. Could I see it? I actually came in especially for it. No time for breakfast even."

"In that case, would you like a cup of coffee while we look at it?"

"Since it's you that made the offer, and the coffee...certainly, a quick cup would help keep the wheel from getting away from me on the drive back."

A bit of a rush? A quick cup for the drive back? Things were happening too fast. April had to slow them down. She was hoping Avery would linger over her father's new discovery, not scamper back off to Oakville. It wasn't even ten o'clock yet.

"It's not the best cup Mr. Coffee's ever made, but if it's an early morning lift you need, this should do it." There it was again, her impish mouth getting the better of her. She wanted Avery to stay, share his many insights with her, not shoot off like an over-caffeinated rabbit.

She offered him her father's desk chair and poured a cup of coffee that was no more than an hour old, then helped herself. Avery seemed a bit more frazzled than usual. A few days growth vied with his usually trimmed mustache and Van Dyck, artfully designed to mask the youthful dimple in his chin. The rest of his complexion was so pasty it seemed bathed in moonlight. Only his dark, sad eyes reminded her of the man she had known for almost six years now.

"You're right. This is strong...but good."

He shook his head to emphasize the point.

Retrieving the manuscript from the vault, she handed it to him. His coffee forgotten in an instant, Professor LeMaster examined the title page, head cocked slightly to one side. Then he inclined it toward the first page, read it and turned to the second. As his fingers gathered speed, he occasionally pronounced words, even entire phrases from the text as he went along. Soon, he was no longer tarrying over individual lines, but taking in whole pages.

Finally he looked up at her. She couldn't quite read Avery LeMaster at this point. His features appeared perplexed and astonished at the same time. As she had expected, the strange *Hamlet* had seized his imagination, perhaps even run away with it.

"Where did you get this?" he asked. She told him the story of the crate her father had sent from England. As she did, she showed him the bound copies of the journal, *The Censor*, and the letters among which she'd found the *Hamlet*.

"I'm not entirely certain what you have here, April. The paper and script might be authentic, I don't know, and the text reads like the early Shakespeare, but it's all too good to be true. I mean, my god, we may have a missing play by Shakespeare, perhaps in his own hand."

"Then you really think it's written by Shakespeare and not a prompt book, or the work of some copyist?"

"Just possibly. If it is, your father's made the discovery of a lifetime. Outside five or six signatures on legal documents, and a debatable manuscript for *Sir Thomas More*, there's nothing that's come down to us in Shakespeare's hand. In this case, of course, experts will be the judge of that.

"Your father may have found a version of *Hamlet* that's troubled scholars for almost a century. You see, early in Shakespeare's career, when he was an actor and writer, there was a version of *Hamlet* kicking around London, maybe by Thomas Kyd or another of Shakespeare's contemporaries. Some think that early *Hamlet's* by Shakespeare himself, perhaps a draft of the great play we know today. No matter which side one comes down on, everybody refers to what your father's got here as the *Ur-Hamlet*, that is, the *Original Hamlet*. Myself, I'm convinced the *Ur-Hamlet's* by Shakespeare.

"If the manuscript is authentic, it could show us how Shakespeare's vision of *Hamlet* changed over a fifteen-year period. Even if it's by one of his contemporaries, it's still invaluable since so few late sixteenth-century plays survive. On the other hand, as you have guessed, it could also have been written out at a later date, and has only now turned up. The letters with it could be helpful in that regard."

"My father's been delayed in England. That's why I called you. I'm not sure when he's getting back, and I haven't been able to reach him by phone. In the meantime, I thought maybe you could tell me something based on the internal evidence?"

LeMaster hesitated, but only for a moment.

"Yes, it would be possible to evaluate your new *Hamlet* based on evidence contained in it, and draw conclusions about the document's authenticity. But that will take time."

"How much time?"

"Days for a superficial evaluation. Far longer, perhaps even years, for something more conclusive. I'm honored that you've chosen to share this with me, April. Does anyone else know about it?"

"No one, except perhaps my father and the people who sold it to him."

"Why do you say *perhaps*?"

"Because it was part of a much larger shipment. I found it tucked away in all those papers. That's why I'm not certain my father or the sellers even knew it was there."

"Intriguing. I assume you'd like me to examine the manuscript, then?"

"Would you, please?" she answered without a moment's hesitation.

"I'd be delighted. I'd have to take it with me, though. Can't risk making a photocopy of it. That might damage the paper or ink, which would be a disaster. And the pages buckle too much to shoot with a camera, even a good one. The old-fashioned, secretary script is going to be difficult enough to decipher as it is without having to contend with blurred lines or whole pages out-of-focus."

"I don't know. My father could be back anytime."

"I see." Avery's eyes wandered the office vacantly as he thought. "The manuscript isn't that long. I might be able to give you a very preliminary opinion in a couple days. As I say, a complete, word-by-word analysis would take far longer. But I could at least start on that after we open at the East Village. I'd love to, in fact."

April had been hoping he'd forget his blessed *Othello* and spend the morning poring over her father's discovery with her. Still he had agreed to return it within a few days, far better than the months that had separated his previous visits. What if her father walked through the door that evening and demanded to see his new discovery? She'd be in trouble so deep she didn't even want to think how she'd get out. She liked Avery LeMaster, but did she like him that much?

Evidently part of her did. Her mouth. "Alright, but please have it back as soon as possible," it said without her permission.

"Of course, and you'll want to have someone analyze the ink and paper."

"I've already send a tiny sample to Dr. Grossman. He's the forensics expert Father uses for old documents like this."

"You're a step ahead of me already. What about a graphologist?"

"We occasionally send letters, things like that out to Elizabeth Duke. I haven't said a thing about it to her yet in case you wanted to see the entire document."

"I see." Avery stopped to think. "The last page has only five or six lines on it. I'll copy them out quickly and you can send her the original, which should be enough to compare against Shakespeare's signatures. This is potentially far too important a find for me not to explore it, no matter how short the time."

April searched for an envelope while he copied out the last lines of the play. As he did, he made what, for him, she supposed was small talk, most of it spent encouraging her to take up acting again. He'd seen her Laura in *Menagerie* at the Roundabout, and thought she was wonderful. Perhaps not wanting to hurt her feelings, he didn't ask why she had quit only two weeks into the run.

Then something utterly unpredictable happened. As he was saying goodbye, she handed him an envelope and he kissed her casually on the forehead, leaving her speechless.

"Thanks. Thanks for this," he said afterwards, as if to explain his actions. "I'll have it back, if not tomorrow, then the next day. Are...are you all right, April?"

"I...if Father gets back and asks for it before then, I'll just tell him that Dr. Duke's analyzing the handwriting. That's not a total lie, anyway."

"It's not even a partial one. Good to see you again. Thanks for the coffee and this."

Holding up the manuscript, Avery LeMaster left the shop, unaware of the utter state of confusion into which he'd plunged her. Only one man, her father, had been that close to her physically in recent memory. There had been times, celebrations mainly, when he, too, had kissed her on the forehead or the cheek. Neither of them derived anything but the mildest satisfaction from that. For him, she was...well, what she was. His daughter, and a *woman*. For her part, she couldn't allow anyone, not even her father, to get that close for more than seconds.

Anyone except, perhaps, Avery LeMaster, and now he was speeding back toward Oakville and Joanna Priestly.

5 A PROPOSAL

"Only two minutes late. Sorry," Joanna apologized to her husband, son, and brother-in-law as she entered the study. Rob sat at the desk, his younger brother, Gene, on the window bench across from him. RJ was hunkered in the one other chair, a wingback, in the room.

She had just come up from the barn where she'd had to soothe Hope Wrightsman's ego about some evidently casual remark Charles Cassidy had made to her. Now, in addition to her role as producer and business manager, Joanna had evidently become the company's resident psychologist. What other unwritten job titles awaited her? Factotum-at-large? Fortune-teller? Fixer-in-chief?

Rob looked at her as if she had just defected to the enemy camp, which made Joanna wish she hadn't given up smoking in the worst way. Thank god the election would be over in ten days. And the new production would go up not much more than two weeks after that.

Lifting RJ's feet from the ottoman, she took a seat on it and focused her attention on Gene, who was an assistant principal and taught political science in the city, and had volunteered as Rob's campaign manager even though everyone knew he was a Democrat. He was different in other ways from his older brother—balding, not quite the looker, though in much better shape. And Gene was a real listener. He let Joanna talk. Didn't interrupt. And always found ways of showing his support, even if he didn't agree with her. As he spoke now, his words washed over her like a lingering hint of tobacco that calmed her nerves, rubbed raw by that morning's rehearsal.

"The Quinnipiac poll has us only four points up on Fortinbras, seven on Mayor Pierson. I don't have to remind anyone here we had this election in the bag until four weeks ago when Hiz Honor reentered the race. He's draining off our conservative base and we've got to do some triage to keep the rest of our supporters in the fold.

Fortunately, there are still enough moderates in the district that we can pull this one out, it's just a matter of getting them to the polls on election day. Now, I want...Rob?"

"I can't figure out why that turncoat mayor decided to run as an independent? He said if he didn't win the primary, he wasn't interested in anything other than his job at city hall. If we don't neutralize him, the district's going to elect its first Democrat in almost a half century."

"You know why. You refused to cave to Leon Brodsky."

"Damn right I did. He'd have me in his pocket along with Pierson, and it's dark and smelly enough in there already."

"You did the right thing," Gene replied. "But now Brodsky's money's going to Pierson through every legal channel he can find. And he's busy inventing new ones, too."

"Can I say something?" RJ asked, running his fingers through his adorable ginger curls.

"Of course."

"I just want to tell you, I've got over ninety volunteers lined up. Lots of students home on summer vacation. All have lists with phone numbers of dad's supporters. And they've got cars. Some have summer jobs, but the ones who don't are willing to give us up to twelve hours September 17th ferrying voters to and from the polls."

Joanna wasn't as shocked by RJ's words as by the force with which he'd spoken them. Over the course of the summer, he'd changed from a college freshman who wasn't even certain of his major into a true political believer. She had hated to see him come under Rob and Gene's influence, especially when RJ loved English and theater so much. She prayed his change of heart was temporary, a show of support for his beleaguered father, but she doubted it. Maybe she'd mention something to Hope Wrightsman about RJ, get her to offer a few words of encouragement about theater to him. Anything to keep him from going over to the dark side.

"That's great, RJ," Gene continued, "we also need to see more of that kind of initiative in the form of outreach to local churches. We can't concede a single vote to Pierson, even if he is a minister's son and thinks he's the keeper of the keys to heaven. If not St. Peter himself. Rob, I've got you scheduled tomorrow at the Catholic Men's Fellowship at...."

At that point, Gene was interrupted by a series of quick raps on the door. Without waiting for a response, Avery LeMaster burst in. Matted clumps of his long, blond hair seemed abuzz with an unseen electrical charge. The Players' resident director hadn't shaved either. His scary, bulging eyes came to rest on Joanna. In almost thirteen years of working together, she had never seen him look quite so agitated.

"Sorry for interrupting," he rasped, "but I've got to talk to Joanna,"

Rob's eyes rolled up, and, if she wasn't mistaken, he was trying suppress a knowing smirk.

"When I'm finished here, I'll...."

"Now!" Avery bellowed in a voice theatrical enough to send RJ deep into the cushioned back of his chair. If the interloper could only perform that minor miracle a couple times a week, there might still be some artistic hope left for her son.

"Go ahead and talk to your Guru," Rob snarled. "Hell, it's only my election we're discussing here."

"I'll just be a second."

Joanna didn't know who she wanted to shut up more just then, her husband or Avery LeMaster. Still, she rose from the ottoman and escorted the wild man out into the corridor.

"What the hell are you...?"

"You've got to read this." Avery thrust a thin stack of pages under her nose.

"I'm in a meeting, Avery. I'm supposed to update the group on women's outreach in Rob's election. I can't be bothered with...."

"*This*, right here! This is women's outreach, in its most powerful form," he said loud enough that everyone inside could hear. She took him by the arm to lead him further down the empty corridor. "What's going on in there, that's just bullshit by comparison."

"That bullshit happens to decide who governs this country," she said bluntly. "It also determines how much money goes to the National Endowment and eventually to us."

"This'll get us millions, bare minimum," he claimed, waving the papers in front of her. "And that's a promise."

"What's got you so worked up?"

"I've been trying to tell you. This is an entirely new...."

"A new romantic comedy by your favorite female playwright of the moment?" she said when he didn't, or couldn't complete his sentence. "How many times do I have to remind you, Avery? We're a classical repertory company. We don't do anything written after 1945."

"How about something written before 1645? Before 1590?"

"What are you talking about?"

"A version of *Hamlet* written...."

"We're doing *Othello*. Not *Hamlet*."

"Read this, then tell me that."

"I don't have time to read it."

"You don't have time *not* to. This is an early version *Hamlet* I've transcribed into modern English. I'm sure it was written by Shakespeare. We've known about it all along, but it's been lost for four hundred years. Miles Oliphant discovered it on a buying trip to England. We have a chance at a premiere of a play by Shakespeare, Joanna! Do you know how long it's been since any company's been able to make that claim? Think what this'll mean for our box office. Donors worldwide will be lining up to fill our coffers."

"Sorry to break the news to you, Avery, but we don't have time to change productions barely three weeks before we open. We don't have enough time to rehearse *Othello* as it is."

"This new *Hamlet's* only nineteen hundred lines long."

"Look," Joanna said, taking Avery by the shoulders, "subscribers are expecting *Othello*. They have their tickets already. Posters are up. Copy for the program is at the printers as we speak. How many other ways can I say 'Don't even think about it'?"

"I dare you even to try and utter those words again after you read this."

He pulled free of her hands, pressed his new *Hamlet* into one of them and closed her fingers around the script. Then stalked out into the living room, stopping perhaps ten paces away and turning to face her.

"Read it, Joanna. You'll never have another opportunity like this in your life."

She stood there motionless, caught between two completely different worlds—the political one of the males in her family, and the very impolitic world of Avery LeMaster. She was committed by blood ties to the former, by personal sympathies to the latter. She had to get back to the study, no way to avoid that or the poorly masked indifference she was certain to confront there even though she was totally on top of the information she was about to present.

Competency was the curse of Joanna Priestly's adult life, one she wouldn't wish on anyone else, not even on Avery LeMaster. It was always difficult to fight him, but she was determined to do precisely that, especially in light of his insane proposal. He had to have gotten his new *Hamlet* from Oliphant's daughter. No matter how great an actor, April was turning into a very big pebble in Joanna's tightly laced boot.

6 A POLICE SUMMONS

Two nights passed before April got any decent sleep after Avery kissed her on the forehead. The next morning, she scrambled an egg, made a slice of whole-wheat toast dry, and an extra large pot of coffee. She was just sitting down to breakfast when the phone rang. Quickly, she looked at her watch and saw that it was almost nine. It might just be her father calling. England was six hours ahead of New York, after all.

"April Oliphant?" inquired a high-pitched voice that made her wonder if she was being addressed by a man or a woman. Certainly it wasn't her father.

"Yes, who is this?"

"Sergeant Cochran, Missing Persons, New York Police, returning your call."

At first, April's sleep-starved memory didn't register that she'd called the police about her father the day before.

"Oh, yes, that's right. I...I want to file a missing person's report."

"That's what your message said. What's the name of the subject?"

"Miles Oliphant."

"Just a second." Cochran paused here. "I hate these new computers. They move slower than a glued turtle, but at least I don't have to chase down files and go through them one by one anymore. Oliphant, you say?"

"That's right. Miles Oliphant."

This time, her response was greeted by a silence so long it seemed the phone had gone dead in her hand.

"Are you still there?"

"I am, this ugly machine still hasn't spit out....Wait, there it is. No Oliphant of any sort, Miles or any other name like Yards or Feet." Cochran laughed at his own bad joke. "Are you a relative?"

"His daughter." The long wait had sparked hopes, which had been doused now. "So what do I do?"

"I'll need some information."

"Go ahead. We don't open 'till ten."

"Sorry, not over the phone. In person."

"In person? Why?"

"Because I'm the only officer in the precinct who works Missing Persons. Plus illegals. Plus you name it, all the strays no one else at the precinct wants to take on. I don't have time to write down all that information. Plus there are forms to sign."

"Maybe you could have someone bring them by?"

"This isn't Domino's, Ms. Oliphant. It's the police. We don't deliver. You want to report a missing person, you've got to come down to the station, fill out the appropriate forms and sign them, then we'll see what happens. It may take a couple weeks."

"Weeks? I thought we could find out something maybe today or tomorrow? It's been four days since he failed to return from London."

"Four days, you say? We've had people missing four years. We treat everyone the same here. You've got to come down and fill out the paperwork. 357 West Thirty-fifth. Second floor. If I'm not here, ask for Rose. Rose Thornhill."

"You don't understand. I can't possibly come there. I'm...." April hesitated. Normally, she resisted the word she was about to use. Not that she was ashamed of it, she just didn't particularly like convenient labels that pigeonholed people. Especially if the person being pigeonholed was April Oliphant, but circumstances had conspired against her. Her father was missing, and the refrigerator was almost empty. Besides, she had never called the police before. It was all the fault of Shakespeare and his so-called *Ur-Hamlet*. No matter how important it might turn out to be, it was upending her life when all she wanted was...? Well, she didn't know, which was the real problem.

"I'm agora...agoraphobic."

"Sorry, you're *what*?"

"I'm agoraphobic. That means I'm someone who has a very entrenched fear of...never mind. I'll get down there somehow. Thanks for taking the time to call."

With that as a good-bye, she hung up, but not in anger. She just set the phone in the cradle, frustrated by her inability to conduct a simple conversation. She'd have to call Art Kass, the industrious limo driver who took her father to and from the airport. She could, of course, forget about filing a report, but what sort of option was that really? She was worried about her father, the one person in the world she could count on. The one person in her immediate family she truly loved. How could she possibly go on without him?

Something had happened to him, she just knew it.

7 A ROOM WITHOUT A VIEW

Enter the light.

And as the encompassing darkness began to fade, the recumbent man perceived a faint wheezing as his lungs slowly emptied and filled. Emptied and filled. Emptied and filled. Somewhere out there in space beyond him, a steady beat also began to seep into the recesses of his consciousness.

His mouth was desert dry, his tongue unable to move, no matter how hard he tried. All he wanted was a drink of water. And then another and another until the overwhelming thirst went away.

He could feel a sheet on top of him, a mattress underneath. His body seemed wedged deep into a groove he himself had created, and there was no way out, no matter how much he might have wanted to escape.

Then he heard a familiar sound...voices, he thought, but he couldn't make out the words. More than anything, he wanted the people who spoke them to come closer. To get him some water. To show him he wasn't lost and abandoned the way he felt he had been almost forever. If only he could open his eyes, at least make contact.

Sometime, he didn't know how much later, he heard something just as regular as the whooshes and beeps around him, but louder. The sound of feet, and words again, though he couldn't quite make them out. Only their warmth and comfort. If he could just respond, tell the person who spoke them that he wanted water.

Next the sheets rustled, followed by a warm hand on his. A gentle squeeze and more words.

He tried to rise up, but couldn't move his arms, not even to let them brace him on the mattress to either side. Concentrating on just one eye, his right, he tried to force it open. Again and again he tried until he felt the lid give way just slightly. He couldn't see anything really, just blinding light filtering through the void within. And he shut it again immediately, thankful for the darkness.

"Wa...water," he murmured through half closed lips. "Water."

He felt the hand on his tighten, at the same time a voice called out.

"He's back with us. He's awake!"

8 THE WORLD OUTSIDE

Too often it took something special, *very* special, to pry April away from the safety of her father's loft. She was all too comfortable now living above Oliphant's. In the beginning, it had been nothing more than a floor of an old factory building in the Garment District. She didn't know how many nimble fingers had sewed there in the decades before her father bought the five-story walkup. Tens of thousands probably. When he converted it, he had put in new appliances, new partitions. New everything. With her encouragement, he even added a new stereo system and large-screen TV. With all that, she asked herself, why leave? Usually she didn't have to because her father did all the shopping. In his absence, that particularly oppressive task had gone undone for almost a week now.

When Nick came into his life, they'd painted everything (except the exposed-fir sub floor) white. Shockingly white. The lamps, couches, tables, rugs, curtains were all white, too. So was the bathroom and as much of the new kitchen as possible.

April hadn't been at all certain she could take the immaculate brightness of it all when she first moved in. She liked it now...sort of.

Her father's place was just so different from the apartment in which she'd grown up in Stuy Town. They were a slowly disintegrating family of five then. Her father worked night and day at Schulte's, where he was always on call. Always unhappy, too, except when daddy's girl somehow managed to charm him unexpectedly. Now he spent most nights at Nick's.

Her mother was the dominant force behind Jarmila's Famous Guláš, the restaurant she still managed almost singlehandedly. With both parents working, baby-sitting fell to Teddy, who was eight years older and the lone source of joy in April's life then. If something had happened at school to make her cry, Teddy always managed to cheer her up. If she needed help with her homework, Teddy was never too busy to nurse an answer from her. If she (almost) never fell for other boys, Teddy was the reason why. Then there was her other brother, Lawrence, with whom she hadn't talked in years.

She had arranged an 8:35 pickup with Art Kass. Whenever she could not avoid going out, she called Kass's Deals On Wheels. This morning it was to take her to the Fourteenth-Precinct station house.

Her back against the windows, she waited inside Oliphant's, counting slowly down from 100 to calm her nerves. She didn't really want to make the trip, but then she never did. Unless Art had problems in traffic, he'd pull up at the scheduled time, or slightly before.

The short beep of a horn told her he was there. That was followed by the all-clear, a slight rap of Art's knuckles against the glass. Fast as she could, she stepped outside and locked up. Art made certain the door was secure, then led her head-down to the waiting limo. All so she would not have to cross an extra inch of urban horror known as the sidewalks of New York.

The inside of the Chrysler 300 was freshly cleaned, just as she knew it would be. The rear windows were tinted so that, with sunglasses, she could see little beyond her confines of glass and metal. Gradually, she began to relax and sink into the leather upholstery of the back seat.

"Still no Mr. O?" Art asked once he pulled into traffic.

"Un uh. I haven't heard from him in almost a week. That's why I'm going to the police. To report him missing."

"You don't think he's, uh...just fooling around some place?"

"You know Father. That's not really like him."

"I'll probably get a call to pick him up at the airport in the middle of the night."

"I wouldn't be surprised."

That morning, Art was his usual talkative self, caught in rush-hour traffic the way they were. He filled April in on the details of a cousin's wedding that past weekend. In the end, she half felt she had been there herself, all without having to find the right dress, the right wedding gift. The right escort! Art was a godsend, that's all she could say. Anywhere she wanted to go, almost any time, he was there to drive her.

"Did you hear?" he asked, stopped dead in a long line of cars waiting for a light. "Estonia declared its independence last week! Grandfather has outlived the curse of the Russian bear. He's free now."

She had never heard Art punch his horn quite the way he did at that moment. She figured it was his way of informing everyone around them of Estonia's newly won freedom. The sentiment behind this pure joy roused a tingling sensation at the base of April's spine. Forced daily to look out for suspicious strangers, she knew just how citizens of Estonia must have felt under Soviet rule. Always on guard for the one person who might spell their undoing.

"That's great news," she half exclaimed, trying to imitate his enthusiasm. "Think you'll ever go back to the old country?"

"Soon as I can, and often. Maybe for good."

"You'd actually leave the U.S.?"

"In a heartbeat."

"Well, you've almost made mine stop."

He pretended to cram down on the brake pedal.

"Should I call 911?"

"Don't even think about it, Mr. Kass. I was just speaking metaphorically. If you went back, what would I...I mean, what would Father do for limo service?"

"I have four other employees."

"All from Estonia!"

"No, just Juri and Alfons. Juri wouldn't go back for all the tea in Japan."

"In China, you mean? If you leave the country, will you give the service to Juri."

"Give? This is America, the land of capitalism. Why should I *give* away my cash machine? I'll keep running it from Tallinn."

"You're just euphoric now. It'll wear off."

"No, Carmen will wear it off for me. Her and the kids. They'll never move."

"I'm glad at least one of you hasn't lost her senses."

Art was too busy now tracking the street numbers to reply. Inwardly, April cheered on Carmen as he continued his upward count. Between Art's wife and his business instincts, he would never move back to Estonia, or so she hoped.

"There it is," he pointed to a drab, three-story brick-and-concrete building, which blended perfectly with that morning's somber sky. He pulled in across the street. Then, just as he had escorted her to the car, he waited until the street was clear and guided her toward the entrance.

"I'll park and wait for you," he told her.

"Shouldn't take long. I just have to fill out a few forms."

"Right. Say hi to your parole officer for me while you're at it."

Art had been watching too many cop shows, but then so had the entire nation. The streets outside were tame compared to the utter chaos that greeted her on entering in the dayroom. Head down, gaze narrowed, April hunted for the stairs to the second floor, trying to steer clear of all human contact. Certainly she wasn't going to ask directions. When she finally found the stairwell and started up, the bedlam of the station house thankfully fell away with each step she took. At the top, she almost collided with an officer who had just turned the corner.

"Sgt. Cochran?" she choked, recoiling from the man in blue as if he were a mugger.

"You mean the short, black cross-dresser in the fourth cubicle past the water cooler. Don't let him get to you. Had a long night. Usually he's not so fussy."

Her informant had turned the corner before April, in a state of near panic, thought to thank him. She slid down the center aisle until she reached the designated cubicle. Back toward her, an impossibly thin man, hair graying at the fringes, sat at the most untidy desk she'd ever seen.

"Sgt. Cochran?" She had tried to whisper, but her question came out like a dislodged cough drop.

"Yes?"

"I'm April Oliphant. I called yesterday about a missing person. You told me I'd have to come in and fill out some forms."

"Ri...ight. About your father, the four-minute Miles man. Oli...?"

"Oliphant."

"That's it, Oliphant." The pink palm of his otherwise bronzed hand shot out toward her. She pulled back automatically, arms frozen at her sides.

"Sorry, most women shake hands these days."

"It's not that."

He looked at her, lower lip receding beneath his overbite. "Yeah, yeah, that's right. You're the one that doesn't like people."

"I wouldn't put it quite that way. It's just...new places with lots of strange people."

Cochran's lips spread into a smile that could have melted the fillings in his teeth. "That's alright. I'm a policeman. I'm used to people steering clear of me. Not because of the color of my skin, but the color of the uniform, which, thank god, I don't have to wear anymore. Maybe we should take an interrogation room, if you'd feel more comfortable there?"

"That would be better."

"Just let me get the forms."

Cochran opened a desk drawer, pulled out some papers and led her down the hall, always out in front and slightly to one side. Somehow he knew instinctively how to handle her. Maybe he had an agoraphobe in the family? Or was he one himself?

The room in which he offered her a chair was barely larger than a closet. One that reeked of cigarette smoke, coffee, with a just hint of aftershave. The lone window was so dirty she couldn't tell where the glass ended and the clouds outside began. He set the forms in front of her, then took a seat on the opposite side of the table.

"It's not exactly St. Patrick's," he admitted, "but at least it's private. I can leave if you'd feel more comfortable filling these out yourself?"

For a cop, Cochran wasn't so bad. In fact, he was more decent than most people she didn't want to meet but had to. The very fact that he'd chosen to sit away from her said more than most politicians did in a lifetime. So what if her Inspector Clouseau was a little too effete with his thin mustache and short, curly gray hair? At least he was going to help find her father.

"No...no, you can stay." April inclined her head to the forms, then looked back up. "Thanks for being so...understanding."

"Mind if I ask a few questions while you write?"

"Certainly. I don't know what kind of answers you'll get, though."

As April cautiously filled in the blanks, she ended up telling Sgt. Cochran pretty much everything important about her father. She even went on at some length about the mysterious *Hamlet*, found by a man who possessed the most uncanny nose for rarities.

"He hasn't called in almost a week," she concluded, her hand cramped from squeezing the life out of her pen. "We usually talk every two or three days."

"Want my opinion, he's probably off on a pub crawl, or at some glitzy spa. Maybe he's spending quality time with a new lady friend?"

"*Lady* friend?"

April didn't know whether to be more offended by the term, or by the unlikely nature of the proposition. She thought her description of her father, while subtle, had made his sexual preferences clear. Especially the part about his estrangement from her mother, Jarmila, then their drawn-out, vindictive divorce. Cochran should have intuited it because he and her father were strange bedfellows perhaps only because they'd never met. Then maybe she had overestimated the man on the other side of the table.

"You mean his new *boy*friend."

"Interesting," the detective replied without a whit of interest animating any part of him. Certainly not his voice. "That makes it even more likely there might be something going on he doesn't want to tell you about."

At first, April thought Cochran was starting to sound like Nick Reed. To keep from telegraphing her feelings, she turned back to the forms, which she'd almost completed.

"What will happen once I'm finished with these?"

"I'll go over them, give them to Rose to enter. Then fax them off to the London police. They'll probably sit on some inspector's desk there for weeks, by which time your father will be happily back in New York running his bookstore."

"Isn't there any way you can speed things up?"

"You know the Brits. They're very thorough, but I'll see what I can do."

That was all April could ask. She felt better, much better, for having come to the precinct despite the ordeal it involved. She thanked Sgt. Cochran, who gave her his card and told her to phone him if she heard from her father. For his part, he promised to call in the unlikely case the London police turned up anything.

All she had to do now was brave her way out the door. Past all the cubicles outside. Find the stairs again. Then flee through the noisy squad room and pray to god Artur Kass was waiting out front in the sanctuary of his limousine.

9 EXIT *OTHELLO*

Huffy Charles Cassidy had been squirming in his folding chair for whole minutes it seemed, but couldn't restrain himself much longer. The object of his disaffection, the script he held in his hand, was an outrage that Avery LeMaster claimed to have been written by Shakespeare, about as likely, say, as Mayor Giuliani writing the Bill of Rights. In an effort to hold his tongue as their director droned on about the supposed virtues of the play, Charles turned his eyes up toward the hayloft, then into the rafters of the imposing old barn, silently praying the pigeon flapping above would decorate the director's golden mane, letting him know what even a dumb bird thought of his new *Hamlet*.

The barn, while not the perfect rehearsal space, was far better than the Players' cramped quarters in the East Village. Pigeons excepted, the air was fresh, the breezes plentiful and the space inside provocative almost to a fault. They also had the living room and library of Joanna's great old house for smaller rehearsals. It was such an ideal complex for a theater company, he wondered if she could somehow be persuaded to make this summer retreat an annual event? Robert, her husband, wasn't the most sympathetic sort, but if he got elected to Congress there might be whole weeks during the early summer when he'd be away in D.C., allowing them the freedom to rehearse well into the wee hours, Charles' favorite time of day, which was, of course, the night.

"Here, in the *Ur-Hamlet*," Avery continued, "we find Shakespeare grappling with a character type that would become so important in his later, more developed work. That is, namely, the affectionate, aging father. That's why we're so fortunate in having Charles with us to play Polonius. It's a perfect role for him with...."

"This Polonius is completely one-dimensional," Charles burst out, no longer able to hold back, "more of a fool, if anything, than he is in *Hamlet*, the real thing, not this absurdist melodrama. If you expect me to play this part, then you really have no idea who I am."

"It's the ham in you that doesn't like the part, Charles," he heard someone whisper behind him, and he hoped it wasn't Hope Wrightsman. "That's because you've only got twenty lines."

"Fifty-seven lines, Hope," he said, swinging around to face her. "Not a single one filled with anything but platitudes."

"Fifty-seven, but then who's counting?" It was Valerie Schneider, *his* Valerie, and not Hope who was speaking. Surely Valerie wasn't the one who had called him a ham, even if in jest. Scowling, he turned back around to face Avery.

"You can claim this is the greatest discovery since sliced Vodka, but I wouldn't buy a bottle even if I were still drinking. There's no way I'm voting to participate in this catastrophe-in-the-making. No way!"

Avery was about to offer some sort of cowardly response when Joanna signaled to him and stepped up onto the makeshift stage, set against the unused stalls of the barn. Charles still couldn't believe she supported the sure fiasco.

"I understand your concerns, Charles. They're very real. We're going out on the proverbial limb...."

"Limb, hell!" he interrupted again. "It's a twig, and a spindly one at that."

"Remember the rules, Charles. We allow others to speak fully and without interruption at company meetings, especially ones as important as this."

"What about Valerie and Hope when they interrupted me?"

"I didn't say a thing," Hope defended herself.

There it was, the truth. Valerie herself had called him a ham. Charles couldn't believe it, not after he'd stolen into her bed, and into her heart, or so he thought. He thrust his hand up to be called on again.

"That was my fault and I accept responsibility," Joanna continued. "The limb, twig if you like, may very well break, but then the entire tree's in danger of falling. You know that as well as I, Charles. We need to save the company, and I'm convinced Avery's found a vehicle to do just that. I've read I don't know how many scripts before, but nothing like this. I promise you we have something unique here, the youthful Shakespeare in highest spirits, full of imagination and wit. We simply cannot *not* put this on.

"To that end, Avery has agreed to set this in medieval Denmark, not in any other place or time such as Kuwait during the Gulf War, the location of our present *Othello*. It was a concession on his part, but he was willing to go along for the good of everyone." Here, Joanna looked around the room as if there were any other hands raised but his. "All right, what is it, Charles?"

"What if it's not by Shakespeare? Worse yet, what if it's the worst-case scenario? A forgery. The company would come away with so much egg in our face all you'd have to do is batter and fry us up at KFC."

"Avery assures me it's not a forgery. And he's an authority on early Shakespeare. We've been thrown a potential life-saver here, Charles. It could take forever to authenticate the manuscript, but this is what I propose and Avery has agreed. We keep all this under wraps until we get reports back from two people, a forensic chemist and a handwriting expert, to tell us if the paper and ink are from Shakespeare's time, and if the handwriting is his. If both reports come back in the affirmative, then we substitute the new *King Hamlet* for *Othello*. At the same time, we'll launch a media blitz the likes of which this company has never seen. It will guarantee we sell out every seat, and, more important, have donors lining up all the way to Newark. This could pull us back from the brink."

Charles was so incredulous he didn't even hear what Joanna had said. He, like the others at The Gables, had donated his services so the company could recreate, with minor insertions like Operation Desert Storm, their triumphant, 1978 *Othello* in an effort to rescue the Players. Charles was supposed to reprise his greatest role, Iago. The chance to do that offered him the possibility of rescuing his career from eight years in obscurity that had ended with a month-long recovery program that past March. Now Avery wanted him to play a light-weight Polonius in a *Hamlet* that had no real heart, no dramatic soul.

"That's no guarantee," he said in response. "What's to say Avery couldn't have written it himself?"

Charles heard a couple gasps go up behind him, telling him that he had perhaps gone a step too far; also that he was in the minority. But was it a minority of one? It just couldn't be.

"I am truly honored, Charles," Avery came to his own defense, "to think you could credit me with something as marvelous as the *Ur-Hamlet*. I can assure you that I did not write it myself. It was discovered by the noted antiquarian, Miles Oliphant, on a recent buying trip to England.

"I have spoken with his daughter, April, whom you all know. She told me she found it in a crate of items her father had purchased from an estate there. Now, here's what we all must do whether this vote succeeds or fails. Keep the new *Hamlet* among ourselves for now. That means we don't tell our husbands or wives, our partners or our friends. And especially not critics like Shawn Kirby. When we've got the reports back from the experts, we'll go public with everything. Whether the play's by Shakespeare or someone else, the publicity alone will provide a coup like the theater world rarely sees. And we'll build on that. Think what this could mean for the company."

At this point, Samuel Pilgrim, who'd come all the way from Hollywood to rejoin them as their Othello for ten weeks, raised his hand. There were few actors Charles Cassidy admired more than himself, and Pilgrim wasn't one, mainly because he had the ability to attract large audiences who knew and loved him for his four Action Jackson films. Still, Charles thought he knew how Samuel must have felt about being hired to play a commanding general only to find himself cast, in the new *Hamlet*, as a conscientious objector in the space of less than a day.

Pilgrim rose from his chair at the end of the front row and turned to make certain he had everyone's approval to speak. Nothing but smiles and nodding heads greeted him.

"I must start off by saying that I was not only miffed, but almost offended when Avery first came to me and laid out the barest of outlines for the new play. As all of you know, I was originally invited to play Othello because...well, because of my natural tan.

"Avery made no promises, didn't try to sway me one way or the other when he handed me the script. I set it aside for hours, almost didn't read it because I was so committed to *Othello*. But then I went through it carefully two times. Afterwards, I asked myself how many chances I'd get to play Othello in my lifetime, as opposed to how many I'd get to do Hamlet and in a totally new version of the play? All of you here know the answer to both questions.

"I agree with you, Charles. There is not a breath of Othello's power or pride or pain in this *Hamlet*, who's more like an over-sexed teenager than a duped, jealous lion of a man. But I do have the chance to create a role that no one alive has seen before. And it will force me to draw on resources I have never employed until now. How could I turn down an opportunity like that? How could anybody turn it down?"

Here, Pilgrim, who stood a good four inches taller than anyone else there, simply bobbed his head once to the company and sat down.

"Thank you for listening," he concluded.

Not much of a vote counter himself, Charles could tell from the greeting Pilgrim had received both before and after he spoke that he, himself, was now a minority of one. He would have packed his bags and left the Priestly estate right then if it hadn't been for the Players' charter that clearly stated: "On any and all matters of importance to the company, a meeting of members shall be called, and a full discussion entertained allowing all the opportunity to voice opinion. Only after this may a vote be taken. Consensus must be achieved on any matter placed before the company in this manner."

Not only was it Charles' right, it was now his solemn obligation to maintain his opposition to the bastard Hamlet, no *matter* the amount of scorn he might face from his fellow actors whom, until this juncture, he had thought level-headed and judicious *in extremis*. Either he was wrong, or they were. And he knew who would win the battle of wills.

10 CASE HALF SOLVED

"If you're ready, you have a visitor, Mr. Reed?"

The man's eyes blinked open. Alice Hall's broad shoulders and huge breasts, both clothed in starchy white, virtually filled his entire field of vision, still somewhat limited by the bandages wrapping his forehead. She had been calling him Mr. Reed all day but he knew that wasn't his real name.

"A visitor, you say, Alice? Even though I look a step away from death, I'm certain, I'd love company."

And he wasn't lying, either. It felt good to have people around once again, all sorts of different people. He didn't feel quite so lonely anymore and that thought buoyed him, though he wasn't certain why. Perhaps he had felt abandoned as a child? Or was that a more recent development in his life? At any rate, he wouldn't be losing his way now, not in a hospital with all these people around.

"You're improving every day, sir. And I'm not just saying that. You're one of the best patients I've ever had."

The man had never thought himself particularly nice, but then he'd been trying particularly hard to be that way, and evidently it was working.

The room in which he found himself was sterile and its whiteness seemed vaguely familiar. It needed something else, though, perhaps pictures to make it more appealing. Yes, that's what it needed, pictures to relieve the dreary sameness of the walls.

"Why, thank you, Alice. Show him in if you would. At least I hope he's a him." Here, the man called Mr. Reed managed a laugh at his own mildly mangled response, even though it still hurt to speak or move his head. She aimed a somewhat puzzled look directly at him.

"Oh, it's a him alright. A gentleman with the police."

"Police?" he repeated in a voice that shocked him with its crispness. "Whatever for?"

"I suspect they want to ask you how you came by the head wounds that brought you to us six days ago."

"Six days? Has it really been that long?"

The man had been told something like that before, but he simply couldn't track days and numbers. They meant nothing but added confusion.

"Yes, sir. The therapist can help you with things like keeping track. She'll be by later this morning."

The man remembered that particular she-devil clearly. Yesterday's session had been pure torture, especially the set of test questions she insisted on asking, questions that he thought would never end. He'd told her to go away, *nicely* of course, but she'd stayed with him a full fifty minutes, trying to rebend his mind in ways it did not wish to be bent.

A knock at the door set Nurse Hill pivoting in that direction. The wedge-shaped head of a man with rosy cheeks and thinning, almost translucent hair poked through the opening.

"Is he ready for me yet?" he asked.

"I said I'd call you," Nurse Hill said in a clipped voice.

"It's been twenty minutes."

"If I'm going to have to face the angel of death, I'd as soon get it over with now," the man told Nurse Hill.

"That's the spirit, sir."

"Detective Neville," the officer introduced himself.

Dressed in a cheap, gray summer suit that had seen its share of wear, he stepped in and approached the man's bedside under the scrutiny of his self-appointed defense counsel. Neville, who wore an easy smile, didn't seem so very intimidating.

"If we might have some privacy?" he asked the nurse.

In reply, she shot him another of her patented looks of disapproval. "Alright, but Mr. Reed's vital signs better not change. I'll be monitoring from the nurse's station."

"Where'd that formidable piece of work come from?" Neville asked once the door shut behind Nurse Hill. "The Sumo Academy?"

"She just likes me. Thinks my name is Reed, but it isn't, is it?"

"You get right to the heart of matters, don't you, sir? Maybe it's not Reed, but that's our best guess right now."

"Why do you say that?"

"Mind if I have a chair?"

"By all means."

Detective Neville's question chagrined the man, who should have offered the one chair in his hospital room to his guest before this. Evidently he was not trying to be nice quite hard enough.

"Please, if you would, tell me why you think my name is Reed?"

"More precisely William N. Reed? Perhaps you go by Bill?"

Neither William or Bill sent a flicker of recognition from the man's brain to his tongue, and he shook his head.

"Then perhaps Will?"

"Sorry."

"Too bad." The detective grimaced a moment here. "Let me try a different approach then. This is important. Do you remember anything that took place on the evening of August twenty-seventh? That would have been seven days ago."

The man tried hard to think, but his mind remained as impenetrable as stone. Finally, he had to shake his head in admission of his own inability to place himself, either in time or space.

"Then let me tell you what we've found out in the course of the past few days. We're virtually certain you were on your way to the Heathrow Guest House that evening. A travel agency in Grand Rapids, Michigan had reserved a room for a Mr. William N. Reed there, but he never arrived. That's why we're calling you William Reed, though, of course, that may not be your name. We've had the Grand Rapids police search the telephone directory there, but there's no William Reed, or Reed family they've been able to contact that recognizes that name. I've left a message with the travel agency, but they haven't yet returned my call, probably because it's a long holiday weekend there. Labor Day, I believe you call it?

"You were found lying on the sidewalk by a neighbor, blood stains on the bottom step of the guest house, where you almost certainly fell. It appears you were struck in the jaw by an unknown assailant. You collapsed and hit your head with considerable force on the step and rolled onto the sidewalk. When they found you, you had no wallet, passport or identification of any sort, and no luggage. In all likelihood, your assailants were thieves, looking for anything readily convertible into cash for a quick fix.

"We've managed to find the cabdriver who let you off at 12:03 a.m. according to his log. You paid with cash, so he didn't get your name, though he made a snide remark about the amount of your tip. Soon as the bandages come off and your face has healed sufficiently, we'll take a picture, publish it in the papers here and in Grand Rapids. Don't worry, sir, we'll find out who you are.

"Now, does any of this seem familiar?"

The man had been thinking precisely that same thought as the detective spoke. One thing Neville said set off an alarm, and that had to do with his missing luggage. He couldn't remember exactly what bothered him about it though, perhaps because his head felt like the inside of a clothes dryer with only a few items in it, and those kept tumbling hopelessly around. Since there was no light inside, he couldn't tell what they were.

If he were going to find out, he'd have to open the dryer door and start grabbing at the darkness.

11 A HOUSE IN THE COUNTRY

Shortly after they turned into the driveway, a huge, old yellow Victorian filled the whole of the windshield. Its shutters and trim were set off in lavender, leaded glass topping the ground-floor windows. Doweled bargeboards ran the length of the wraparound porch and under the eaves on all three levels. That same fussy ornament crowned the corner turret, though a lost piece stuck out like a missing front tooth. It would take a year of summers to restore the fading paint on the west side alone.

From April's vantage point in the backseat, she could see the side of the red barn the East Village Players used for rehearsals. Avery had mentioned it when he'd invited her to The Gables. If he had wanted to tell her the *Hamlet* manuscript was a fake, he could have done that over the phone. There had to be another reason he'd asked her to join him when they broke for dinner. She had not thought to tell him she couldn't possibly go inside.

"Would you do something for me, Art?"

"Who do you want me to get?"

What was the eastern-European gene that allowed Artur Kass to read minds so well? Perhaps he had some Gypsy blood in him? Then, too, he had grown accustomed to her various needs.

"Go inside, get Avery LeMaster and bring him to the car."

She went on to tell Art how to recognize the well-known director. He was tall and thoroughly distinguished with flowing, blond hair. Almost certainly he would be dressed all in black. Impossible to miss really.

While Art was gone, she surveyed cast members who'd carried dinner plates onto the porch to enjoy the warm summer evening. She recognized almost all of them, but the one big surprise was Samuel Pilgrim. He was standing there now, just like she'd remembered him in *The Heilmann Affair* on the big screen. Actually, no screen was big enough to contain Pilgrim. For that and many other reasons he was Hollywood's second largest grossing actor of 1989.

She was still staring at Pilgrim when Avery's gaunt, dark-clad torso cut off her view. If anything, he was even thinner than she remembered him. He hesitated before opening the door, then leaned inside to speak with her.

"Your driver tells me you want to meet in here," he said. "I was hoping you might come inside and say hello to some old friends of yours. They were excited when I told them you might be stopping by."

"Excited?" she gulped in disbelief, realizing as she spoke she could never do as he requested. The thought that they might want to see her again was simply too great a lie to believe. "Please get in, would you?"

"Of course, if you'll consider my request?"

She acknowledged his appeal with a brief nod.

"It's such beautiful country here, Art," she called out to the limo driver who stood just behind Avery. "Don't you think it would be nice to go for a little walk?"

"Sure. Know who I saw up there? Samuel Pilgrim. Maybe I'll try my Brando impersonation out on him. See if he won't slip my name to Scorsese or Cameron."

"Sorry," she apologized to Avery after the door shut and Art started toward the porch.

"That's okay. It's just like a Scorsese film anyway, asking the driver to take a walk while we talk. 'Com' inda the caar wid me. Wha' kinda deal ya wanna make, huh?'"

April couldn't help but smile at Avery's gangsterspeak. Even though he wasn't sitting particularly close to her, she drew up hard against the door on her side.

"Do you really want to know why I asked you to drive all the way up here?"

"Yes." That lone word escaped April's mouth before she had chance to consider.

"I've finished going through your manuscript."

"Yes, and...?"

"It's in my room. I forgot all about it when your driver told me you were waiting out here. You can take it back with you when you go."

April tried to restrain her anger, but couldn't. Too much had happened in the course of the last week to keep her bottled frustrations from spilling over.

"When I *go*? You mean you had me come all the way out here just to pick up my father's manuscript? Surely there was someone who could bring it to the city so I didn't have to hire a driver?" She paused, but only for a moment. "And another thing, *Professor* LeMaster. Have you ever considered the way you treat people who like...people who are your friends?"

"Alright, April. Alright," he cut into her little tirade. "You're right. I could have had someone deliver the manuscript to you. And, yes, I could treat people better. I do have character flaws, many of them. That's why I do theater. And if I'm the least bit successful at it, it's because I let those flaws drive the pieces I create. In reality, I had you come out here because, in addition to picking up your manuscript, I have a very special question to ask you, one that could only be made in person."

"What is it?" she asked, still angry at him. She felt as if The Gables were an amusement park and she was on a roller-coaster ride there. The build-up Avery had so skillfully created had made her more hopeful than she had been in years.

"Would you be our Ophelia?"

"Ophelia?" she gulped in reply. Avery LeMaster didn't often make verbal gaffes, but this was one of those rare blunders. "I thought the Players were performing *Othello*?"

"We were, but not anymore. That's what I've been trying to tell you. I'm convinced your manuscript is the real thing, probably written early in Shakespeare's career before *Henry the Sixth* or *Comedy of Errors*. The language, the nascent human insight, the well-shaped characters–they're all Shakespeare's. I don't know about the handwriting. I'm no expert. It could be his. No matter, your father has unearthed an amazing document. Far more important that the Players give the world a totally new, previously lost *Hamlet* than yet another *Othello*.

"You know the company bylaws. Charles refused to grant his consent for the longest time. I finally won him over by offering him the role of King Hamlet instead of Polonius. He's been brilliant so far."

April didn't know what to say. Her anger had not abated, but Avery had diffused it with this new information. In his estimation, the manuscript was the real thing. The play it preserved was indeed written by Shakespeare himself, and the man in the car with her intended to stage it. What was more, he wanted her to play Ophelia. It was all so far beyond anything she had imagined, she didn't know how to get there from where she was sitting. On the backseat of Art Kass's limousine beside Avery LeMaster.

"You actually want me to play Ophelia?"

"I do."

"That's so unreal."

No, it wasn't unreal. It was utterly impossible. That was the word she should have used. Impossible because she had not acted in almost two years, and for good reason. Fear. Cowardice. Perfectionism. People. All those people, onstage and off. She'd never told Avery about her little problem in that regard. She hoped he'd guess it.

If that weren't enough, there was Samuel Pilgrim. April could still hear the echo of her mother's words from summers she had worked in the Guláš kitchen. "Never alone with Horace in the back room. You hear?" "Don' share your tips with the black girl, okay?" "Why you want to be friends with them for, anyway?" If the thought of rejoining *all* the others wasn't already too much, now Avery wanted her to play opposite Samuel Pilgrim! Then April thought of a way out of her dilemma that would require no gushing confession of all those inadequacies.

"You can't put on the *Ur-Hamlet*. It doesn't belong to you."

He drew his head back and looked at her in dismay.

"Copyright protects the playwright, not the person who found the manuscript, or the owner. And, anyway, it doesn't apply to a play that's four-hundred-years-old. I was hoping you'd see the brilliance in this, April?"

"When do you open? In three weeks, right? I could never get the role down in that time."

"Twenty-two days actually, and I promise you could memorize your part in four or five. Even fewer, knowing you. It's not that long, as Shakespeare's plays go. And you'll be back working with some of the finest Shakespearians in New York. Richard Marz will be playing Polonius. I don't need to tell you, he's a true professional. Valerie, of course, will be our Gertrude. She'll do everything she can to help bring you along. And there's our Hamlet, Samuel Pilgrim."

"What about Hope Wrightsman? She'd make the perfect Ophelia."

"She broke her foot out riding with Joanna's son, RJ, day before yesterday."

There it was. Avery hadn't asked her to be Ophelia because he thought she was perfect for the role. He'd done it because Hope had broken her foot, and he had to replace her on short notice. Then, too, he'd probably offered her the part to assuage any qualms she might have about letting them use her father's new *Hamlet*. All this was more than enough to put him off the real reason she couldn't accept his offer.

"You have too much confidence in me."

"All of it justified. I saw how quickly you got to the source of Rosalind's being. How absolutely mercurial, yet controlled you were in *Menagerie*. You'd be the perfect love object for Hamlet."

"Love object?" The concept stunned April. How could he possibly think that she, the daughter of the most bigoted woman on earth, could play adequately opposite a black man? An icon of blaxploitation movies no less, movies like *Black Trash* and *Honkey Heaven*. It was unfathomable, and yet...yet at the same time redemptive. Which would have been so very beautiful if only Avery had known something about her mother, which he didn't. What was motivating this strange man on the seat beside her?

"Look, you've made your pitch," she told him. "I've listened. The truth is, no matter how strongly you feel I can do this, I can't. Now, please, I don't want to discuss it anymore."

At that point, Avery leaned forward, elbows on his knees, about to come back at her. Instead, he simply grimaced and reached for the door handle.

"I'm sorry. Very sorry. This is the perfect comeback role for you, but I respect your decision. I'll just run upstairs and get the manuscript for you so you won't have come all this way in vain."

Once the door closed behind him, April wondered if she'd done the right thing. Avery had given her an opportunity that would almost certainly never come along again. He'd offered her a chance to perform in the premiere of a newly discovered play by William Shakespeare. Not only that, she'd said no to something she'd often dreamed about. If only she knew why he'd offered her the role of Ophelia in the first place. She wasn't *that* good an actor.

She looked absently out toward the porch, which was vacant now. Avery would be down with the manuscript anytime. The moment she had it in hand, she wanted to drive off so temptation didn't overtake her. Cautiously she got out of the car, walked up the drive to the wraparound porch and peered in the windows, looking for Art to drive her home.

Avery had not lied on the phone when he told her about the interior of the Priestly place. The pocket doors downstairs had been opened so that the dining and living rooms ran together. Clamped to the balcony railing, lights angled toward the intimate stage used for smaller rehearsals below. A cardboard maquette of water-colored, castle walls ran around the perimeter. In all, a perfect little rehearsal space. Just moments from the actors' bedrooms upstairs and intimate enough to remove any hint of an audience, and the threat it posed.

A door to one end of the dining room opened to the kitchen where the actors stood around drinking coffee. A peal of laughter rang out from somewhere. Through the windows she caught sight of a crowd of about a dozen, most of the actors in the company. Memories of past *bonhomie* half paralyzed April as she stood there. All too soon she remembered how those times had lost their appeal and turned first awkward, then downright painful.

Finally, Avery appeared on the balcony landing, a manila folder tucked under his arm. His face had gone long, skin as pale as the walls behind him. When he started down the stairs, he grabbed the railing to steady himself. Something was wrong.

"I don't know what happened," he mumbled when he stepped through the doorway. His voice was so weak she could barely make out his words. "It's gone."

"What's gone? Not the *Hamlet?*"

He nodded, but just barely, to confirm her suspicion.

"But the folder?"

"A copy of the transcription I made from Elizabethan English to something more intelligible to modern ears."

How could she ever have been so stupid to let something as valuable as that manuscript out of her hands? The answer to that question was simple, of course. Avery LeMaster knew Shakespeare better than most people knew their own children. That was not the only thing. April had let her feelings for her former professor overcome her so-called good judgment. What would her father say? His old anger would rise up when he realized the enormity of his loss, and she'd be out on the street again.

"Could you have misplaced it?"

"Hardly. I know the value of that manuscript better than almost anyone. I did not just leave it sitting idly around. I kept it locked in my room, hidden to the rear of a bookshelf whenever I was out, at rehearsal...at dinner. Wherever. I took it out only to make necessary changes in my transcription."

"Who else knew about it besides you and me?"

"Everyone in the cast. That would be eleven...no, twelve others."

"That many?"

"Yes. More if you include Joanna and her family."

"If you didn't misplace it, one of them must have taken it?"

Avery LeMaster was, himself, among those staying at The Gables, but what motive would he, or any of them, have in stealing it? Only money and fame, life's two greatest aphrodisiacs.

"Perhaps."

"So what do we do? Call the police?"

"Not that. It would be in all the newspapers the next day, and we want to keep the project under wraps until we have more proof it's the real thing. I don't know how, but Shawn Kirby–you know, the *Chronicle's* critic–already has an inkling, I believe. If Joanna finds out someone here leaked news to him, there will be blood, you can count on that."

"We've *got* to find that manuscript."

"Don't worry, I will. It can't have been gone more than an hour. I consulted it for some small changes in the banquet scene we were rehearsing just before dinner. I'll gather the entire cast after you leave and tell them about it. If no one steps forward with information, I'll announce that they're not allowed to leave here until it's returned."

As Avery spoke, April heard footsteps on the creaky boards of the porch. She turned to see Art approaching them.

"Here's my driver," she said.

"This is for you," Avery said, handing her the manila folder he'd brought with him. "Just in case you change your mind about taking that part."

"I might as well be frank with you, Avery. I can never go out on stage again. I just can't."

"And I understand, perhaps more than you think I do. I promise you this. If you rejoin us, you'll have a room to yourself here. You and I will go through your lines one-on-one, then ease into rehearsals. Start you on scenes in which there is just one other person. You have two of them with Hamlet. One each with your father and brother. It won't be easy, I know, but I'll be with you the entire time."

"I...I simply can't."

"If that's the way you want it. Take the copy with you anyway. Without you, after all, we wouldn't have it. Read it and see if you don't think your father's discovery is sublime, remembering, of course, that it's the work of a very young Shake...n'bake."

Avery corrected himself comically because Art was on them now, and Joanna didn't want news of the *Ur-Hamlet* leaking out. April put her hand out formally, forcing Avery to shake it, then she scuttled down the stairs onto the sidewalk. How had Avery guessed her secret? He must have, or why else would he have offered to give her a separate room? Run through her lines alone with her? Ease her into rehearsals? All that when she had accused him, in her own mind, of stealing the manuscript himself. No one was in a better position to do that than the man who had talked her into loaning it to him in the first place.

If her father knew she'd let someone walk off with his discovery, he'd...well, she didn't know what he'd do, but it would be ugly.

As April closed the limo door, Charles Cassidy stepped out onto the porch and looked her way. Sinking into the back seat, she prayed he couldn't see her through the tinted glass. Much as she admired the great man on stage, their last fleeting real-life encounter had ended in complete disaster.

12 A NASTY HABIT

Sitting on the edge of his bed, Charles staunched a sniffle, righted his head from the lone remaining thin white line on the framed photograph of an old covered bridge he'd taken off the wall. It was the last of his stardust, and the thought terrified him. He needed it to endure the demands everyone was making on him, Joanna and that bugger-fuck Avery LeMaster especially. Scoring wasn't a problem. He'd found a source in town, but Freddie wanted money, which Charles burned through these days like fire through tinder-dry autumn leaves.

He had just survived an afternoon so awful that saying it came from hell trivialized the damage it had done to his ego. Avery had insisted that he was playing the king as if he were already dead, then encouraged Charles to think of Hamlet as his own son, but didn't realize that, in real life, he and Christopher had been estranged for months now.

It had all come about on family day at the end of his recovery ordeal. Christopher, who had come with his mother, stood up in front of everyone and told them how very much Charles was like his father, the great actor Desmond Cassidy, who'd come over from Dublin and torn through the New York theater world like a drunken storm. Married four times in his last twenty years, Grandfather Desmond had been an inveterate story-teller, who could talk his way out of any predicament, into any bed, through any mental lapse.

Charles had refused to speak to Christopher ever since that twenty-minute monologue had dragged him through the mud of his past. Refused to speak to him even now, though he loved his son in a way that often baffled him because he did not know how to deal with it, or his own stubborn refusal to talk to the only real piece of himself he had given the world.

Then there'd been Valerie Schneider. She'd been feeling terribly depressed after Avery had broken off with her during that past spring's *Dr. Faustus*, and that had made her vulnerable to his advances. The evening before, when they were in bed together, she'd told Charles she was still in love with Avery.

He had just inclined his head to the last line when two penetrating knocks almost broke down his door. No choice remaining, he sucked up what was left of the fine, white powder and dusted all traces from the glass surface of the photograph.

"Please don't come in. I'm dressing now," he called out perhaps twice as loud as need be as he slipped into his freshly laundered, white linen short-sleeve.

"Group meeting downstairs in two minutes," Avery informed him through the door.

"I thought I was rehearsing the denial scene with Valerie and Lenny?"

"There'll be time for that afterwards," Avery called to him, his voice already trailing off as he slipped off toward Samuel Pilgrim's room.

Taking a few deep breaths after that close call, Charles hurried down the balcony hallway in the other direction, just beating Craig Sommers to the bathroom. He threw himself through the door and locked it without apology to the startled, long-time company member. He turned on the cold water, grabbed some toilet paper and blew into it until he could clear no more phlegm. He'd have to do something about the running sinuses, but then remembered the Sudafed back in his room. Perfect. He doused his head in cold water, patted his cheeks until they were pink, repeated the process three or four more times, blew his nose again, then stepped out to find Craig still waiting for the bathroom.

"You didn't even flush the toilet," Sommers said.

"Didn't need to," he snarled back. The nerve of Craig, assuming he was unsanitary.

Fortified with three Sudafed, Charles descended the stairs. Everyone but Craig and Joanna had assembled in the front room where Avery had just finished setting out two rows of folding chairs. As people chatted, Charles found the perfect seat at the end of an aisle, and consumed whole minutes arranging it and preparing to sit down until Avery singled him out.

"I think everyone's here now, Charles."

"What about Craig?"

"In case you hadn't noticed, he's sitting right beside you. Unfortunately, Joanna can't be with us. She opted to play Lady Macbeth tonight, out campaigning with Rob. I've had to call this unscheduled meeting because of a disaster, one that threatens to ruin everything. The manuscript of the *Ur-Hamlet* appears to be missing. If anyone knows the least thing about it, step forward this evening, please. I won't ask any embarrassing questions, I just want it returned."

While Avery's eyes searched the room, apparently for someone to admit taking the precious manuscript, Charles wiped his nose and blinked back a few unwanted tears.

"Until it's returned, no one's to leave The Gables just to make certain...."

"No one's to leave?" Charles objected, thinking about the meet he'd already set with Freddie, his dealer. "That's preposterous. We're actors, not prisoners."

Avery ignored him.

"If it isn't returned by tomorrow morning, believe me, there will be questions asked. And Joanna will be the one asking them."

Even though more than sufficiently fortified against almost all shocks, Charles felt gooseflesh rise on parts of him that didn't know what gooseflesh was before Avery's last remark. A chill rippled through the whole room, in fact, causing a few to slouch an inch or two lower in their chairs.

"Sorry to have to bother you about this," Avery half apologized. "Now, let's get on with the schedule for the....Yes, Charles, do you want to tell us something about the manuscript?"

"Heavens no. This is about April Oliphant. You're not thinking of having her replace Hope?"

"I did offer her the role, but she seems inclined not to accept. I think everyone agrees by now that we're working with a rather remarkable script. We need an Ophelia with all the potential April can bring to the role. I'm willing to give her a day, two at the most, to sign on with us. If she doesn't, I have the perfect backup in mind. Someone almost as good."

At this point, Charles' head began to throb and the silhouette of Avery's body, no more than twenty feet away, was little more than a blur of black against the light, which hurt his eyes. He didn't really care now if young April came to their rescue or not. Or if the new *Hamlet* was the greatest play ever, which he remembered being fairly certain it was not. All he wanted to do was go back to his room, crawl into bed and pull the covers over his head. But he had rehearsal to go to, and no way to back out of it without giving away his own dark secret. His much-heralded recovery was little more than an illusion, fading rapidly into the past.

13 FACSIMILE

"There, now. What do you think?" Doctor Marshall asked as he held up a mirror for Miles to examine himself, but he pushed it away with unaccustomed haste. The face he saw there appalled him. Mottled dark greenish-blue to black, a bruise spread to both sides of the large bandage over his left eyebrow and forehead. Discoloration bled into his temple, around the socket and down his cheek. Lacerations from his fall still scarred that same side of his face, which he wanted to belong to somebody else. Anybody else. And he offered a silent prayer to that effect.

The now-familiar, wedge-shaped head of a man with rosy cheeks poked through the door.

"You're busy," Detective Neville said. "I'll wait."

"No, come in," Doctor Marshall replied. "I've finished with our patient for now. He is scheduled for additional tests in...." Here he looked at his watch. "In twenty-five minutes."

Having said that, he started to withdraw, but his progress was halted when the detective caught him by the arm.

"If you would stay just a few additional seconds, sir?" Neville requested. "I'd like you here at least for the start of my conversation with Mr. Oliphant. It won't require much of your time."

"Of course."

"How are you this morning, Miles?" Detective Neville asked.

"Confused."

And that's the way Miles wanted to appear. First the bandage had come off revealing the most hideous face he could imagine. Now it seemed the detective had somehow discovered the name Miles had known went with that face for the last day at least. He'd recalled it with remarkable clarity on waking the previous morning.

"Does the name Miles Oliphant mean anything to you?"

"Not really," he lied.

"I thought perhaps the shock of hearing it," the detective continued, "might just stimulate some of that uncooperative gray matter."

"At first you thought I was William Reed. Now I'm Miles Oliphant. Who will it be next? Margaret Thatcher?"

"I don't think you're quite ready to fill her shoes just yet. Besides, they might pinch a little. You see, we're certain Miles Oliphant's your name. Take a look at this. It was faxed last night. The quality of the image isn't the best, but it's definitely you."

The detective held up a blurry, black-and-white photo that, at first, was difficult for Miles to decipher. On closer inspection, he saw his own rather pleasant face staring out at him. A slightly lined forehead slid into unbruised temples, then to full cheeks and something of a weak jaw. Even though the photograph was old, he liked his face and hoped he would look half as good when the bandages were removed permanently and the bruises healed.

"You see?" the detective said.

"Yes, I believe I do," Miles replied.

"But still the name Miles Oliphant means nothing to you?"

"You don't know how badly I wish I could say yes."

"Let me tell you how we pieced all this together. That may help. Your daughter, whose name is April, went to my counterpart, a Sergeant Terrill Cochran, in Missing Persons in New York City. She told him that you were on a buying trip in England. So Sgt. Cochran faxed me a copy of this photo.

"From all appearances, you truly are Miles Oliphant. Sixty-one years of age. Five feet eleven inches tall. Weight 195. You were born in Milwaukee, Wisconsin August 22nd, 1930, and live in a flat above the store you own and run, Oliphant's Rare Books, at 13 West Thirty-ninth Street, that specializes in theater books. I have other poor photographs, again faxed from New York, that may help jog your memory."

At this point, Neville reached into his briefcase and extracted a loose stack of faxes–ten, eleven, perhaps twelve in all. They were entirely predictable, the very ones Miles himself would have included–the store and the loft above where he and April lived, other members of his family, Nick and then Nick's apartment. Through all of them, he played along with the English detective's show-and-tell. He could not afford to let anyone, especially Neville, know his memory was returning clearer than ever. He tarried perhaps a few moments too long over the photo of Nick in swim trunks taken at Bar Harbor the summer before.

"That's the person we thought you were at first, William Nicholas Reed. Actually, he goes by Nick. Nick Reed." Neville paused here as if waiting for Miles to say something. When he did not, the detective continued. "That caused a spot of confusion initially. You see, it was this William Reed in whose name the reservation at the Heathrow Guest House was made. When you were found unconscious and bleeding on the sidewalk outside, we wrongly assumed you were Mr. Reed. We know otherwise now."

"And this Nick Reed recognizes me?"

"We haven't sent any photographs of you yet. We were waiting for the bandages to come off. Then we'll send...."

"Don't" Miles interrupted rather brusquely. "I mean, if I truly am who you say I am, and I know this Nick Reed, I certainly don't want him seeing me the way I look now."

"We need confirmation to make certain you are indeed Miles Oliphant."

"Wait a few days until my face clears up."

"It will take at least another week," Dr. Marshall cut in, "perhaps as many as two for it to heal more or less completely."

"Two weeks!" Miles protested, feeling utterly defeated.

"I need to send photos to New York now," the detective insisted.

"What about my fingerprints?" Miles countered. "Can't you use them?"

"Of course we took them when we were first trying to identify you, but you must have committed a crime for your prints to be on file in New York. And you have no criminal record. All we need is one quick, painless photograph."

Miles was forced to think. "All right. If you let Nurse Hill apply some make-up to hide the worst of the bruising."

"And I suppose I could remove the bandage temporarily," the doctor conceded.

"That's alright," Miles said. "Maybe that will stir this Nick Reed's sympathy."

There were three or four more faxed sheets, one with the older of his two sons, Lawrence, looking rather defiant with his bull-nose and straight, perfectly cut, black hair. April hadn't sent photos either of his mother or of his wife, perhaps because one was dead and he'd divorced the other. Nor had she sent one of young Teddy.

"There's no photograph of my younger son," he said to Neville.

"Your daughter, who's very anxious about your condition, was probably in a hurry to get these to us. Maybe she didn't have a photo of him, or she simply forgot to include one."

Miles didn't recognize either of the last two photographs in the pile, perhaps because they were mug shots. Neville had slipped them in, either to trick him, or to produce a spark of recognition. Even though the ploy hadn't worked, Miles could have guessed who they were. The drug-addled teens who'd mugged him. "These don't look like family members," he said innocently enough.

"You're right, of course. The top one is Mick Hubbard, and that's Barry Brisco. We're certain they're the two youths who assaulted you outside the guest house."

"What makes you say that?"

"For one thing, they confessed. For another, a fence sold this to a jeweler on Portobello Road." Here Neville pulled a watch from his jacket pocket and handed it to Miles, who recognized it immediately by its off-color, gold case. It was the antique Rolex Nick had given him, engraved on the back "To M. O. On His 60th. Love N. R.."

"I promised the jeweler you'd pay the fifty pounds he laid out for it. Plus a finder's fee. A bargain at that price, I gather."

"Of course," said Miles hopefully. "Did you find anything else from that evening?"

"Yes, but nothing of yours, I'm afraid. The wallet, passport, anything else of immediate value went to fuel the pair's habit. Hubbard's been apprehended four times before and he's only eighteen."

The news unsettled Miles, but he didn't know why. If the police couldn't tell him anything more, he'd have to find out for himself, which further convinced him amnesia was the best cover he could adopt for his coming journey into the past.

"Any other encouraging news?" he asked somewhat cynically.

"There is one thing. Your daughter would like to speak with you about a matter of some importance, I gather, but only when you feel up to it."

14 REPRIEVE

"You look tired, Joanna," her brother-in-law Gene said. "Why don't you let me do that?"

She righted herself from loading the dishwasher. A sudden, sharp pain stabbed at her lower back, which she tried inexpertly to massage with her right hand. She was tired, dead tired, but refused to let that slow her down. It was the trip into Manhattan that morning that had done it.

She couldn't imagine how the handsome, impeccably dressed Lars Carlsson could be so unresponsive and yet smile through the whole of their ninety-minute meeting. By the end, he had the dollar-hardened Joanna thinking the East Village Players would be fortunate if the Eldridge Street Settlement House raised their rent only five percent for the coming season. And in the middle of a recession when theater companies were going belly-up faster than tropical fish in an overheated aquarium.

Even though Gene was an expert campaign manager, it sometimes seemed to her she was running her husband's bid for Congress, at least on the home front, at the same time she was trying to keep a dysfunctional family of actors together for the coming year. Perhaps neither absolutely needed her minute-by-minute ministrations, but she couldn't quite admit that to herself.

"RJ could volunteer," she said in reply, looking across the table at her son who was wistfully watching the rehearsal of the garden scene taking place in the living room just then. RJ had had one of his pieces published in *The Wittenberg Review* his first year in college. He could write like Poe without the dark streak, precisely the reason he was so valuable to his father's campaign.

"I said you could finish loading the dishwasher for me, RJ."

"Sure, mom, I will. Just give me a minute."

By this time, Gene was at Joanna's side, literally taking the dishes from her hands to set them in the bottom rack.

"If you insist," she told him. "I'm going into the study for a badly needed Virginia Slim."

That got the attention of RJ, who, more than his father, had kept goading her until she had quit six weeks earlier. About twenty times a day, she wished she hadn't listened to either of them. There was nothing like a cigarette, just one, to put a little distance between her and the rough spots in the road that she, and only she, could patch over.

"I'm coming with you," he threatened. "If I even see you reach for a match, I'm blowing it out."

"Just help your uncle. Check the study anytime you want. You won't smell a whiff of smoke. I'll just be lying on the floor, getting in a catnap. I promise."

That seemed to satisfy RJ, who picked up his plates and carried them to the sink. On her way down the hall, Joanna glanced briefly at Samuel Pilgrim as he pleaded to go to war with Charles, their King Hamlet. For the first time, she thought, things were starting to come together. Despite his tendency to act the part of drama queen, Charles was holding up to the challenge of his new role remarkably well, showing an intensity and focus she'd rarely seen in him before. She thought she knew what was behind it, but hoped her instincts were wrong.

She slipped past both actors and into the study, where she lay down, stomach first, on the thick, cradling wool fibers of the carpet. About to doze off, she thought about Gene and how, for a moment, she'd wished he'd followed her into the study, but then there was RJ.

As Joanna drifted off, she realized how little she knew about April Oliphant since she'd left the company. Little except for the buzz about her, which was considerable. She trusted Avery's unfailing instincts about actors, which had, with the exception of his initial coolness toward Samuel Pilgrim, always been to the Players' benefit. This time, however, he'd been so insistent about April, and Joanna hoped that wouldn't light a match to Valerie's increasingly short fuse.

She awoke to the sensation of fingers gently, but expertly kneading the muscles at the base of her spine. It had to be Gene touching just those parts of her back that needed touching. She often thought what would have happened if she hadn't fallen in love with Rob before she'd met his brother. Rob was certainly the more handsome of the two, but his looks got him in continual trouble. She was certain he'd had affairs on the side; how many, she didn't know. And now this new receptionist of his. On the other hand, she could always count on Gene for a little moral lift, just at the right time. She'd married an eagle when she really needed a robin.

"That feels so good. Keep doing it," she moaned almost sexually, startling herself. "I mean...." Well, what did she really mean? "You make it seem like everything's fine when, in fact, it's not."

"You're not worried about the election, are you?"

"No, not really. I'm invested in it only because Rob wants it so badly. Money, a nice home, marriage, all that doesn't seem enough for him somehow. Even if he wins the election, I wonder how long he'll be satisfied being a mere Congressman?"

"Men. You know how we are?" Gene said, letting his fingers continue to say what words couldn't.

"I suppose. You're not like that, though."

"You're worried about the new play, aren't you?"

There it was. Gene knew things Rob could never guess, perhaps never care about. What's more, he gave her a chance to talk about them when there was no one else she could tell her doubts about the Players' new production.

"How did you know?"

"A lucky guess, I suppose."

"It's just that we're taking such a gamble with...with this play. It's far riskier than Rob's bid for Congress. After all, someone has to lose elections. But in theater, especially in this economy, a loss could mean the end of so many dreams. Every time I think about it, I just...."

15 REMEMBRANCE OF THINGS PAST

"Is that you, Miss Oliphant?"

"Yes."

"This is Dr. Standish Marshall. I'm ringing from your father's room here at Middlesex Hospital. Didn't know if I would find you in at this hour. Let me just step outside if the cord will reach that far."

"Thank you so much for calling, doctor," April said, pivoting away from her computer screen. She focused instead on a blank patch of wall below the poster of Vanessa to help her concentrate.

"Yes, well, I'm just outside now. I'm pleased to report that your father's been making steady progress, physically speaking. Indeed, his motor skills are excellent and he can already walk fair distances up and down the corridor here. I wish I could say the same neurologically. As you know, we've been testing him daily with a set of questions, the same ones really. 'Who are you?' 'Where are you?' 'What day is it?' That sort of thing. His score improved steadily the first two days, telling me he's definitely over the disorientation, the lack of concentration and attention that generally accompany traumatic brain injury. At one point, he could even remember things like his nurses' names, the hospital he's in, how long he'd been here. But now...now I'm afraid sometimes he can't recall even his own name. It's most unusual really. His last MRI was normal. Physiologically, there doesn't seem to be anything wrong with his brain. I just don't know why he sometimes can't answer the simplest questions when he could before."

"Can amnesia be temporary, or fluctuate?" April asked.

"Indeed it can. In your father's case, I'm not certain it really is amnesia. And, if it is, that it hasn't somehow interacted with his early onset Alzheimer's. Maybe you can help? I'd like you to talk with him about familiar things...you know, family, business, anything that might interest him, really. See what he tells you."

"I'd be happy to."

"Before I take the phone back inside, however, something you mentioned last time could be of real assistance. You said that your brother might be in a position to help facilitate getting Mr. Oliphant a new passport to replace the one that was stolen. The consulate here has informed us that process could take as long as three weeks going through the usual channels. Perhaps you could inquire with your brother, see what he can do? The sooner your father gets back to familiar surroundings, the faster his recovery will be, I suspect. Maybe you could bring the new passport with you when you come to take him home?"

Her father's British doctor presumed too much. Far too much! He didn't know how difficult it would be to ask Lawrence for help. Hadn't even asked if she'd come to get her father, just assumed that she would. The English were not nearly as polite as they were said to be.

"I'm afraid I won't be coming myself," she told him. "There's far too much to do here at the store. Perhaps I could prevail on my brother, or Father's friend, Nick Reed?"

"As I say, there's nothing wrong with your father physically. But he will need someone to accompany him on the return trip to the U.S.."

"And for that a passport is essential?"

April knew the answer to that question without asking. Her brother ran the office of councilman Raphael Leroy, who sat on the city's Committee on Immigration. If anyone could speed up their father's passport renewal, it was Lawrence. April hadn't spoken to him in the longest time, but she'd do almost anything to help her father.

"It is."

"I'll see what I can do then. It may take a couple days."

"Your father wouldn't be ready to leave before then anyway. I'll put him on if that's alright?"

It was more than alright. April hadn't spoken with him in almost two weeks now. She had to think what to say. The doctor had given her no real hints.

"It that you, Dad?"

"That's who they say I am anyway."

"Do you know who I am?"

"Dr. Marshall tells me you're my daughter. Until a couple days ago, I didn't even know I had one."

"Well, you do, and there's Lawrence, too. He's your son. He's thirty-eight and has a good job working for a city councilman. And your friend Nick...Nick Reed."

"Yes, I've seen a picture of him, you and Lawrence too. But there's not one of Teddy. Why?"

She would have to tell him about Teddy sometime, but that was the last thing he needed to hear in his present condition. Something like that could set back his recovery for years, and she had no intention of letting that happen. So she lied conveniently.

"I couldn't find any."

"Well, fax one to me when you do. I hope he looks better in real life than you and Lawrence did in those awful photographs. The machine they used to send them does a pretty good job of making monkeys out of the both of you."

At least her father hadn't lost his sense of humor, or his bossiness. She thought it strange how he, anyone really, could lose his memory, and yet some aspects of personality remained pretty much intact. So she decided to start in with that.

"I probably looked the same way the day you welcomed me home. Do you remember? That was almost five months after I quit *Menagerie*. Lost my apartment, too. I'd ridden the subway to stay warm, a horrible experience really. Thankfully there was almost no one else on the train. In the morning, I got off to clean up at the library. It hadn't opened yet, so I walked the neighborhood to keep from freezing. I found myself looking in your window at a display you'd arranged on Brecht.

"You walked right up behind me to open early. I ran off toward Fifth Avenue, but you caught up with me. Invited me back inside. We had coffee and a muffin. Both were nice and warm and I didn't want to leave. Then you told me every production you'd seen me in. That's how our life together began all over again. We didn't get off to the smoothest start, but thank god you weren't mother. I could have never moved back in with her. You must remember some of that?"

It took forever, it seemed to April, before her father responded that he thought he did. His voice was so hesitant, so distant, though, she felt certain he was lying.

"Your store, on Thirty-ninth Street, is the second you've owned. There's a display room on the ground floor where a previous owner had partially blocked the windows with an ugly stucco facade. Originally, women's blouses were sewn upstairs. A psychic was renting an office on the second floor when you bought the building. The first floor holds upwards of 4,000 titles. You restored the original facade and converted the top floors into apartments where you...."

"Enough!" her father protested. "I...I can't keep up with all that." April had overwhelmed him. All because she had wanted to help so much, and there was still one question she had to ask.

"Don't worry. It will all come back to you."

"I think that's probably enough for this afternoon, Miss Oliphant," Doctor Marshall cut in. "Progress in cases like this never takes a straight line. Thank you so very...."

"Could I ask just one question?" she half pleaded. "No more information about Miles Oliphant, his family or the store, I promise."

In the pause that followed, the doctor had evidently covered the mouthpiece. He must have been asking her father if he thought he was up to another round with his daughter.

"Here he is," Marshall said. "Please make your question brief."

There was almost no way April could be brief, but, for her father's sake, she had to try. That meant eliminating all details surrounding the manuscript she had found in the shipment he'd sent from England.

"You bought some old family letters, and a complete run of a periodical, *The Censor*, right before your accident. Do you remember anything about a manuscript among them? A manuscript of an early version of Shakespeare's *Hamlet*?"

In the silence that followed, April prayed her father would say yes. Any piece of information, no matter how trivial, would help her. She had a decision to make, an important one. She badly wanted an excuse, any excuse really, to decline Avery's offer to join the Players at The Gables. That way, she could go on living a comfortable life, comfortable for her at any rate, and be there to help her father when he got back to New York.

"A manuscript by Shakespeare, you say?" he replied. "I...I wish I could help you. Is it valuable?"

"It could be, yes."

"Then you're keeping it in the vault?"

April hadn't expected that question.

"Actually, I've sent it out to Elizabeth Duke," she tried to sound convincing, "to have her analyze the handwriting."

"Just checking. I'll want to see it when I get back. It might help me...remember some things. You have no idea what it's like...."

His voice fell away. Then Dr. Marshall came back on.

"I think that's enough for today, Miss Oliphant. Thank you for your assistance. Good-bye."

He hung up without waiting for April's reply. Phone in hand, she sat at her desk wondering if her father even remembered the sale? Where it had taken place? From whom he had purchased the collection? Had he spotted the manuscript, unrecognized by its owner, amidst all the papers? Perhaps, too, it had been buried among them, unseen even by the usually observant Miles Oliphant?

Then there was another, far worse problem. Her lie about the location of the manuscript. When her father got back and found it wasn't at Dr. Duke's, he'd start asking questions. When she couldn't answer them he would, of course, blame her for its theft. Then she'd be out on the streets again, and she feared that more than anything.

Her fears, his anger. Those two things about April and her father, each circling around and biting the other by the tail, would never change.

Avery had to find that manuscript!

16 KNOTTING THE NOOSE

"Almost, Charles. *Almost*," Avery said in his usual diplomatic way. "But I want you to remember that King Hamlet is leaving home to fight a valiant opponent, Fortinbras of Norway, who may well dash your ambitions. Even kill you in battle. In that case, you will never see your wife or son again. I want you to bring the King's predicament home to the audience. He knows this may be the last time he sees his beloved family, but he doesn't want to convey that to them. Now, again from 'I leave thee for a brief time....'"

Without a moment's hesitation, Charles leaned back from the table, as if in conversation with Polonius, then slid off his improvised, apple-crate throne, put one hand on the Queen's exposed neck and began caressing it almost erotically while placing the other squarely on his son's shoulder. Charles fought to keep a chill from rippling the muscles of his lower spine. He had to admit it was not a bad effect, even if it was Avery LeMaster who had inspired it.

They had been rehearsing the departure scene in the barn for almost forty minutes now, Steve Benedict, the stage manager, taking notes. The new play generously included not one, but two banquet scenes, including virtually everyone in the cast, which was a sure sign of Shakespeare's youthful, exuberant spirit, or so their director claimed. Big scenes, not intimate ones. Life at full-tilt, not in its poisonous decline, a course which Charles, himself, had experienced too fully for his own good.

This time Avery let the action continue as the king drew his son toward the front of the makeshift stage. It didn't matter that their Hamlet, Samuel Pilgrim, was twice Charles' size. In hiring the Hollywood hunk, Joanna had skillfully tried to load the dice in the Players' favor. This time, perhaps, she would crap out on her first roll. A decent Hamlet could always play Othello; not so easy the other way around.

Hamlet. I do not understand why you will not
　　Let me take arms and fight beside you, sire?"
King. You are a youth of brain made more....

Those first few words came out sounding like so much crowcaw, hardly the voice of a forceful monarch. Charles did not wait for Avery to stop him. Instead, he held up his hand in acknowledgment of his miscalculation, and started over again.

King. You are a youth of brain made more than might
　　Your place must be in Wittenberg with peers
　　For scholars play at combat with their words
　　Not with such metal as turns flesh to blood.
Hamlet. Do not accuse me with such unjust words
　　For students follow in their teachers' ways
　　With voices strong but actions weak indeed
　　The books they praise do armor me in ice.
　　Do take me with you, Father.
King.　　　　　　　　　　　I cannot
　　Offend your mother and her gentle kin
　　In truth, you are far better liked by them
　　Than by the troops that follow me to Norway

Seeing the king arguing with his son, Richard Metz, their new Polonius, stepped forward and intervened, consummate courtier that he was.

Polonius. Your absence from the table pains the queen
　　For she would see you two more closely bound
　　In this a time that draws one from his books
　　Before the other's deeds will fill them full.
King. The queen's place in my heart is deep and true
　　No more of this, we must return to her.

With that, the director's entire body arched backward as he launched a look at Charles that seemed intended to chastise him by means of visual power alone. He thought he knew every gesture in Avery's directorial repertoire, but he could have sworn he'd seen nothing quite like this before. The man-in-black never said a thing, not one word, leaving it to his victim, who was never at a loss for them, to fill the dead space that caught everyone in the barn struggling to escape its gravitational pull.

"A couple lines are hardly sufficient to end an argument between these two forces of nature, the king and prince," Charles struggled to explain himself with a sniffle that forced him to search his pockets for tissue that he carried with him continually now, even though it was summer. "Look, Avery, I've done *Hamlet* under four different directors in my brief lifetime, twice in the title role, to no small acclaim I might add. So I know more than a flipping thing or two about the play. Shakespeare, even in his early years, would have given the king a far stronger way to end the scene."

"Thank you, Charles," LeMaster replied. "Now, if we may get back to...."

"And another thing," Charles went on, incapable of shutting his mouth. But this time he was looking up at Samuel Pilgrim who seemed somehow shorter now than he was in reality. "Your Hamlet's too timid, Sam. Not nearly brash or daring enough. Yes, he's everything his father says he is. Bookish. Peaceable. More comfortable in the company of women. You should make the audience feel that Hamlet's also a man. Fire should rage beneath his introverted ways. Remember, he's been put in school and kept there by his family. And overshadowed by his forceful, angry father. The son's in rebellion against all of this, so, if he's deferential, his is a deference with balls. If he's attracted to Ophelia, it's not only because he senses a kindred spirit in her. He's got a hard-on for her. Even in this version, Hamlet's a real person, a mix of mama's boy and Father's sword."

"You're so full'a shit, Charles, your hair's starting to smell like an outhouse," Pilgrim replied, the tip of his powerful index finger coming to rest on Charles' runny nose. "Avery didn't hire you to play Hamlet; he hired me. I can motivate my character just fine without your thick-Mick help. I don't believe in picking on someone who's had two too many, but if you ever call me Sam again, I'll rivet your tongue to the roof of your mouth. The name is Samuel."

"I haven't had a thing to drink, nor am I a thick-Mick. If you want to engage in racial epithets, I'll...."

"Alright, you two. *Alright*!" Avery stepped in to break up the impending fight he had ignited, and Pilgrim seemed more than willing to finish. Backing down as gracelessly as possible, Charles finally saw what Avery was really doing, or thought he did. He was allowing Charles to spin the hemp, weave it into rope, then tie the noose around his own neck. All the clever director would have to do was press the lever for the trap door, and Charles would go tumbling into an oblivion he had willed upon himself.

He had stopped a pace, perhaps two, short of that precipice. No coward, Charles could step off at any time, or so he told himself. He simply would not give LeMaster the satisfaction of making him take the plunge. Someone was going to have to push him.

At that moment, he figured, most of the cast would eagerly volunteer for that assignment, with Valerie Schneider, his own Valerie, in the lead.

Charles tried to dredge his mind for ways out of his dilemma, but if there were any his vision was too blurred to see, let alone embrace them.

17 BROTHER LAWRENCE

April hadn't seen her older brother since Teddy's funeral, and then it had been only from the rear. He didn't even know she was in attendance, which was the way she had wanted it. She had waited to enter until the service had begun, tried to keep from sobbing so she wouldn't give herself away. Snuck out before it was over. She hadn't even gone to the cemetery, for which she would feel eternally damned.

Thank god for Art Kass or she never would have found the new, yuppie corner mall where her brother had his office now. The new quarters were sleekly modern. Everyone but the receptionist–a young black man with short, curly hair and tapered sideburns–seemed to have an office. It took not much more than a second for April to spot her brother's. The prominent nameplate on the door read LAWRENCE OLIPHANT, CHIEF-OF-STAFF. Even without that, she could have guessed where he hung his hat. The distinctive, raucous bite of his voice easily penetrated the thin walls. Pictures of Councilman Leroy with mayors going all the way back to John Lindsay hung behind the receptionist's desk.

"I'm Hector Ortiz," he introduced himself.

"April Symonds," she replied, trying to sound at ease with the pseudonym she'd used in making her appointment. She was certain her brother would duck out if he were to know in advance she was coming.

"Any trouble finding us?"

"Not the least."

"You're here about a problem with your landlord?"

"That's right." April had spoken truthfully this time. Her father *was* her landlord, and had a problem that had become hers now.

"And you've already spoken the city's department of housing?"

"That wouldn't help in this particular matter, I'm afraid."

"I see. Well...you're here already. It might be a few minutes. Someone slipped in ahead of you."

April could tell as much by the sound of her brother's voice. It had risen in the short time she'd been there so that she could make out almost everything the two men were saying through the cheap walls. It would have been foolish for her to expect anything other than angry words. He was, after all, Miles Oliphant's son.

"Who is he with?" she couldn't help asking when the profanities that carried into the outer office got to be too much.

"Assemblyman Lutz. Things between them can get heated sometimes. My vocabulary's improved about a thousand percent since I started working here. Unfortunately the words I've learned won't get me into Harvard."

"You might be surprised."

"Not much surprises me after working here thirteen months."

Suddenly, the chief-of-staff's door flew open and a beefy man in a limp, seersucker wash-n-wear burst into the reception area.

"You need a shrink, Lawrence," he suggested angrily. "A *good* one."

"I got no use for those brain-twisting mindfucks. I've paid them thousands over the years, and what's it got me? Prescriptions for drugs with names like a bunch of tropical fish. Put me in an aquarium anytime."

"An aquarium with padded glass so you don't break the walls every time you crash into them. If the councilman doesn't want to support the listing of Newton Creek for cleanup with CDEP, we'll go around him. It's that simple."

April's brother said nothing further as Lutz waded out the front door. Instead, he stood frozen just inside his office, staring at April. Ortiz nodded that it was her turn.

"April," Lawrence managed, holding his arms out toward her. "I didn't know you were here."

Awkwardly she evaded his attempted embrace, entered and sat in a chair that still retained Lutz's warmth.

If the office manager suspected she was someone other than April Symonds, she couldn't tell. Her back was toward him. The door shut without complaint from him.

"To what do I owe this unexpected surprise?" Lawrence asked, attempting a misplaced smile.

"Business...purely business," she replied crisply. "I need a favor. Believe me, if I knew a better way of going about it, I wouldn't be here."

By now, the chief-of-staff had assumed his place behind his desk. He leaned forward on his elbows to take his sister in. He had aged since Teddy's funeral, the last time she had seen him. His hair had thinned. The flesh of his face had gathered, but in the wrong places, making him look almost sinister. He sported his usual summer tan from time on the Sound. All this was set off by a maroon bow-tie, the real thing, she was certain, not a clip-on.

"How can I help?" he asked, all business now.

"Dad's stuck in London without a passport. His was stolen in a mugging that left him in a coma for six days."

"My god, I didn't know!"

"I didn't want to trouble you. He's recovering, but has some memory loss."

"I'll pack my bags tonight, go right over."

"He would prefer that you didn't."

Their father hadn't exactly said as much, but April knew how he felt. If she was wrong, it didn't matter. She didn't want Lawrence going. Too many old, bad memories for her father to deal with. Besides, Nick had already volunteered to make the trip.

"I need your help in getting him another passport as soon as possible," she continued. "The doctors think familiar surroundings will help his memory."

"This is not the fucking State...sorry, the State Department, April. I can grease some wheels, yes, but others are beyond my sphere of influence."

She pushed herself up from her chair. "If there's nothing you can do, then there's nothing you can do. Sorry I wasted your time, Lawrence." She turned to leave.

"Wait a minute, April. Please! I didn't say I couldn't, just that it's a stretch. I'll call in some old markers. See what I can do. I'll need the particulars, though."

"You sure it isn't too much of a stretch?"

"Positive."

"There." She set an expired passport of her father's, a copy of his birth certificate tucked under the front cover, on her brother's desk.

"Tell him to keep checking with the embassy," he advised. "It could take a couple days, minimum."

"Thanks." Without looking directly at him, April continued toward the door and opened it.

"Don't go, not yet," he pleaded. "I haven't seen you in two years. I've missed you."

"Help get Father back into the country and maybe I'll believe you. Another thing, I don't want you going anywhere near him. No calls either. And certainly nothing about Teddy. I don't want you setting back his recovery."

With that, she strode out into the front office, passing Hector Ortiz almost on a run.

"Oh my god," he exclaimed. "So you're *that* April. Your brother talks about you all the...."

She was out the front door before he finished, which was just as well. She dashed to Art's waiting limousine and threw herself inside, burying her head in leather of the back seat to keep Art from hearing her cry.

18 DANGEROUS INTERSECTION

Charles turned his head toward the sky and exhaled. He felt so cold, he swore he could see his own breath. Or was it his vaporous, weary soul escaping his mouth that momentarily made the stars overhead go blurry? He'd borrowed one of Rob Priestly's golf jackets from the front closet, but, no matter how tightly he pressed his wrapped arms over the precious package he'd tucked under his waistband, he just couldn't keep warm, even on a summer night.

A pair of headlights appeared over a rise in the road, then dipped below it just as quickly. He glanced at his watch again. 4:21 a.-goddamn-m.. In the morning. A little too late for night owls like him, too early for *morning* birds like Joanna, part of the reason he'd sneaked out of the house and hiked he didn't know how far to the intersection with U. S. 9. He didn't want her or anyone else to know he'd taken a brief leave of absence from the rural penitentiary which their warden called, ever so quaintly, "The Gables." As if the number of the house's pointy peaks somehow made up for all the torture and confinement below that had necessitated his escape. What Joanna initially advertised to them as a "month's vacation in the country" had turned into an eternity in a Siberian gulag where it was so cold on summer nights not even ten golf jackets would keep him warm. Charles needed something else to do that, which was the only reason he was standing there at that god-forsaken intersection.

Twin beams of light again fanned out in brief, V-shaped patterns as they crested the next hill, then settled back to the asphalt. The vehicle behind them was certainly going fast enough to be driven by Harold Forsyth, which raised Charles' hopes. Warmth. A little friendly banter. Cash. But the prospect of all those things went speeding by. And he raised his fist in the direction of the reckless, retreating driver.

Then he heard a little chirp, and for a heart-seizing moment he thought Joanna MorningBird had come up behind him warbling a mating call. But when he turned back around, he saw the shimmying break lights of the speeding car. Then the glaring backups flashed on beside them, and the car started coming toward him in reverse almost as rapidly as it had approached from the opposite direction. The driver slowed and the passenger door swung open.

"That you, Good-Time Charlie?" Harold's voice cut through the air, quiet now except for the Beamer's purring engine.

"Who the hell else would you expect standing at a country crossroads, four-thirty in the morning? You're half an hour late."

"Ease up. Remember who you're talking to. The art doctor making house calls at this godawful hour. And you're the patient who called him. Get in. You'd better have something good for me."

Before Harry had finished speaking, Charles had the door shut behind him.

"Mind turning up the heat?"

"Heat? Jeeesus, Charles. You weren't lying on the phone, were you? You really are bad off."

Still, the dealer's hand snaked in front of the dashboard lights, turned a knob and Charles experienced an almost instantaneous surge of warmth. Gradually, he relaxed into the plush comfort of the bucket seat.

"Thanks."

"So what are you doing all the way out here in the country? I had you figured for a city boy?"

"You figured correctly. To explain what I'm doing in Oakville would require an eternity, and it feels I've been stuck here at least that long."

"The meter's running."

"I wouldn't expect anything less, but some other time. If my R.A. finds I'm not in my bed, it'll be a week in solitary on bread and water. And she gets up when most of the rest of us are just going to bed. Or at least I am anyway. I've gotta get back."

"Then let's get on with things. What fabulous painting do you have for me this time?"

"Something far better than the one you practically stole from me last April, that's for sure. But, well...you see, it's not a painting."

"Too bad. But if it's better than that Sergeant, it's got to be something like a Rembrandt etching? Maybe a drawing by van Gogh?"

"Better than that even," Charles said, forgetting entirely about Joanna in the warmth of the car.

"So tell me?"

"It's this."

As Charles spoke, he drew a plastic envelope with a sheaf of very old papers from under his belt.

Eagerly, Harold switched on the overhead light, and took the packet from Charles.

"What's this?" he said after flipping through four or five pages. "There aren't any drawings here."

"You're right. It's something far more valuable."

"I sell art, Charles. Expensive, unreportable, untraceable art, not your Grandma Mabel's letters, even if they were written to Franklin Socialist Roosevelt. That's not my métier. You said over the phone you had something worth millions. Why the hell do you think I drove all the way out here?"

"This is worth millions. This is a manuscript by...."

"I don't care if it's by Shakespeare," Harold interrupted, "if it hasn't got pictures, I don't handle it."

"No, it doesn't have any of the pretty pictures you get from me for pennies on the dollar. But it so happens that it *is* by Shakespeare, Harry."

"Really?" the dealer said, backing off a little.

"You know how many manuscripts there are today in Shakespeare's hand?"

"No, but I've got a hunch you're going to give me a sneak preview."

"None. Zero. *Nada*. That is, not until this one."

"I don't know a thing about manuscripts. How do I know this is not some bodice ripper by Shakespeare's wife, Anne What's-her name?"

"Hathaway. Here. Check it out. For starters, call the library and ask them to look up a play under the title *Ur-Hamlet*. Better yet, go there and look it up yourself. Then make an appointment with any antiquarian bookstore in the city, any store but Oliphant's. They'll give you ten thousand down for it, sight unseen just to have skin in the game."

"A manuscript of *Hamlet*, you say?"

"Something like that."

"And you want your normal percentage?"

"For starters. And if your man manages to sell it for more...and he will, I'll expect my usual twenty percent. There are ways of checking the sales too, Harry."

"You don't have a provenance for me, do you?"

"Sure. William Shakespeare, Esquire. Will Shakespeare, Jr. Shakespeare the Third. The Duke of Fuckingham. Somebody Oliphant. The Commander-in-Chief, then Charles Cassidy."

"More likely the cokehead-and-thief."

Charles simply glared at him in the greenish light.

"Okay, so you don't have one," Harold went on. "I'll give you a thousand."

"Two, or it's no deal."

"You yourself just admitted you stole it. It's not like the usual stuff you sell me from your mother's house. And it has no provenance."

"I'm not backing down. Two thousand as an advance on millions, Harry. Millions."

"Fifteen hundred. Cold, hard cash."

"I don't have time to argue. Count it out. I've gotta get back before the cock crows."

Harry drew out his wallet and started thumbing through hundred-dollar bills. "What if it turns out you found some old paper and just scribbled out gobbledygook because you needed a quick fix?"

"You still haven't paid me what you owe on the Sergeant."

"Yeah...yeah...yeah. Tell me, where do you manage to get coke out here?"

"Wake up, Harry," Charles said, taking the fistful of bills and sliding out into the nighttime cold again. "Look at the houses you drove past the last few miles. This place is Fort Knox-on-the-Hudson. And where there's money, there's snow. Even in summer. It's cold enough for it, that's for sure."

"Check your source. You never know what they cut that stuff with."

"This guy's cool. Trust me."

"Stay in touch, okay, Charlie?"

"If I don't get my head handed to me going back in the front door. Remember, you can call anyplace about Grandma Mabel's letters there. Just not Oliphant's bookstore."

Charles shut the door, waved once, and stuffed the roll of bills in his pocket without counting them. He could do that back in his room. At least it would be warm there. Besides, Harry wouldn't dare short him for fear of losing access to the paintings in his family's collection.

Scuffling into the closest approximation to a run he'd attempted in months, Charles set off toward the Priestlys', praying he wouldn't see a light on in their bedroom, or worse yet in the kitchen. He'd never be able to sneak back in then and call Freddie Jeffers to set a meeting time to make the cold deep down inside go away.

19 A NEW OLD FACE

"Do you know who I am, Miles?"

He certainly did, but he wasn't going to admit that to the young Apollo, face beaming like the sun, who stood with a monstrous array of brilliant flowers—reds and oranges and purples and yellows—tucked under one arm. Nick carried perhaps an extra pound or two around his mid-section and had slight wingtips denting his blond hair, but he still looked as good as he did when they first met. Perhaps it was his hesitant smile, his sultry blue eyes that completely collapsed the distance between bed and door. Certainly Nick was the most appealing thing that sterile hospital room had seen in weeks.

"Sort of," Miles faked forgetfulness. "You're Nick. Nick Reed."

"You do!" the younger man said, approaching the bed with flowers outstretched. "You remember my name. From the way April described your condition, I thought it was far worse."

Within seconds, Miles found himself wrapped in inviting arms and debilitating odors. Nick had forgotten his allergies. As gently as possible, he eased the arm with the bouquet away from his face.

"I know you're allergic to scent," Nick went on, "in case you've forgotten, you love the colors, too, as long as I keep the flowers away from your side of the table. You actually remember me!"

"I've seen your picture. And they told me you were coming."

"Oh." The ends of Nick's lips, previously jutting well into his cheeks, fell until they threatened his tapered chin. "I should have known. I suppose I was expecting a miracle."

"Don't worry. You are precisely that. A miracle come into my life from nowhere."

Miles wasn't exaggerating either. Ever since first seeing Nick in the doorway, he felt something rising in him that he hadn't felt in the longest time. He would have fallen in love with the man beside his bed in very short order if they weren't already in love.

"You're so kind. You've changed somehow." Nick propped the flowers on the far corner of the window sill. As he turned back around, Miles rose from his bed and held his arms out, as if to embrace his lover, who walked right into the trap. In no time, Miles had the bed's top sheet wrapped tightly around Nick's neck from behind.

"Move the chair in front of the door, if you would please," he requested.

"What's come over you, Miles?"

"You've figured that out already. As you said, I've changed. Now, the chair."

"Alright, alright."

Sheet still firmly around his neck, Nick pushed the lone chair toward the door, propping its back under the handle. Next, Miles guided him toward the sink so he could see Nick's face in the mirror.

"I need some answers," he said with a hint of menace in his voice. "Honest answers. Tell me what you're doing here?"

"They gave me compassionate leave at work. I had to go all the way to Ed Ryder, but in the end he saw how it would look, an employee bringing suit against a firm that specializes in domestic law."

"No, I mean who sent you?"

"No one. I came because...because I love you."

"April didn't ask you to come?"

"Well, yes...she did, kind of. You know how she is. The thought of flying to London was too much for her, I'm certain. What's wrong with you, Miles?"

Nothing in Nick's handsome face told Miles he was lying, and he loosened his grip on the sheet, but just a little.

"Did she say anything to you about a manuscript?"

"Yes, something by Shakespeare. She made a big deal of it, wants me to take you by Reg Sloane's before we fly home to see what he can tell us about it."

"Why?"

"Because you don't remember anything about it. You know how you were before? And now you've got amnesia, too."

"That's precisely what I want the doctors, everyone to think until I find out what's going on."

"Then you remember buying that manuscript?"

"Actually, I don't...not everything anyway. April said she found it buried among all the papers in a crate I sent, and I do at least recall the hurried sale. You know how I was before my accident, a little forgetful...well, maybe more than a little. Now I can remember everything since I woke from my coma. The names of nurses, doctors, even from the paper. And I used to be so awful with them. Things that happened before I was mugged, like the time we went up to Bar Harbor last summer, are starting to come back. The wake-up call I got in that coma has helped me far better than any drugs the doctors prescribed."

"I brought them with me."

"Well, throw them away," he said as he released the sheet and folded Nick into his arms. "I don't need them anymore."

"You don't?"

The excitement that colored Nick's face just then persuaded Miles he could be trusted. And he needed someone he could rely on, someone who wouldn't give away his secret, if he was to find out what lay behind the manuscript he had theoretically discovered, but couldn't remember. His lover had responded to a totally unexpected set of questions, not in anger but with empathy. And he hadn't put up a struggle, though he did still seem mildly incredulous.

How had Miles had been so lucky to meet someone like Nick, fall in love with him, and then fall in love with him all over again in that hospital-room mirror? The first time, Miles had probably been blinded by lust. The second time, blinded by an honest face. He hoped he would never have to fall in love again a third time, because three times was a curse.

And he liked Nicholas Reed far too much to let any curse like that catch up with them.

20 HOW NOW, OPHELIA!

The ringing phone rescued April from the uncooperative Amiga on her desk. She'd been trying to balance the books for August the last two hours. The month's sales figures had been so weak she could have penciled out the numbers herself in half the time. Instead, she'd sat there berating the computer that was supposed to be so fool-proof. Well, she was the fool, and the spreadsheet in front of her proof of it.

The call, a brief one, was from Nick Reed to thank her for getting Miles' passport. Unfortunately, early reports of her father's improved memory were premature. He didn't seem to remember all that much about Nick, his legal practice, or the condo he owned. He had only a vague idea about the manuscript that concerned April so much. Then came the real shocker. The doctors were releasing Miles into Nick's care. He'd be home in two days.

Just two days? April hadn't thought it possible. She didn't really know how to pose her next question.

"Do you think Dad could stay with you the first couple weeks or so after you get back, Nick? You see, the opportunity of a lifetime has come along, and I'm tempted to take it. The East Village Players have asked me to rejoin them for their season opener. I'd have to go upstate where they're rehearsing." She couldn't really tell him she'd be playing Ophelia in the new *Hamlet* her father had discovered. "It's an important part in an American premiere. I'll be back in the city by September 30th for the opening. Is that asking too much?"

"I don't know why, but I'm surprised, April. You mean, you're actually going to do it?"

"I'm not really sure. It would be pretty bold, wouldn't it, leaving my comfort zone?"

"I think it's just the thing for you. It will take real courage, but if you don't do it, you'll hate yourself forever.

In fact, Miles and I had already talked about him staying with me when we get back. I'm afraid if he's too close to the store, he'll spend all his time working when he's supposed to be recovering. I think he'll be fine with the idea."

Even before the conversation ended, April had begun to feel sorry for herself. She had hoped Nick would say no, which would have told her she simply couldn't rejoin Avery and the rest of the company at The Gables. As it turned out, her father didn't really want to come home at all, and he'd certainly recover faster with Nick to care for him. She had what she thought she wanted, their approval to go upstate, but now she wasn't at all sure that was the smartest thing to do.

She shut down her computer and closed up for the evening. Then climbed the stairs to their apartment and ran a tub of warm water for a long soak and a chance to reconsider her momentous decision. No hesitating, the moment she emerged from the tub, she'd call Avery and let him know one way or the other. She slid into the water and let it peel away her doubts. They lingered on the surface like a layer of dirt, just waiting to cling to her when she got out again. So she stayed under until the water got tepid, then almost cold.

Finally she climbed out, drained the tub and toweled off. By the time she finished drying her hair, it was stick-out frizzy. No other excuses left, she plopped down on the kitchen stool in her bathrobe. Avery LeMaster's number in Oakville was right there on the counter where she'd left it. Normally she'd have spent whole minutes working up the nerve to dial. This time her fingers punched the touchpad as if she really knew what she wanted to do.

"Priestly's," a young woman's voice finally greeted her.

"I'd like to speak to Avery LeMaster, please."

"I'm afraid he's in rehearsal now."

April hadn't thought she'd have to leave a message, and on this, the most important phone call she'd made in months.

"I see. This is very important. I need to tell him something. It will just take a minute."

"I'm afraid he can't be interrupted."

"Look, this is April Oliphant. Professor LeMaster wants me to...." She knew then it was no use. Why leave a message with someone whose voice she didn't recognize? Someone Avery might well have cast as Ophelia after she herself had initially turned down the role. She was just about to hang up when the young woman's voice came back over the line.

"Just a second, I see him coming up the hill now."

This was it, April told herself. No more excuses. No putting off Avery any longer. At such a crucial juncture, she was in no mood for small talk.

"Is that you, April?"

"Yes. I called to tell you I've made up my mind about your offer."

"My offer?"

Didn't he remember? Worse yet, he'd probably given the part to the young Gucci girl who'd answered the phone.

"You asked me to play Ophelia in your new *Hamlet*."

The pause that followed seemed to go on forever, or at least long enough for her to switch the phone to her better ear.

"I didn't expect you to accept, quite frankly."

"I certainly put you off long enough." Only after that did she intuit what she thought he was trying to tell her. "You've offered the part to someone else, haven't you?"

"Not really."

"But you have. I can tell."

"It's nothing for you to worry about, April. I want you as my Ophelia."

She let the faint sense of excitement she detected in his voice overcome any remaining doubts. "You're sure?"

"I am."

"Then I guess we've got an understanding."

"Excellent. We rehearse act two, scene four tomorrow afternoon. Can you make it?"

Just like that? Rehearsal in less than twenty-four hours. She hadn't cracked the transcription of the *Ur-Hamlet* he'd given her. Memorization wasn't the problem. She was good at that. It was the people. Actors. So many of them when she was used to living alone most of the time.

Even when her father came home for a night or two from Nick's, the walls of the apartment seemed to close in, and that was with just one other person there. April couldn't possibly do it.

"I have something on tomorrow afternoon."

"You do? What?"

She'd never known Avery to be a bullying director. Who was he to challenge her that way?

"What is it you're doing tomorrow afternoon, April?" he asked again when she didn't answer. "Or is it just an excuse because you're afraid of working with other people...being with others?"

Of course she was, and she came right out and told him so.

"You can do it," he reassured her, "and both of us know you can."

"I wish I had your faith in me."

"Look, I've got an idea, a stepping stone of sorts. Why don't I come into the city tonight after we wrap here? We can run through your lines in scene four together. Go through them again in the morning to get you used to working with someone else. Then we'll drive back up together. How does that sound?"

"Intimidating," April offered the first word that came to her. It sounded as if he planned to spend the night at her place. He couldn't, and she had the perfect excuse why not. "Besides, it's not safe here."

"April...really!"

"You'd be coming in late. Parking's impossible and you'd have to walk blocks."

"Look, I don't doubt your fear is real, but that's not going to get you where I think you want to be."

"I could come to your place downtown?" she suggested as if she did that all the time. "Just to rehearse. I wouldn't spend the night."

"Are you serious?"

"I think I am."

"I'll be there by midnight. Do you have the address?" After he gave it to her, the two of them said fewer than ten words, including good-byes. April hovered over the phone for minutes. She didn't know what could have possibly inspired her to be bolder, far bolder than she'd ever been with any man in her life. Was it fear, or desperation? Either way, she'd reached out just when life, or happiness, seemed out of reach.

She had less than six hours to read scene four and get it down. Nail it as she had never nailed another dramatic role in her life.

Before that, though, she had to give Art Kass a call.

21 ONE-ON-ONE

As they approached the address on Charles that Avery had given her, Art slowed the car. She didn't know why, but she had expected Avery's building to be a nondescript apartment block. Instead, the director lived in a cute, two-and-a-half story brick building with dormer windows poking out from the roof. The names on the mail boxes informed her that he occupied the only apartment on the top floor. She pressed the bell and he rang her in almost immediately. The hallway didn't appear to have been swept in months, and the worn, wooden stairs were in even worse condition.

"Any trouble getting here?" he asked when she reached the top landing.

"None."

Inside, his apartment was small but comfortable. One of the windows she'd seen from below looked directly into trees that flanked the street outside. Theater posters decorated the plaster walls. A heterogeneous collection of sofa and a couple easy chairs sat atop a braided rug that covered more than half the front room. She recognized Sonny Rollins' "Tenor Madness" playing in the background which surprised her almost as much as the apartment. Astonishing as it was, she felt strangely at-home there.

"Your place is adorable. How'd you find it?"

"I got lucky. Sandra Parker–you know, the costume designer–decided to give it up when she got married. I was the first person she told about it. Something to drink?"

"Better not. This is a working session."

"You're right. I just thought a little wine might make this easier for you. You look...how should I put it? Anxious."

She was. Doubly anxious, in fact. He knew one of the reasons. Her first rehearsal in two years. She had no intention of telling him the other.

"I am, a little."

"That'll disappear once we get started."

"I hope so," she said as she wrestled the transcript from her purse self-consciously. Then she thought better of having declined his offer. "If you don't mind, maybe I will have something to drink."

"What would you like?"

"You said something about wine. Red, if you've got it."

"I have a nice Chateauneuf-du-Pape. You'll like it, that's a promise."

April would have liked anything just then. Anything that prevented the inevitable debacle in which Avery would see how creaky her acting skills had grown with disuse.

"I'm sure I will."

"If you don't mind my asking?" he called from the kitchen. "What changed your mind about taking the part?"

She should have lied and told him it was a great professional opportunity, which it was. How many actors had a chance to perform in a new play by Shakespeare these days? Somehow, with every last safety net in her little world gone, she just couldn't lie.

"I really don't know how much longer I can go on living the way I am. All my trusted standbys have deserted me. My best friend Shelly's moved in with this man she met just last month and she never calls. My father's still in London, though he's due back in two days. When he gets here he'll go nuclear the moment he finds out his manuscript is missing. I just couldn't wait around for that happen."

"It's all my fault for being so careless."

"No. It happened for a reason. To get me out the front door and acting again."

"If that's really true, then this is an auspicious occasion," he told her and held his wine glass up to hers. "Look, tomorrow I'll pick you up at your place, but I have to make a stop beforehand. Joanna wants me to talk to the president of the Settlement House board. She thinks I'm diplomat enough to persuade him to see things our way when it comes to this year's lease."

"You mean it hasn't been signed yet?"

"That was supposed to happen before the first of the month, but negotiations fell through. They gave us an extension, though, which is a good sign. It's all a matter of money. I don't understand why she thinks I can sweet-talk this Carlsson fellow."

"You can do it, I know you can. After all, I'm here, aren't I?"

"Meaning?"

"The obvious. You talked me into playing Ophelia, even though I haven't acted in two bloody years." What was she saying? The wine truly was already having its way with her tongue. Two sips into it and her well-honed inhibitions had already begun to lose their hold. "Sorry. Maybe we should get started with scene four? Before I let the wine do any more with my mouth than just drink it."

"Why not?" He nodded toward the typescript April had set on the coffee table, then slid closer to her on the couch. Before starting, he set his glass down and leaned forward, propping his elbows on his knees.

"I'll take Hamlet's lines. Now, set the scene for me, if you would please?"

Fortunately, April did not voice the string of additional epithets that shot through her mind at his request. She wasn't the director. *He* was. He had to know how difficult the next few days were going to be for her and reassure her. Why was he making her do his work, and not helping ease her into their little rehearsal?

"Let's see?" she began. "Uh...we're in Elsinore, of course. King Hamlet has just gone off to fight the Geats in Sweden. Hamlet, who's something of a party boy, has spoken...."

"Sorry to interrupt, but I think Hamlet's more an apathetic youth than a party boy in the *Ur-Hamlet*. Today, I suppose you'd say he's laid back or something of the sort. He's not without charm or intelligence, but lacks direction in a very big way. He thinks he wants to go off and fight with his father's army, but not really. Nor is he happy about going away to university in spite of his mother's urging. He just wants to hang out in Elsinore with his friends, Ophelia chief among them, though he clearly thinks of her as more than just a friend."

If that wasn't a description of a party boy, April wouldn't be able to find one on any fraternity row in the country. She wasn't going to contradict Avery though. In fact, his characterization filled out her mental impression of the young prince.

"Thanks. That helps. Anyway, he's asked his mother to invite me...Ophelia, for a ride in the country. The queen refuses, saying there are far too many other pretty girls at court. She doesn't want Hamlet to concern himself with one as relatively low-born and high-strung as Ophelia. So, on his own, Hamlet sets out to ensnare Ophelia in the garden outside her father's house."

"Just so," Avery said, smiling. "Now, as we're going to stage scene four, Hamlet has created a curving path, just a line really, of roses of all different colors, set against the grim backdrop of the castle walls. Ophelia wanders in and starts gathering them up, only half-surprised when they lead to a gateway behind which Hamlet has hidden himself. Then she says...?

Ophelia. Lord Hamlet, you have given me such fright.
    Is there a reason for this?
Hamlet.   None. If reason
    Knew itself, there'd be no reason in it.
    For roses will put curves in straightest paths
    To add delight to home where there is none.
Ophelia. If it is of my home you speak, then know
    Delight has no reward, for our departed
    Mother still draws hearts down that same path
    As the unrosed one you curved for me.
    It's true my father loves me far too well
    My brother too, though he loves none like you.
    For if delight must make its entrance, it
    Will do so like a player with no part
    Who waits on words that he will never speak
    Till darkness has arrived, the stage is bare
    And he returns to house to act out there.

Through the later part of her lament, April could see Avery shifting his weight ever so slightly on his 1950s beige sofa bed. He was unhappy, but didn't want to show it. Why had she ever agreed to read through her lines with him when she could have stayed comfortably at her father's place?

"You've got the lines down, but then I would have expected no less. Let me ask this. Who's speaking here?"

"Ophelia...."

"Of course it's Ophelia, but...?"

"Let me finish, please." She drew herself forward until her face was no more than inches from his. "It is a surprised Ophelia who speaks. A mere girl really, who has no other woman in the house except servants. She's modeled herself on her nanny and doesn't know the ways of the world. That's why she's completely unmoored by the way Hamlet devours her with his eyes at court. Now this, roses that lead to a hiding suitor, Prince Hamlet. She doesn't know how to respond to such an impetuous, poetic gesture."

LeMaster pulled back as she spoke, his restless hips now motionless, his head cocked.

"That wouldn't be my reading," he said, then paused long enough for a freight train pass. "I think it's *better* than mine. Go with it, but consider where your Ophelia's going to end up. Sounds to me as if she's fifteen going on fifty. Let's take it from Hamlet's response where he says, "That will be my task in life, to brighten yours."

April spoke her next lines but never heard herself utter them. It wasn't that Avery's response overwhelmed her. She simply hadn't expected him to see Ophelia her way, and that sparked an unusual response. Perhaps admiration. Perhaps something more.

They worked the scene another half hour. When he drew close again and once touched her knee, she barely recoiled. In fact, she felt a faint moisture between her thighs that sent blood to her face, and she hoped he didn't notice. When he poured her another glass of wine, she exhaled the last of the tension that had built up from events of the day.

"Let's go through it just one more time," he said.

She looked at her watch. "It's almost two."

Avery slid away from her, shocked. "I had no idea. I'll drive you back to your place. My car's just around the corner."

"You'll lose your parking place and an hour's sleep. I'll take a cab."

The thought made him pause. "You do that all the time, take cabs?"

"Whenever I need to," she said evasively.

"I hope this doesn't come out sounding too forward," he began. "I've got to be on Rector Street at nine to speak to Carlsson. I'd be happy to drive you back tonight, then come by for you on the way upstate."

"You'd hardly get any sleep that way."

"That's true. You know, we're sitting on a comfortable hide-a-bed? We could make it up in five minutes. You can sleep in in the morning while I'm talking to Carlsson. I'll pick you up, then we can stop by your place to get your things. That way, we'll both get almost enough sleep for the grueling day ahead. Does that sound too awful?"

Avery's proposal didn't make April nearly as happy as it should have. If she said yes, she'd be sharing an apartment with someone else, if only for one night. It was true, she lived with her father, but he spent most nights at Nick's, and Avery's couch was very different from her bed at home. Just a thin wall would separate her from a man she'd be working with intensely for weeks, perhaps months. A man she was attracted to.

"I'd better not."

"I understand. Let's get the car. I'll drive you back and pick you up, say at eleven?"

"You don't think I'm being too silly?"

"Not at all. I just need to get the keys."

He turned and disappeared into his bedroom.

"If you don't think I'm too wishy-washy," she heard herself call to him, "we'll both get more sleep if we stay here."

Honestly, April didn't know where those words had come from, but there they were. She had spoken them, or rather her heart had. If she'd thought about it just a second, she'd have overruled herself. Now she'd have to live with the consequences. After all, she was talking about just plain sleep. Not sleeping *with* someone. They'd both be in separate beds, in separate rooms. It would be just like a night at home with Father.

"Are you certain?"

"Positive."

She enunciated her one-word response forcefully. It felt as if she were on stage and had just reached a major plot point the director wanted to impress upon the audience. In this case, an audience of two, and she was not at all certain that wasn't one too many.

"Great. I think it's the right decision."

Avery got out a light blanket, a set of sheets, and together they made up the sofa bed in the front room. He volunteered to let her use his toothbrush, which she declined. It was one thing to sleep in someone else's apartment. Quite another to use a toothbrush that had been in his mouth hundreds of times. When he offered a tee-shirt to take the place of a night gown, however, she accepted and asked for a second one. False modesty, she supposed, but it might hide some of her shape in case they met on the way to the bathroom in the night.

She hadn't counted on the softness of her improvised nightie. The slightly sweet smell left by the fabric softener could not hide the unmistakable scent of aftershave. Old Spice, she thought, just like Teddy used.

22 A DAY PASS

Hand on Nick's firm, guiding arm, Miles turned the corner to Cecil Court and halted not six paces down the narrow street. It wasn't the heat, soaring already at that hour of the morning, that stopped him however. He stood there half paralyzed by the feeling that he was an escaped prisoner who'd just broken out of that awful hospital room he'd been confined to for almost two weeks. The pleasant green and white facades, the brick and masonry upper stories around him were just so appealing. So very British.

"Remember," he prompted Nick, "we're here to see how much Reg knows about the manuscript."

With the hand that held a gift bag, Miles then pointed to the display window of Reginald Sloan's Rare Books, which, he knew, specialized in literature, first editions, and, above all, the performing arts. It was not yet ten and a CLOSED sign still hung in the window, but the owner, a long-time friend, had agreed to meet them early on the one free day they had before flying home.

Miles knocked but got no answer, then he tried the handle and the door opened.

"Reg didn't say a thing about leaving the door unlocked when I called," he said to Nick. "Maybe he's working in back?" They entered a rather long, narrow space, books crowding shelves that reached from floor to ceiling, a staircase to a second floor off to one side. A single, white door to Reg's office at the rear swung open and a wafer-thin man walked out, a smile of recognition adding one more set of angles to an already angular face. As he approached, Miles could see rib bones visible through the cotton turtleneck he wore to keep cool in the unusual, early September heat. His prominent Adam's apple led to crane-bill jaw, topped by a nose every bit as bony as the rest of him. That flesh which wasn't drawn tightly over his protruding features sank into pockets made even more shadowy by the overhead lighting.

"Sorry, I just had some last-minute tidying to do," Reg said. "I hoped you'd try the door. Come on back. Except for a bruise or two, you don't look the least bit different, Miles."

"How have you been keeping, Reg?"

"Cool is the operative word, or trying to keep cool at any rate. An impossible task without that American Rube Goldberg of yours, air conditioning. 364 days a year, you wouldn't catch me with one of those noisy, unsightly devices. Today is the one day I'd gladly renounce those Puritan principles. Wouldn't be an air conditioner you've got in that sack you're carrying, would it?"

"It's a bit too small for that. We stopped at an Off-License on the way. This is for you." Miles handed him the bottle bag. "Sorry for being so rude. You remember my friend, Nick Reed? He's come all this way just to take me back to the States."

"You've talked about him often, but this is the first time I've had the honor," Reg said, shaking Nick's hand. "Come on back to the office. I'm brewing a pot of coffee right now, another American luxury, but one I've grown accustomed to, thanks to you, Miles."

Quite unlike the shop itself, the office looked as if Reg were just straightening up after a minor disaster, papers deposited in precarious piles on the desk and floor, old, valuable books lying about in different arrangements on the surrounding shelves. One of them, bound in smooth chocolate brown leather, snared Miles' attention for a moment.

Reg extracted the bottle from the gift bag.

"Ah, I see you've brought along another friend, Captain Morgan. The perfect rum for morning coffee really. Since it's early yet, I'll add no more than a touch."

"None for me, thanks," Nick said. "And Miles better not. His medication and all that. The gift's really for you."

"Then you don't mind if I...?

"Not at all."

After cups were poured, and Reg's amended, Miles gestured toward the bottle.

"I'm not going to have any," he informed Nick. "Just a quick whiff, if I might?"

Nose over the top of the bottle, Miles inhaled and almost immediately thought he could sense whole symphonies he had once heard, beaches visited, holidays past. Having them linger there tantalizingly in his nostrils was enough to summon sounds and places, whether fact or fiction didn't seem important just then. Doctors be damned, he'd have taken a little of that Caribbean sweetener in his coffee if Nick hadn't been there to look after him. He envied Reg, oh, how he envied the unsupervised bookstore owner.

"Here's to you, Reg," he said, handing back the bottle and hoisting his cup.

"Sorry I didn't visit you in the hospital, Miles," his host said after a slow, appreciative taste. "The story was all over the papers one day, but they called you by a different name, Nick's in fact. I should have made the connection, but didn't."

"Don't worry. I'm not at my best in hospital rooms, as Nick can attest."

"But still I could have helped on this end somehow."

"I think we've got things covered pretty well now," Nick said. "All we have to do is get Miles on that plane tomorrow."

Reg took another, longer sip.

"You do remember some things, don't you, Miles?"

"Some, I suppose, yes."

"What about the day you stopped by almost three weeks ago now? You said you were going to hire a car to go out to an old estate I told you about in Somerset. Anything about that strike a familiar chord?"

Behind that question, Miles sensed an interest in his manuscript. Did Reg know there was one involved in that sale in Somerset, and that it was by Shakespeare? Had he perhaps had a larger role in it than that? That's what they had come to find out.

"Does a town called Marston...Marston Bigot, I believe, mean anything to you, Miles?"

He shook his head.

"Wait a moment. I've got an atlas out front. I'll get it and show you." He rose. "Now, don't you go sneaking any of my coffee while I'm gone."

"Do you think we can trust Reg?" Nick asked once the door shut behind the shop owner.

"That's the real question, isn't it?"

They fell silent after that, waiting for Reg to return. Miles pulled himself upright in his chair, and, after a few moments, drifted toward the shelves behind Reg's desk where he picked up the book that had attracted his attention when he first entered the office. The title page told him he was holding *A Plot and No Plot*, a comedy he'd never heard of previously. There was no date on it, but everything about the book–its cover, the quality of the print, the color and texture of the pages–told him it was valuable.

Miles thumbed through, concentrating not on the words or the individual pages, but on the heft and feel of the book which was indeed elegant, there was no other word to describe it. The surface of the cover had been burnished by all the hands that had opened it before, some perhaps even lovingly. He lifted it to his nose and detected, in addition to the lingering scent of calfskin, a hint of tobacco, and, unfortunately, dust. Inexplicably, the volume spoke to all his senses, every last one of them enthralled by the experience. Even more certainly than he knew he loved Nick, he truly loved this book, and others like it that somehow carried the imprint of the years with them.

"You must have had a deuce of a time finding Marston that day," Reg proclaimed as he walked back into the office.

Miles hastily put the book back into position on the shelf, though he didn't really know why he did so. Reg obviously loved books, too, and set two of them down on his desk.

"It's a tiny town, no more than a hamlet really, in east Somerset. I doubt anybody knows it, though I should have. See, here in Pevsner there's a manor there that's terribly old, even by British standards. But this is the part that really piqued my interest. In the early eighteenth century, Charles Boyle, Fourth Earl of Orrery, lived there and was responsible for rebuilding much of the manor and planning the gardens."

Then Reg placed the second book, an encyclopedia Miles thought, on top of the first and, without even consulting it, went on.

"Boyle conducted a lively correspondence with Lewis Theobald, who staged at least one of Shakespeare's so-called lost plays, *Cardenio*."

"One?" Miles repeated, trying to make his question sound as casual as possible. "You mean there are others?"

"There's also *Love's Labors Won*, which may either be lost or one of the comedies that, for a time, went by that title. And an early version of *Hamlet*, perhaps by Shakespeare. You might have discovered a treasure trove at Marston Bigot, Miles. Perhaps you made a purchase? Had it sent back to the States?"

"I don't think Miles remembers much about his trip to Marston," Nick said, "do you, Miles?"

"Unfortunately, no. But I'm wondering how you found out about the sale, Reg?"

"Through an old family friend of mother's. Loren Pritchard. He's a former employee of Marston Manor."

"Loren Pritchard, you say? Thanks, Reg. That's helpful. Very helpful indeed."

"I was so hoping that little excursion would turn out for you. Perhaps you shouldn't think too much about it. Give it a rest for a while and the details will come back. Or take a jaunt out to Marston, see if someone at the manor doesn't remember you."

"Unfortunately, the doctors won't allow it," Nick spoke up. "They're releasing Miles because they think going home is best for him. Not for him to go dumpster diving in some small town in Somerset."

"It's almost due west of....Of course, you're right, Nick. It's the wildest of goose chases anyway. Maybe I'll go out on a Monday when the shop is closed and make some gentle inquiries myself, let you know if I learn anything. In the meantime, by all means take Miles back home until he's completely well again."

They remained at Sloane's another quarter hour, talking primarily about the book trade. Miles asked an occasional question or two of Reg, but their only real consequence was to grate on Nick. He hoped Reg, who was trying his best to help, didn't take offense. Relief played across his companion's features when they said their farewells, Miles promising to stop by on his next visit to England when he was more *in mens sana.*

"What were you doing in there?" Nick asked in a transparently tempered voice, not ten steps down Cecil's Court from the bookstore. "Trying to give away the candy store? No, more than that. Every damn candy shop on the block?"

"Just trying to fit together a few pieces of the puzzle, that's all."

"Pieces of the puzzle?" Nick repeated in exasperation. "For God's sake, Miles, let's let this lie for a while. That's the best thing Reg said the whole time we were there. I don't know why April ever suggested we visit him. I can see now all it did was get you stirred up. That's the last thing you need."

As they continued down the street, Miles knew Nick was right. He also knew he had experienced something in Reg Sloane's office that ignited a mental burner, one that had fluttered off some time ago. Was it all that talk about books, the touch of them? Or something else?

Miles didn't know, but for the first time in recent memory, he felt alive again. Truly alive.

23 SAINT FOR A NIGHT

The man certainly looked like LeMaster, The Master, who was also clearly a saint based on the halo that April saw surrounding his head. His light beard and unkempt hair looked just like Avery's. He had been drinking out of a lion's head spigot when she came upon him at the well, where he helped fill her water jug. In thanks, she invited him to take the evening meal at her house. The scent of something in the kitchen permeated her house, just like another scent she remembered from earlier that night.

A holy man, he was carrying a message to all who would accept him, as few were prone to do. She, the woman at the well, was different. She had recognized him for the unique man among men he truly was. A man who brought love into other's hearts. A man who knew the way to those hearts, which was through a door he deftly unlocked and entered. Then snuggled like a dog in its mistress's lap.

Fearing he might leave, she held him ever closer. Then felt him stir in her arms. Opening her eyes, she saw it really wasn't a dream at all. Avery LeMaster lay in bed beside her. His bed, not the foldout in the front room.

April tensed and pulled away, stifling a scream. Had she drunk so much wine that she allowed him to cajole her into bed? No, she distinctly remembered struggling to fall asleep on the freshly made sofa bed in the front room. Only afterwards had she gone to The Master's bed.

She couldn't blame the wine really. It was all her own doing. Her own fault. She had become a horror, taking advantage of Avery that way, ultimately at her own expense. Soon her tears were draining from one eye to the other and onto the sheet. At the same time her body began to quake. All because she had fallen in love with a man who probably hadn't the least idea what she felt toward him.

"What's wrong, April? You're crying."

"I...I don't know," she tried to put him off.

By this time he was facing her in bed, blotting her cheek with the hem of a sheet. He took her face in his hands and went to kiss her eyelids, forcing her to close them. Was he trying to kiss away her tears?

"You're not crying about what you did?"

"What *I* did?"

"What we both did, but you're the only one of us who has regrets."

"It's not that." It wasn't, either. Regret was a surface emotion that passed in hours. Days at most. Making love with Avery was a watershed event, one that would change her life forever. He had no way of knowing the depth of feeling he had roused in her.

"No, I guess not. I was totally surprised, and delighted when you crawled into bed and hugged me. I didn't expect you would ever allow yourself to get that close to anybody. I think that took real courage."

"In spite of myself, I have this underlying need to connect with a few people, and very deeply. So beware."

"I feel honored. Still I think it's remarkably brave of you."

April could tell he was sloughing off her warning. That wasn't necessarily wrong. Knowing what she did about herself, she'd have said something even more innocuous in his place. She was about to ask if he loved her, at least a little bit, but then pulled back. Of course he'd say that he did, but what would she learn from such a predictable lie? Precisely nothing, so she tacked into a different wind.

"Don't say I didn't warn you."

"It's the most delicious warning I've ever had."

He was still making light of the situation. No sense continuing down the same slippery path she had chosen for herself.

"You have my permission to kick me out of bed if I ever impose myself on you like that again."

"Kick you out? Are you kidding? I'd like to keep you here all morning. Or at least another hour. What do you say to that?"

She'd love it, that's what she would say. As he drew her closer, all thought of living in the company of more than a dozen other people for the next week vanished. It didn't matter if the prospect frightened her beyond belief. That was then and this was now.

"How'd it go on Wall Street?" April asked as Avery finished passing an impossibly long eighteen wheeler.

"I hoped you wouldn't ask."

"That bad?"

"As it turns out, I'm simply not very good at negotiations. Carlsson was reasonable, saw our point of view...to a degree anyway. But he wouldn't budge. He's adamant about getting the back rent before even discussing a new lease. And Joanna told me she can't take a cent from their joint account without setting off a tripwire with Rob."

"At least you tried."

Avery didn't say anything more. They continued the drive north until April decided she needed to cheer up her handsome chauffeur.

"Let's stop!" she proposed in her best dramatic voice, pointing to the motel sign ahead of them on the right.

"April!?"

"Don't be shocked. It's just a short detour. No, maybe a long one."

"To a motel? What's come over you? The April Oliphant I knew led the life of a cloistered nun. Now she's turned into a sex fiend."

"For all of about ten hours."

Avery didn't even pretend to take his foot off the gas pedal of the old Subaru as the low-slung sixties motel swooshed past April's window. She hadn't really expected him to stop, but didn't regret her suggestion either. The previous night had been such a revelation she could barely keep her reawakened libido from taking over her life.

This, her second trip up the Saw Mill Parkway in as many weeks, seemed a totally new experience. Nothing intruded on the beauty of the drive. Not the whine of the car's tires. The grinding of its worn transmission. The dull roar of passing vehicles. The sun, which baked right through the hanging humidity, glared off the pitted, silver hood and streaked the windshield. Stirred by passing cars, flickering leaves half-mesmerized her. She drifted between the afterglow of the past evening and the gnawing anxiety that awaited her at the end of the achingly gorgeous drive. She would have done anything to preserve the bliss of that brief journey between two points of desperation, New York and Oakville.

"Oh, God, I guess we're doing it then," she said. "Going directly into the lion's den. Do not pass go. Do not collect two-hundred lashes."

"It's going to be fine. I saw the way you handled the material in scene four last night. You'll collect so much respect by the time we leave Oakville, you'll be able to open the First National Bank of Broadway and loan the excess to less confident actors."

"Clever. Very clever, Avery, which just shows that, despite all your words of support, you don't appreciate how truly vulnerable I am right now." April tried to stifle the insecurity she felt by asking a question she'd wanted to for months now. "What happened between you and your wife?"

His head turned briefly toward her, a scrabbled smile tightening his lips. "Oh, didn't I tell you? She wanted to stop at every motel we came to and...you know?"

April hammered his shoulder. Hard.

"Damnit, that hurt."

"Be serious. I want to know what happened between you two?"

When he looked over at her this time his smile had wilted, leaving his features limp with pain. "I honestly don't know. I was so busy, I guess, teaching, directing, trying to do a little writing, our marriage simply imploded from inertia. It was my fault. I ignored her, hurt her really, for which I'll be forever damned. No matter how much I tried to make it up to her, nothing seemed to work. Eventually, we both got lawyers and...and a divorce."

April got the answer she deserved. She had been utterly naïve to pose the question in the first place.

"Do you still miss her?" she asked to make herself feel worse.

"Still? I don't know. I miss being really close to someone, I suppose."

"But surely there've been other women to take her place? I mean, it's not as if you don't have mountains of appeal, and venues to show it off, teaching and directing flocks of ingénues."

"There haven't been nearly as many as you'd expect."

She swore she wasn't going to ask him how many women there had been. She just wasn't.

"How many?"

"Please, April."

"All you have to do is tell me and I'll shut up about your love life forever."

"Promise?"

"I promise."

He paused here, raising his fingers on the steering wheel as he counted. The number reached sixteen and his fingers kept rising in time to the dull throbs of the ailing transmission.

"Enough!" she whimpered. "Sorry I asked."

"There have only been two or three."

"Two *or* three?" she repeated, horrified at the word *or*. Things were even worse than she thought. "You mean you don't remember how many?"

"Alright, just three."

So there had been three rivals in less than a year, which was about what April had figured. She wanted to ask their names, but then she might know them and that would make comparison invidious. Far more important, she wanted him to tell her how serious the relationships had been. This time, however, she managed to restrain her self-destructive impulses by humming *sotto voce* the rest of the way to Oakville.

They pulled into the circular drive outside The Gables ahead of schedule. April told herself she had nothing to fear but fear of herself as she went to open the car door.

"Let's go in through the kitchen," Avery suggested.

She reached around for her handbag, then followed Avery in through the screen door on the back porch.

Inside, he opened another door which led to a small, well-lighted stairwell and headed upstairs. How many other, pleasant little surprises like this back staircase, April wondered, would the marvelous house contain?

To the sound of echoing voices below, he tiptoed down the corridor toward the rear of the house, then stopped before a rectangular patch of sunlight. When April caught up, she saw that she was standing at the entrance to a converted sun porch. Peering inside, she could see that it looked out in two directions. In one, the yard merged in the distance with an orchard of some sort, planted on a gently sloping hillside. The other was almost totally engulfed by a giant oak.

Covered with a simple summer blanket, a double bed sat beside a dresser against a wainscoted wall. Another door, either to a closet or bathroom, had been cut into the opposite wall. An old, uncomfortable-looking mission style rocker angled out from the corner where the windows came together. The floor was bare except for a scatter rug beside the bed.

April simply could not believe her extreme good fortune. Here she was, not two hours from New York, in a simple yet charming room. She hated the word *charming* but nothing else conveyed the impression left by her surroundings. The countryside with grass and flowers and fruit trees seemed so completely boundless. Especially compared to the confines of her apartment in the city. She could barely keep from throwing herself at Avery in joy. Instead she wrapped her arms around him, drew him close and kissed him.

"I wonder if the mattress is firm enough?" she said in a honeyed voice. "Let's see?"

Avery played along for all of three or four seconds. Then scruples, such as only a director could have, tugged at his mental reins.

"This isn't the best time," he whispered back. "Others might hear."

April wanted to say so what, but she knew that wouldn't get her what she wanted. In fact, it might possibly alienate the very person who was responsible for the new, rosier view she had of the world.

"I understand. Maybe tonight?"

"Definitely tonight. After we put everything to bed." He turned toward the door. "I've got to get rehearsal started. If you feel like taking a walk during free time, you can go along the fields this side of the road, especially to the north. They're all part of the Priestly property."

"North?" April half joked.

"City girls!" Avery played along, pointing in the direction of the shorter of the two solarium walls. "Better be careful if you go out. There are all sorts of rabbit holes out there."

"I think I'll just stay here. I need to go over my lines for this afternoon."

April could not let him leave without hurrying over to him and pulling his head down to her lips. He was not in such a hurry to join the others downstairs that he couldn't return her loving, good-bye kiss.

25 A FEW ANNOUNCEMENTS

"Please, please. If I may have your attention!" Avery called out to those assembled in the great hall downstairs. Within seconds, competing voices fell off, then grew quiet altogether. There was a certain drill sergeant's resonance in their director's voice that Charles hadn't detected in their earlier dust up when Avery came barging into his room, theoretically to borrow his script. But he'd been left with the distinct impression it wasn't the script that had brought Avery by. After all, how many other copies were lying around the huge old house if he'd lost his? That lame ploy could mean only one thing. Well, maybe two. Either he suspected something between Valerie and himself, or, far worse, that Charles was using again. He'd have to come up with some way of sending Avery's dog sniffing up another tree.

"A few announcements before we begin. I've already checked with Charles, Craig, and Randolph. We're going to switch tonight's rehearsal from act three, scene three to the same scene in act four."

Avery broke off and glanced briefly toward the balcony before continuing. Charles alone traced the direction of the speaker's eyes and thought he detected a pretty female head in the shadows there, the same one he had seen on the porch a few days before. That could mean only one thing, which brightened Charles' outlook considerably. They had their new Ophelia, April Oliphant, who could take his mind off the fickle, dithering Valerie Schneider faster than a python could snap up a small bunny.

"Now Joanna would like a word."

If Charles wasn't mistaken, Joanna had been to the hairdresser's recently. Now tightly coiffed and freshly colored, her black hair neatly framed her rather longish face as she took her place beside Avery at the front of the room.

"All of you know the importance of keeping word about the *Ur-Hamlet* to ourselves until we have further proof of its authenticity," she said, the slightest trace of a New York accent in her clipped voice.

Charles thought he knew where this line of reasoning would take Joanna, and averted his eyes. There was no way, however, that he could avoid her words short of jamming his fingers in his ears. And that would be just too obvious.

"I will not name names, but I saw one of our number in town this morning in a phone booth. I'm ninety-nine per cent certain that individual said nothing to even hint at the unusual nature of our new undertaking. But remember what we all agreed? No one leaves The Gables. All outside calls are to be made from the kitchen phone until we get the results of the handwriting and forensic analyses.

"Now, when I see someone in a phone booth in Oakville, I can't help asking myself why this unnamed individual would want to use a phone in town? So let me reiterate. Please, if you have to make a call, use the kitchen phone. And don't leave the property. After all, it's only for another few days. Remember, it's for the good of the East Village Players."

Charles did not keep his attention averted from Joanna for long during her brief admonition. He couldn't afford to because Avery, the only other person in front with her, looked at him long and hard the entire time she spoke. They were all ganging up on him, Avery looking for Charles' newly replenished stash, and now Joanna accusing him indirectly of violating not one, but two of the rules she had arbitrarily laid down to keep them virtual prisoners there. The persecution was getting to be too much.

Avery took over from Joanna again, speaking in a slightly more understated manner, "I'd like to welcome April Oliphant back into the fold. All of us, except Samuel I believe, already know April."

That was precisely the announcement Charles had been waiting for. Now the real fun would begin. No more of the frustrated foreplay Hope had put him through, or Valerie's open vendetta against Avery, who directed their attention to the balcony where the young April stepped forward, leaned out no more than an inch or two over the railing, and waved to all below, at the same time closing her eyes tightly, a gesture that struck Charles as a perfect, if slightly coy display of modesty. Everyone applauded enthusiastically.

April's response to all that was curious, the product really of the extreme shyness Avery had warned them about earlier. She said nothing, not a single word, just offered a fleeting wave of her hand over the balcony railing before retreating into the shadows. Charles' heart–and contrary to what most thought, he did have a heart, a very big, though unhealthy one–went out to April in a way it could never go out to Hope or Valerie.

Yes, he was definitely going to enjoy having April Oliphant among them, even though she herself didn't really seem to like being there.

26 BACK TO WORK

Miles propped an elbow on the front counter. He was utterly exhausted. They'd landed at JFK at 3:45 the previous afternoon, gone out to dinner, and he'd been in bed by nine that same evening, three a.m. London time. And he'd awakened in the morning at the same time he normally did in England, which meant he'd had only four hours sleep. It wouldn't have been so bad, but he'd agreed to let April take off work because she'd won a part in some obscure Off-Broadway production. Nick had told him it was a real opportunity for her, so Miles went along. More than that, he wished her well. So far it had meant leaving the shop shuttered only two days. He wanted to go in himself that morning to make certain things were alright. Nick agreed reluctantly, but insisted that he come along.

Miles let his eyes circle the store. Out front, rows of handmade, cherry bookshelves stretched all the way to office. The artfully exposed brick walls were studded with posters, autographed celebrity photos, framed reviews, a couple old prints. Much as Miles wanted to see the apartment above, he just wasn't up to climbing the stairs at the moment. Barely sixty-years-old, a little jet lag, a bump on the head and too little sleep had debilitated him in ways he had never thought possible.

"Nothing's changed in my absence," he announced.

"That's good, isn't it?" Nick replied.

"I'm not sure, let's see the office."

Once inside, Miles dropped into his desk chair. Two walls of windows, hung with silhouette blinds, looked out toward the store. The same light color as the blinds, bookshelves lined the remaining walls, just enough room left for a poster of Vanessa Redgrave.

"April's left everything in immaculate order, as you'd expect," Nick commented.

Ignoring the bound volumes, at least two or three of which looked almost as inviting as the one he'd examined at Reg's, Miles began to inspect two shelves that were piled high with an assortment of papers, most with friable, yellowish to brown edges. After he'd exhausted the first shelf, he bent over the one below. It held five or six thin stacks of letters, which April had neatly arranged by year, starting with 1723. He didn't expect to find the manuscript, either there or in the vault. April had sent it out to Elizabeth Duke, the handwriting expert they used, for authentication. First thing that morning, Miles had called her office from Nick's, but, according to her receptionist, Dr. Duke had not yet finished examining it.

When Miles first purchased the lot at Marston Bigot, he had no real opportunity to inspect the contents individually, so he picked up the first stack and carried it to his desk. The script in which the letters had been written was so florid he could not decipher it initially. Retrieving a magnifying glass from the top drawer of his desk, he began to work through the earliest.

London
October 3, 1723

Your Most Esteemed Lordship,

I wish to thank you for your letter of September 25, of which I am now in possession. It was such pure pleasure to read, and then reread those kind words. I, too, enjoyed my sojourn at Marston House, which is filled with every sort of splendor imaginable. I felt privileged to be allowed free use of your lordship's library, which is so sensibly organized, with the largest of its three rooms dedicated to the Greeks and Romans. It is a reader's, indeed a scholar's Eden. The very thought that I might have access to it in the future keeps me awake nights in eager contemplation.

The return journey was not nearly as tedious as the one that brought me to Marston, in no small part thanks to your excellent coachman, who went to every extreme to see to my comfort, despite the inhospitable roads.

I find myself, at present, working on another of the pantomimes that keeps me barely solvent. I will, of course, continue my examination of the poems and plays of Shakespeare, which you encouraged. If that work comes to a fruitful end, I intend to dedicate it to you, sir, in thanks for your largesse and generosity of spirit, both of which still stir marvel in my breast.

I await only word from you when I may conveniently return to Marston to continue my translations in your library.

Most appreciatively,

L.

As Miles was about to lower the magnifying glass, he summoned up a perfectly clear picture of a rather long, low-slung manor house in the French style. It had spanned almost the whole of his visual field the first time he had approached it across acres of gently sloping gardens. He'd passed by a conservatory, in ruins, attached to one end, then by two wings of rooms before entering under a series of arches that led to a formerly ornate doorway.

There, he was met by a proper gentleman, Loren Pritchard, who escorted him up a circular staircase to the ballroom above, in almost the same ruinous condition as the conservatory. He and his host continued climbing to an attic room located over one of the wings, that, in earlier times, must have served as servants' quarters. In that cramped room, Pritchard showed Miles various papers that had been stored in a locked trunk, but he remembered nothing about a manuscript that might possibly have been buried somewhere among them.

All this must have shown on his face, because Nick looked at him as if he were some sort of genie, miraculously sprung from a bottle of bad dreams.

"What is it, Miles? Something's wrong?"

"It's just the manuscript. I have an unsettling feeling about it. Anybody involved with it along the way–Reg, Loren Pritchard, even April–might see something in it that isn't there. Something that was never there, even at the start."

27 A SCONE ANYONE?

Exhausted, Joanna switched sides, holding the bowl in her right hand, flailing at the batter with her left. It didn't matter that she was making scones that were supposed to be stirred only for seconds. If they came out of the oven charred and hard, they would show Rob just how angry she was. She wouldn't have to say a thing to communicate the wound in her heart into which he continued to rub salt. All he had to do was ask her to participate in yet another candidate forum or pose for a new TV ad to find out how fast she could say no.

He'd gotten a phone call from his nubile receptionist, Alicia (who drew out each and every vowel almost erotically when she pronounced her name), at 2:20 in the morning. That had been all Joanna needed to bake a kitchen full of inedible scones. And she would have kept stirring the batter more had she not spotted a pair of black jeans descending the stairs. Avery was up and ready for another day. Quickly, she began to spoon the curdled dough out onto a cookie sheet.

"Scones! My favorite breakfast treat," he said cheerfully enough. "I'm hungry already."

"Sorry." And Joanna truly was. If only she hadn't taken her anger out on breakfast, Avery could have had a warm scone in a few minutes. "You wouldn't want these, believe me."

"Why?" he asked, heading for the coffee pot. "The scones you made last week were the best."

"I'm afraid I've taken my frustrations out on the batter."

"I see. Things not so rosy in Lala land?"

"Don't you dare trivialize my husband's campaign with that Lala name." The moment the words were out of her mouth, she wondered why she was defending Rob.

"With your permission," Avery said, "I think I'll step outside for a little fresh air before the others come down."

Knowing her fits of pique only too well, he beat a hasty retreat out the patio doors, coffee cup in hand. Joanna finished filling a second cookie sheet and put it in the oven on the rack below its siblings. She went to refill her own cup, but decided against it. Her system could handle only so much caffeine. And she wanted her scones, not her mouth to tell Rob what she thought of his receptionist. Instead of coffee, she got a box of Captain Crunch from the pantry.

She was just pouring a bowl when she heard the distinctive echo of penny-loafers on tile. Rob would have slowed to a dead halt had he known what lay in wait for him. She hoped she could spare the others the bloodshed. But if they came downstairs early, they might as well see the food chain of the political world in action. That would be enough to make anyone a vegetarian. She turned down the oven so the scones didn't start to burn. No sense making them *look* inedible, too.

"GooooOOOD morning," a suspiciously cheerful Robert Priestly greeted her. And she knew why. That phone call from AAAliiiciiiaaa.

"And I know why you think it's so good, too."

Having said too much already, Joanna shoveled a spoonful of the Captain into her mouth. God, she wished the scones were done.

"You're still angry about last night? I tried to tell you...."

"Me? Angry? About that...that...that....?" This time she caught herself before she pronounced his receptionist's name with far more vowels than it deserved. Why was she getting so worked up about this particular affair of Rob's when she knew he'd had others before?

"You're upset over nothing."

That did it.

"Over *nothing*, you say? That may be the way you think about our...our....Here, have a scone."

She opened the oven door and, with a hot pad, pitched Rob a scone, then reached in for the entire cookie sheet as his arched up toward the ceiling.

"Hot!" he said a second after catching it.

"But scrumptious. Just take a bite and see."

Instead, the coward tried to break his open to cool the insides.

"Jesus, Joanna. These are incredibly...durable. Perhaps I could use them skeet shooting?"

By this time, Rob had finally managed to split off a vulnerable corner of his scone. As if he knew what lay in store, he sensibly dipped it in coffee before popping it into his mouth and rendering judgment.

"Delicious," he proclaimed as he proceeded to dunk the whole scone, broken corner first.

"Delicious, you say, you cheating liar!" Nothing, not Captain Crunch, coffee or hot scone could stop Joanna now. She rose and backed Rob against the wall between the pantry door and the stove. "You're supposed to hate the scone just like you hate me, treating me...."

"I don't hate you the least bit, Joanna. In fact, I...."

"What do you mean? I suppose those calls from your new receptionist are your way of saying thank you, Joanna, for going with me to all those impossibly boring, predictable campaign events?

"Have you ever stopped to consider the way you treat the people you supposedly love, Rob? I bet your mother beat you unmercifully when you were young. Or was it your first girlfriend who left you for some jock? Is that why you decided on a career in politics, so you could get back at the women who had wounded you so deeply when you were growing up?

"I don't know what the reasons were, but they stop right now. No more campaign rallies. No more women's outreach. No more ...."

"I've never asked you to...."

"If you don't mind, I haven't finished," Joanna said. "I don't know why you asked Alicia to come up here unless...?"

"Excuse me," RJ interrupted tentatively, poking his head through the kitchen door. "I'm ready, Dad. We need to get going."

Joanna hadn't even heard him open the door to his room or come down the hall. Where was her head anyway? Apparently in another parallel and very angry universe.

"Not without breakfast, sweetie," Joanna said in her best mommy voice.

"Oh, man, scones."

"They're not very good," Joanna said. "I'll fix you...."

"Not very good?" Rob said. "They're fantastic, the best your mom's made."

Joanna braced herself on the counter. Rob actually liked the scones. She was on the verge of crying, but absolutely refused to break down in front of the two lame excuses for manhood now violating her kitchen space.

"Gotta go," RJ announced.

Dutifully, Joanna got out the tin foil and ripped three pieces across the serrated edge of the container with a vengeance, then wrapped as many scones and handed them to RJ.

"Don't bite down too hard," she warned. "Better yet, dunk them in coffee."

"Don't wait up. I'll be back late," Rob said as he left.

Joanna stood there, staring after them in defeat until she heard the engine of the F250 reverberate through that end of the house. Moments later she spotted April come down the stairs and start toward the kitchen, then, on seeing Joanna, she retreated in the direction of the front door. If their new Ophelia couldn't handle one person alone, how would it be when they rehearsed the whole of act one the following afternoon, or was it on Saturday?

Before starting breakfast, Joanna had sensed a storm of loneliness brewing. Thank god she had the Players to carry her through. If only she had been an actor, not a front-office shill, she could occasionally slip into someone else's life and forget the hollow one she was living.

Soon, the rest of the company would be joining her around the table and she'd have no time to think about RJ leaving to go back to college, and Rob who'd already left her in almost every way except the crumpled sheets she found beside her in the morning.

There had to be a better way to live, if only she knew what it was.

28 PASSING CHASTE

"Hi, Dad. It's April."

"It took long enough," he bristled the way he always had when angered by some little thing she'd said or done.

He'd called the day before and someone had scrawled his name and number on the message board. It had taken almost twenty-four hours to work up the courage to call back because she knew he'd have questions for her. Questions she couldn't answer.

So she had poured herself a cup of coffee, and after some hesitation dialed, then taken a seat at the refinished kitchen table. Through the French windows in front of her she could see the sun beginning to burn through the tops of the trees in the apple orchard outside.

"How are you feeling?"

As her father answered somewhat haltingly, April heard the sound of approaching footfalls. Someone was crossing the front room. At all costs, she had to avoid the approaching stranger. She thought first about the back porch, but the cord wouldn't reach that far. Looking around frantically, she noticed a door beside the refrigerator. Thinking it led to the basement, she opened it to find herself in a pantry, cans of vegetables and spaghetti sauce and soup all around her. She shut the door before she was able to find the light switch with her hand. It must have been located on the wall outside, so she continued the conversation in the dark.

"Truth is," her father went on, "I've grown tired of lying around in hospital beds and at Nick's, doing things the doctors think I should because they may help my memory. So I went in to work for the first time alone yesterday."

"Was that wise? The doctors aren't telling you to take it easy just to make themselves feel better. They're telling you that for your sake. I wish you'd listen."

April knew that would only anger him more, but she couldn't help it. She was concerned about his health, even though it might not appear that way, she rehearsing in Oakville while Nick cared for him in the city. There was another matter, too. The manuscript. If he found out Dr. Duke had only one page of it and not the whole thing, she'd be the first person he'd ask about it, which was undoubtedly the reason he'd called. She dreaded the answer she was going to have to give him.

"You're starting to sound just like Nick."

"I know. I'm sorry."

"Apology accepted. I called for another reason. Dr. Duke hasn't finished analyzing the manuscript yet. How long ago did you get it to her?"

Closing her eyes, April tilted her head toward the ceiling in thanks. Elizabeth Duke's procrastination had given her a little breathing room, but, knowing her father, that wouldn't last long.

"I don't remember."

"Of course you do, April. I'm the one with the amnesia, remember?"

"Around the first of the month, I guess," she fudged.

Just then the light came on and the pantry door began to open. April wished she was a soup can on the highest shelf. No place to hide, she had only one possible defense. To back into the furthest corner.

"Oh, hello."

Of all people, it was Samuel Pilgrim. Things couldn't get any worse.

"Just a sec," April told her father, covering the mouthpiece. Then croaked to Pilgrim, "a private call, please."

"I just want the Wheaties...there to your left."

When he went to reach for the box, April emitted a high-pitched squawk, like that of a blue jay, then scrabbled to the other corner, still far too close to Pilgrim's huge hand for comfort. He regarded her with a look that seemed more curious than threatening.

"Remember what Joanna said about the phone," he warned her, backing out the open door, cereal box in hand. "I'll be ready soon as I finish this."

In the confusion of the moment, April had forgotten the two of them were supposed to rehearse their first scene together that morning, the worst way Avery could possibly ease her into rehearsals.

"What was that all about?" her father wanted to know.

"I...I can't really talk about it. In fact, I've got to go, unless there's something else?"

"Nothing, except that I love you."

That parting remark left April not knowing what to say in response except good-bye. She couldn't remember the last time her father had ever said anything vaguely similar to her. That knock on the head, the resulting brain injury had changed him somehow.

She opened the door to see Pilgrim standing in front of the French windows wearing black silk basketball shorts and a UCLA muscle shirt. When he turned toward her, April gasped at his well-defined torso, so macho that she would have been disgusted if he didn't look so good. Everything about Pilgrim was just so out there.

"Sorry about the phone," she apologized from a distance. "It was a personal matter. Nothing to do with *Hamlet* or the Players."

"I know," he said, coffee cup in hand. "From what I heard, it sounds like you need help?"

April knew what was coming next. "You need Action Jackson," a tag line identified with Jackson Gunn, the hero he'd portrayed in his *Enforcer* movies. Had he heard everything she'd said, or just intuited her problems with her father? Either way, she didn't like it at all. She had brought enough personal baggage to Oakville without injecting overheard telephone conversations into the mix.

"Just talking to my father, that's all."

"Your father, huh? That's *very* interesting," he replied in a psychologist's dulcet tones. "We're supposed to rehearse on the front porch."

April took a deep breath, then followed Pilgrim down the hall. The great room was being used for the scene between Claudius and Gertrude. When Avery was finished there, he and Steve were supposed to join them in front.

"You still look frightened," Pilgrim said once they were outside. "Your father must be a scary man. Or is it something else?"

"No, not really. Why don't we get started?"

Pilgrim began pushing porch chairs back against the windows. For her part, April raised the wicker curtain that sheltered the porch from the afternoon sun. In front of her lay a postcard scene of marigolds and zinnias in the front yard, and the winding, tree-lined road beyond. Still trying to recover from her initial exchange with Pilgrim, she let the curtain cord get away from her. It caught her left wrist when it failed to hold and came tumbling toward the porch railing.

"Freaking hell." Those words leaked through her lips before she could stop them. She was letting Samuel Pilgrim get to her.

"Here, let me," he said stepping to her side to free her.

"No, *no!*" she shouted, pulling away as far as the tangled cord would allow. Instead of backing off the way he should have, he stood there, no more than a foot away, seeming to enjoy her predicament. She struggled with the cord until her hand turned pink. Then she realized she needed slack to free herself, so she waved Pilgrim back.

"A little room, please," she said when he didn't comply with her unspoken wishes. He waited a few more annoying seconds before he took a couple steps toward the windows.

"I'm worried about Charles Cassidy," he made idle conversation while she tried to untangle herself from the cord. "Maybe it's his medication or something, but he's been distracted lately. If he doesn't pull out of it soon, our scenes together are going to have all the flow of drying glue. My relationship with him is the most important in the play.

"I didn't even know my own father when I was growing up. He just wasn't around. How am I supposed to behave in the presence of my stage father, who's a king, a hero on the battlefield, a master of court intrigue when, in reality, I barely know what the concept of a father is?"

By this time, April had freed herself. Rubbing her rope-burned wrist, she backed a safe distance away.

"Something's wrong, April. What are you so afraid of?" he asked again, looking at her searchingly. "Is it because we're alone out here?"

"It's not just that."

"Then it must be because you're alone with me?"

April didn't understand. Why on earth had he said that unless...unless he was a mind reader.

"I...I...what do you mean?"

"It's pretty clear, isn't it? You're out here alone with a black man."

April had not yet managed to recover her composure. It appeared Samuel Pilgrim could see right through her prejudices.

"There's another choice, you know?" she said finally.

"What's that?"

"Maybe because you're a *person* and you're black." She still couldn't come right out and use the A-word to describe herself.

"Men and women, too, huh? Man, are you fucked up, but at least you're honest about it. That's better than most white people."

Given Pilgrim's powers of perception, she couldn't help wondering if he saw right through her to Avery too? After all, she'd shared his bed for almost two glorious hours the night before. Pilgrim didn't know that. Nobody did, which told her they'd have to be careful about future after-hours meetings, all that much more difficult now that they'd opened the hothouse door.

She was still rubbing her wrists when Avery stepped out onto the porch. He was dressed in casual attire she'd never seen him wear before—sandals, cutoffs, a Spuds Mackenzie Party Animal sweatshirt and baseball cap. The outfit, if it could be called that, didn't really appeal to her, but still it was hard to keep from running over and throwing her arms around him, exactly the wrong thing to do in front of Pilgrim, or anyone else there at The Gables.

"Morning, you two," he greeted them. "Steve's gone off to the bathroom. He'll be joining us in a second. Let's see, April, why don't you stand over by the railing? You can use the door for your entrance, Samuel. You've followed her from the banquet hall to an ante room after you

144

slipped her the potion. It's already started to affect her feelings toward you."

The moment Steve walked through the screen door, Pilgrim turned away. When he swung around again, his face bore the imprint of a pleasantly surprised, rash young Hamlet, who spoke aside.

Hamlet. Is that our sweet Ophelia with me now

Who once was dressed in children's clothes?

April gathered herself to voice lines that were utterly alien to her own feelings.

Ophelia. The same, my lord, I know not who I am.

An hour ago my mind was passing chaste

Yet now its fires cannot contain their heat.

I must escape the crowd to quench the coals.

Pilgrim removed an imaginary hat and stepped forward to fan her with it. Avery did nothing to stop the improvised gesture. It was all April could do to remain in character, and in place, tempted as she was to back away as he advanced.

Hamlet. Then let me happily unfire those flames

Though that runs counter to my own desires

For hide I cannot their excess from you

And do not wish to as you are so dear.

Ophelia. Then you too feel their heat, 'tis not just me?

By this time, their two foreheads were within inches of each other. April could not hide her reaction. Ophelia's trembling would have been from love, induced by the potion Hamlet had stirred into her drink. April, on the other hand, felt only fear.

Hamlet. Not just their heat but their proximity

To one alone who fuels its flames well high

To lap the skies and thus consume the stars

That can no brighter burn than my own heart.

Hamlet's brief speech unmoored April even further, not so much in fear as from surprise. She knew his words from the script, but not the restrained passion with which Pilgrim infused them. His tensed forehead and limpid eyes said almost as much as Shakespeare's words. She could hardly believe the Hamlet opposite her was Samuel Pilgrim in gym clothes, but that's precisely who he was.

His extraordinary reading kept her close to him until she realized how he had affected her and pulled away.

Avery stopped them.

"No, no, April. You've just swallowed a love potion. Any scruples you have about Hamlet's affection toward you are wilting as you look at him. You should, at very least, be inclining toward him, not standing back like a painter sizing up a model. Remember, you feel an attraction for him the likes of which you've never felt before. Now again."

Even as they started over, April silently cursed Avery for not understanding her feelings at all, or did he understand them too well? Either way, he was determined to peel away her defenses layer by infinite layer until she herself became all but invisible. Didn't he understand that, with time, she could construct a complex character for Ophelia out of who she, April Oliphant, was? A stranger in a society of friends. An outsider in a world run by inside players. They went through the scene twice more, then Avery left, still dissatisfied with Ophelia's apparent aloofness toward Hamlet.

"Don't you think he's just awful?" she couldn't help asking the moment the he was gone.

"Not awful in the sense that he doesn't know what he's doing," Pilgrim opened up immediately to April's unexpected question, "or that he's got a Jehovah complex. I just want him to bring out the real passion in the play. In this scene, for instance, why not have us do something that will galvanize the audience? Something it's never seen before. Ophelia's already drunk the love potion. Why not have her put her downstage hand around my waist, caress my butt? Better yet, slip it under my codpiece. That's real theater."

April barely heard this last remark, mainly because she didn't want to. She was shaking her head so violently the rustling of her hair nearly drowned out Pilgrim's words. Both men were too much, far too much for her just then.

"Avery may be known as an actor's director," Pilgrim went on, "but there's only one of us he truly understands."

"Who? Charles maybe?" April said, praying he wasn't thinking about her.

"Charles? Hardly. Our Gertrude, Valerie Schneider."

At first, April didn't understand what he was saying. There could be no mistaking his inflection however, which told her he thought there was something between Avery and Valerie. The others had been at The Gables almost four weeks now. That meant Pilgrim certainly knew more about what was going on there than she did. On the drive up, Avery had admitted having several girlfriends since his divorce. Perhaps Valerie had been one of them, or was she still?

April had gone through so much in the last forty-eight hours. Now this.

Pleading a migraine, she hurried to her room. She had made it successfully through one rehearsal, and with the most challenging cast member. Panic hadn't completely overtaken her and made her run off mid-scene, which was, in itself, a major accomplishment. No, it was Pilgrim's causal remark about one of Avery's former girlfriends that had sent her scurrying to her room.

Sitting on the edge of her bed, she realized there was an elevated cadence in Pilgrim's voice when he spoke of Avery and Valerie. Had their Hamlet already read her so well he knew the worst thing he could possibly say to her? At very least, he realized there was something between Avery and her. If others found out, it would be disastrous for both of them, but especially for Avery, who could ill afford cast members thinking their director was favoring one of them because he was having an affair with her.

That he might be having an affair with two of them, however, was too much for April to comprehend.

29 THE *KING* RETURNS

Miles locked the door behind him and didn't bother to turn on the store lights. No sense alerting passersby that he might be in. He had not the slightest intention of handling foot traffic until he resolved questions that had left him churning in his sleep much of the night.

As he was leaving home, bagel in hand, he had run into Nick, who tried to persuade him not to go in to work alone, but Miles insisted. He was intent on reading through Lewis Theobald's letters to see if there was any mention, no matter how small, of another play besides *Cardenio*, perhaps in manuscript form, on which Theobald and Charles Boyle had collaborated.

He'd just finished making coffee when the buzzer interrupted him. Even though he didn't want to be interrupted, he looked up at the security monitor to see a large NYPD police shield, clutched in an outstretched hand, held in front of the camera lens. Immediately, Miles buzzed in the wiry man, a mulatto he guessed from the grainy image on the screen. The suit jacket he wore looked a size too small for his bony frame, giving him the appearance of a police detective who'd just put himself through the permanent-press cycle, clothes and all. The briefcase at his side looked as if it, too, had been sufficiently battered on the bumpy ride inside the washer.

"Good to meet you in person, Mr. Oliphant," the agile little man said when Miles greeted him out front. "Sergeant Terrill Cochran, Missing Persons and other things, Fourteenth Precinct. I'm here mainly about other things this time, but I'm happy to see you safely back at work."

Miles remembered the name. Another detective, David Neville, had mentioned it several times in London. Cochran had been Neville's New York contact.

"Thanks for all your effort on my behalf, Sgt. Cochran. Come in, please. I've got some coffee going in the office if you'd care for some?"

"Why not, since we may be spending time together."

Miles didn't exactly know what the detective meant by that, but still he led the way to his office and offered Cochran a seat at April's desk.

"I see you're a Vanessa Redgrave fan?" the detective observed, nodding at the office poster.

"Not so much me as my daughter. April loves her. Wanted to grow up to be just like her," Miles said, handing his unexpected guest a Bibliomania mug three-quarters full. "I'm afraid all we have is sugar and creamer."

"Black is fine."

"You said you came because of other things, not to check up on a former missing person. Seems the only thing this person's missing anymore is large chunks of his memory."

"Much of the time after major brain trauma that's only temporary. I'm sure your memory will return."

"I certainly hope so."

"I was kind of hoping to find April here?"

"She's upstate rehearsing a play that opens, end of the month."

"So she really does take after Redgrave?"

"Judge for yourself at the Eldridge Street Theater."

"I'll do that. I was hoping to talk to her."

"I can give you her number. She's hard to reach, rehearsals and all. They've got only one line at the place where she's staying."

Sgt. Cochran stared down at his coffee a long time before looking back up.

"Maybe you can help me then? The first time I spoke with your daughter in person, she mentioned you'd discovered a valuable manuscript in England."

"She's told me as much herself."

"You don't remember it?"

"Only vaguely," Miles lied. He had to maintain appearances, especially with a policeman he barely knew.

"Maybe this will help then."

Cochran reached down, opened his briefcase and drew out a sealed plastic bag with a thin stack of slightly burnished pages with deckle edges. On top of the first, Miles could make out the title: HAMLET, KING OF DENMARKE. He didn't know for certain, but it appeared he was looking at the manuscript he thought Elizabeth Duke was examining. What was a New York City detective, of all people, doing with it? A question that perhaps he should have kept to himself, but which, in his astonishment, he couldn't help posing out loud.

"That's a rather complicated story," Cochran replied, "the details of which I don't fully know myself. Does the name Walter Dinsmoor mean anything to you?"

"I...I can't say," Miles replied, even though he recognized the name immediately.

"He's an antiquarian bookseller on Madison Avenue. I got a blanket email from the detective in charge of art theft for the city. When I read it, I was fairly certain I knew what he was talking about from a conversation I'd had with your daughter. It was about a manuscript of *Hamlet*, like the one you found in England. Evidently, a somewhat shady art dealer walked into Dinsmoor's store and tried to sell it to him for a hundred-thousand dollars. Knowing what he was looking at was too good to be true, Dinsmoor said he'd have to authenticate it, gave the dealer a receipt and voila. I was hoping April could identify it for me before we proceed further. But maybe you could?"

Miles didn't know quite how to respond. There he was, looking at something he thought was in the hands of a respected graphologist. It wasn't possible there were two manuscripts anywhere in the world like the one sitting in front of him. He'd have to call Elizabeth Duke the first moment he could.

"I would need time with it."

"How much time?"

"In my condition, that's hard to say."

"You can have the rest of the day. I need to get it back to the evidence room before they close tonight, or the sergeant-in-charge is going to chew my ass."

"But I'm the rightful owner."

"You know that, Miles, and I believe you. But there's the matter of your memory, and police-department evidence rules. I brought some gloves with me."

"I've got a whole boxful in my desk."

"Good. Use them while you're examining your little baby there. In the process, maybe you'll recall some things that could help us both. If you can tell us how and where you found the manuscript, maybe we can use that information against the thief."

"What about fingerprints?" Miles asked tentatively. "Wouldn't they be of some help?"

"Of course. We've dusted and lifted every latent print we can find, no small task for thirty-six pieces of paper. The lab's working on them now, if that's what you're asking."

"But you haven't fingerprinted me?"

"No need to."

"Won't you want to eliminate me from consideration, based on my prints?"

"They're already on file. The London police took them in the process of trying to identify you. Now, if you don't mind, I brought some work with me. I'll just sit here at your daughter's desk."

With that, the sergeant took some papers from his briefcase and set them on the desk in front of him. More confused than at any time since he'd first regained consciousness in the hospital, Miles couldn't figure out why the manuscript had come full circle back to him. There must have been a break-in at Dr. Duke's, but, in that case, surely she would have called and told him.

He dipped into his desk drawer and pulled out a pair of disposable gloves. Inside Cochran's Ziploc bag, he found thirty-six individual sheets of foolscap, covered top to bottom in tiny secretary hand, so finely written he could make out only the title initially.

His hands were trembling, either in anticipation or because he'd had nothing to eat but a bagel all day. Still, he poured himself and Sgt. Cochran more coffee, then took out his magnifying glass and began going through the manuscript, a task that grew only slightly easier as he became accustomed to the handwriting.

The characters and setting of the play were the same as those immortalized by Shakespeare, but the action was far different. Miles was, it seemed, reading something of a prelude to the all-too-well-known *Hamlet*, an impostor pretending to be the prince, but in king's clothing this time.

Hungry, discouraged and only partway through, he pushed the packet aside for a moment, wondering if he wasn't being taken in somehow? His last time at the office, he'd read enough of Lewis Theobald's letters to realize their author was a true Shakespeare scholar. A call to the research desk at the public library had further informed him that Theobald was, by training, an attorney, who had given up law to try his hand at translations from Greek and Latin. Later he'd written poetry, plays, librettos and even pantomime, almost every type of literature except the novel, all to eke out a rather tenuous living.

Theobald had, as well, discovered no less than three copies of *Cardenio*, then adapted and presented them under the title *Double Falsehood* to the London public, only to have the play pronounced a hoax by some. One of the three copies of *Cardenio* had almost certainly been provided by the recipient of the letters now in Miles' possession, Sir Charles Boyle, a talented intellectual, who lent Theobald unstinting support for almost twenty years. Was it possible that Theobald, Boyle, or both of them had concocted the manuscript in front of him?

With Cochran's permission, he took Theobald's letters from the shelf and compared their open, elegant cursive to the tight, compact lines of the *King Hamlet*. They were as different as English and Arabic. Theobald, or Boyle, could have written out the play only with studied effort. Perhaps one or the other was ambidextrous, used one hand for the letters, the other for his so-called *Hamlet*? Or could Theobald have had someone else copy it out? Of the two men, he had by far the greater motive. Money.

Further into his reading, Miles shot up from his chair so rapidly that blood drained from his head, leaving him dizzy and weak-kneed. Steadying himself on the edge of his desk, he hurried to the front of the store the moment he recovered. There, he located an example of Shakespeare's hand in the plates accompanying *Sir Thomas More*. Clearly, the handwriting in the manuscript was similar, perhaps even identical to that in the *More*. Either Theobald (or Boyle?) was a skilled imitator, who had a copy of something in Shakespeare's hand on which to base his forgery. Or Miles had stumbled on the find of the century—an extant manuscript in the hand of none other than William Shakespeare himself.

He glanced at his watch to see that it was already 3:37. He had been in his office over six hours with nothing to eat, and hadn't thought it any later than noon. He called Elizabeth Duke only to get a recorded message. No other choice, he simply asked her to return his call.

Famished, he realized that Sgt. Cochran would be taking the *King Hamlet* back to the evidence room soon. He still needed to comb Theobald's letters for any mention of a manuscript he might have sent to Sir Charles Boyle, perhaps seeking patronage for yet another of the editor's literary adventures. If Miles indeed found something to that effect, he would have further reason to suspect that Lewis Theobald, not Shakespeare, was the author of the new *Hamlet*.

But when he rose to get more coffee, his knees grew weak, his head dizzy. He remembered nothing else before crumpling to the office floor.

30 AFTER HOURS

The bed went crashing into the wall again with a dull thud.

"Oh, God, that's soooo good!"

The bedsprings continued to heave and fall like a thrashing machine.

"That's it. More. Give me MORE!"

"Quiet. You'll wake the others."

"Don't stop now. Please, don't stop."

They didn't, of course. The bed kept grinding and slapping the wall. The breathing got heavier, the groans louder until it became almost unbearable.

"Yes. YES! YYYEEEEEEEEEESSSS!"

There it was. Finally.

April had tried plugging her ears with tissue at first. When that didn't work, she jammed them with her index fingers, but it was even harder to fall asleep that way. How long she lay in bed awake she didn't really know. It seemed like hours. Then, just when she removed her fingers and began to doze off, the commotion in the adjoining room started up all over again.

In anger this time, she knocked on the wall, timidly at first, then louder until there could be no mistaking they heard her next door. Things grew so quiet suddenly she could hear the exhaust fan in the attic, and hoped she hadn't offended Valerie too much. Except for Samuel Pilgrim, she was the Players' biggest star. Even so, her bedroom antics were just too much.

As April lay there, she couldn't help wondering who was in bed with Valerie? She prayed it wasn't Avery. It just couldn't be, she told herself, even though he had promised to come by her room that night, but never showed.

Unable to sleep, she slipped on her robe and out into the dimly lit hallway. Counting the number of doors carefully, she drew up outside Avery's and knocked softly at first, then a little more loudly. After she whispered his name more times than she should have, she leaned back against the wall to reconsider. He'd had a hard day. Perhaps, he'd slept right through their planned late-night rendezvous.

She went back to her room and moved the rocker to the door, which she left slightly ajar, determined to see who came out of Valerie's room. If it was Avery, she'd leave the next morning and never set foot on stage again.

This time, she intended to keep that promise.

31 ROAD TRIP

In the headlights, the white lines of the highway flashed by the windshield before disappearing into space beside the gray Mercedes. When the road veered left, Rob slowed excessively even before the approach, and Joanna didn't know why. He wasn't that drunk, nor was the curve that sharp. Yes, they'd all undoubtedly had a sip or two too much Champagne, but the solidly built 500 SE would take a sturdy oak with it if it went off the road. And leave them without a scratch. Of all evenings, this was one when Rob could afford to loosen up a little, and he wasn't slurring more than an occasional word.

"We'll never get home at this rate, honey," she said sweetly.

"That's precisely the point. Getting home. I'll have wasted the entire summer if we get killed in an accident tonight."

"You're right, of course," she conceded. "But you've got to get RJ to the airport by eight in the morning."

"He's dead asleep in back. And I can get by on three hours for one more night."

"I know you can. It's just not good for you."

"I appreciate the show of concern."

"It's not show, Rob. It's for real, my big strong Congressman husband from the Twentieth District."

"I not a Congressman yet. I'm a Congressman-elect until the vote is certified and I'm sworn in."

"Don't be like that. This is one night in your life when you've earned the right to celebrate."

Rob tightened his grip on the wheel and leaned forward as if carefully studying the next turn when there was nothing but bright lights and absolutely straight highway ahead, all under a canopy of trees. In the glow of the dashboard, Joanna could see him blinking his eyes open. Maybe he was in worse shape than she thought.

"Why don't you let me drive?"

"I'm perfectly okay," he protested. "In fact, I'm feeling great." Having said that, he took his hands off the wheel and pummeled the padded roof with his fists. "I did it! I won," he shouted. "I beat that sanctimonious Democrat by a good four points and Hiz Dipstick, Karl Pierson by even more. Now he can go back to mayoring his podunk town and cry in his beer all day long. I still can't believe I did it!"

"Not so loud. We don't want to wake RJ."

"You were the one who told me to celebrate."

"Maybe we should have driven to Albany, gotten a motel room for the night? That way we'd all get a couple hours more sleep before going to the airport."

"That'd be a welcome change. At least I wouldn't have to wake up to Samuel Pilgrim grunting his way through his weight training program at six a.m.."

"It's only for another week. Besides, you two are buddies now. You get along famously."

"You're right. He's a decent guy, unlike some of the...."

"Let's not go through that again, Rob. You were the one who thought it would be a good idea for everyone to come to The Gables since you were going to be out campaigning all the time anyway."

"Yeah, well the campaign's over now."

"So are rehearsals...almost."

"It's your *almosts* that get me, Joanna. Every time you utter that word, I know I'm going to get ambushed worse than when you start a sentence with a *but*."

"Then don't be a butt head like you're being right now."

Rob mashed the brake pedal and Joanna shot forward so sharply she almost struck the dashboard. At first she thought he must have seen a deer in the road, but there was nothing ahead except a pair of approaching headlights. He eased the car onto the shoulder.

"What's wrong, Rob?"

"I wouldn't go calling me a butt head if I were you, Joanna. Not after what you did tonight."

"What do you mean?"

"You know very well what I mean."

"We spent all night at your victory party at the Sheraton. We watched the election results come in, and you won. You made a great speech. We both drank champagne. And we danced."

"Once, Joanna. You and I danced together *once*."

"You were busy shaking hands, accepting everyone's congratulations."

"And you were busy, too. With Gene. On the dance floor and at the bar."

"What's that supposed to mean?"

"You were kissing him, Joanna."

"Maybe a little peck on the cheek. He was your campaign manager. I was congratulating him on your victory. He was the one who helped you win, remember?"

"Not with him sucking your mouth like that. His hand all over your ass."

"You're making that up!"

"I am like hell. I saw it with my own eyes. And don't go telling me I was seeing things. I've still got perfect vision at fifty-one. What the hell were you thinking?"

Johanna honestly didn't remember anything like the kind of kiss Rob had described. Maybe she'd had a little too much Champagne, on top of a couple highballs. She'd talked with Gene, of course. He deserved congratulations, too, even more than that for helping Rob pull the election out in the end. Maybe she had given him a little kiss, but nothing like the one Rob made up, and with such explicit detail.

Only then did she realize what Rob was up to. He was trying to strike first.

"You haven't answered me, Joanna?"

"I know why you're doing this, Rob. You've made the whole thing up because you're having an affair with that strumpet receptionist in your front office."

"Get out of the car!" he whispered harshly.

The demand shocked Joanna into sudden, very necessary sobriety. "You're not serious?"

"I'm dead serious. Get out!"

"We're miles from home, Rob," she half shouted in panic. "And it's dark out."

As she was speaking, he reached in front of her and unlatched her door. He *was* serious.

"The walk'll sober you up. While you're at it, think about the good life I've provided all these years. Twenty-five-hundred square feet on Fifth Avenue. A landmarked house in the country with over half a section of land. All the trips to Europe, the Caribbean. Some of the best wine and liquor around. Ask yourself if my fucking brother can provide any of that. My god, he's just a high-school teacher."

"You're crazy, Rob. Drunk and talking crazy. I didn't do anything wrong with...."

"Quiet, you'll wake RJ."

"I'm already awake, Dad," RJ's sleep-edged voice crept in between the cracks in the argument. "You're not making mom walk home."

"Shut-up, RJ," Rob yelled. "This argument doesn't involve you."

"Yes, it does. If mom walks home, I walk with her."

"Okay, then *both* of you get out. And walk to the airport in the morning while you're at it, why don't you?"

"You don't really mean that, Rob," Joanna tried to reason. "I know you don't."

"Oh, yes I do."

He yanked the keys from the ignition, got out and started a little unsteadily around to her side of the car. In a flash, Joanna slammed the door and depressed the lock. She heard the automatic lock click open, then the door. Rob reached in and started tugging her by the arm.

"Stop it, Dad. I mean it," RJ said.

The warning served only to make Rob pull harder. Joanna grabbed the steering wheel with her left hand, but she was no match for her husband. After he yanked her from the car, she had only one defense left.

"It isn't going to look very good next Tuesday when the *Standard* runs the story of newly elected Congressman Robert Priestly forcing his wife and son to walk home on State 237 after his victory party."

"You wouldn't?"

"Oh, yes I would. It's a long walk, Rob. Try it yourself."

As she spoke, RJ struggled to get out of the car, but his father stiff-armed him into the backseat. The eighteen-year-old was far too fast for him and got out the other side before Rob could stop him.

"You two! What am I going to do with you?" he bellowed in anguish.

"Drive us home, that's what," RJ replied evenly, all signs of sleepiness having vanished from his voice. In fact, it had grown serious in little more than a minute. Joanna wanted to run around and hug him, but sensed that was the worst thing she could do just then. Rob's head slumped forward.

"Nothing in the paper?" he asked almost sheepishly.

Joanna had to think, but it didn't take long for her to come up with an answer. "If you agree to take RJ to the airport in the morning?"

"I intended to in the first place."

"And forget that foolishness about your brother?"

"That was your foolishness, Joanna, not mine. Now, get in!"

She could have held out, but it was very late, and she had forced Rob to back down this far. She knew she'd still have to deal with his accusations about her brief kiss with Gene, but that would come sometime in the future. RJ had already climbed in back, leaving her no choice really.

Silently, she slipped into the front seat. Rob got in the other side, put the key back in the ignition, and they drove off as if nothing had happened there by the side of State Highway 237. Certainly nothing any of them wanted the outside world to know.

32 THE UNANSWERED QUESTION

Miles still didn't feel entirely comfortable living at Nick's. The rugs, the paintings and old maps, the antique furniture, bone china place settings, the crystal and silver, the canopy bed, all were a bit much. Miles liked older things, but sometimes it was hard to breathe in there without being overwhelmed. Perhaps he had been an Indian ascetic in another, former life, and his soul's transmigration to the present, graceless era had been fast forwarded when he'd been mugged by Karmic outriders in London.

Nick had been the best nurse a man could possibly have. He was strict but not overbearing, encouraging, and a decent cook who took only mild offense when Miles didn't feel like eating. With all this, he didn't know how he could want more, yet he did.

And the more he wanted was actually less. Definitely less food. Less art. Less encouragement. The painful truth was, he really didn't want or need much except Nick's love. He hated to keep saying no to things for fear of pushing Nick away and perhaps losing him. And—after fourteen hours in bed the day after he'd fainted in the store, plus a few good meals—he was beginning to recover his strength. That morning, he'd walked to Central Park and back, and not felt completely exhausted. All thanks to Nick, who even retrieved Lewis Theobald's letters from the store for Miles to read while recovering at home.

In part, they read like the letters of an improvident writer sucking up to his patron. In part, like a pedant trying to impress a thoughtful aristocrat. Despite the abiding formality in tone that seemed a product of the times, there was an underlying, almost repressed sense of true affection between males, whether of pure friendship or something more, that compelled Miles to move on to the next, and then the next as little other correspondence did. The letters indeed told a tale of a love that could never be, and yet was, he was certain of that.

In all of them, Miles had found only two passages that hinted somewhat vaguely at the manuscript April had found among the letters. In the first, written September 2, 1728, Theobald spoke of sending his benefactor "something that might be of interest for a future joint endeavor." Nothing more than that, certainly no mention of *Hamlet* or Shakespeare, just an unspecified "joint endeavor." Then, almost a year later, Theobald entreated Boyle to "...come to some decision about our project. The time will not soon be so ripe again."

It sounded suspiciously as if Theobald were proposing a project much like *Double Falsehood* on which the two men had collaborated the year before. If that were indeed the case, then how had Theobald come by the manuscript for a second play by Shakespeare? Had it, and the others, perhaps been preserved by a member of the King's Men, Shakespeare's company? Or passed down through his family? Perhaps by some other means? There weren't that many possibilities really, which made it all the more unlikely Theobald should have owned or had access to it.

Certainly he had some other project in which he wanted Boyle to participate, and, more importantly, wanted Boyle to fund. Would Theobald really be willing to perpetrate a hoax, in the form of the *Ur-Hamlet* manuscript, just to make a few extra guineas?

That seemed unlikely to Miles, but, one way or the other, it would help explain how the priceless, or not-so-priceless, manuscript, now being held for evidence by the police, had first come into being.

When Miles next phoned the office to retrieve his messages, there was only one on his machine. It was from Elizabeth Duke, returning his call. Taking a deep breath, he dialed her number.

"Dr. Duke's office, Karla speaking," the receptionist answered promptly after the first ring.

"This is Miles Oliphant. I'm returning Dr. Duke's call. Is she in?"

"Just a second, I'll put her on."

"Miles, how are you?" Elizabeth said only moments later.

He gave her his own, rather upbeat assessment of his condition, then, trying to be diplomatic, told her about Sgt. Terrill Cochran's visit two days earlier.

"He had the *Ur-Hamlet* manuscript with him, said it had been brought to Walter Dinsmoor by some art dealer. I thought you had it?"

"Only the last page."

"The last page?"

"That's all April sent me. I'm positive she kept the rest. Have you checked the vault?"

Of course Miles had. It wasn't there because the police had it, all except one page. April must have known what had happened to the other thirty-six. No wonder she'd been so reluctant to return his calls. And she would get another the moment he hung up with Dr. Duke, who, after another expression of surprise, launched into her conclusions about the lone page of writing with no more than sixty words on it April had sent her.

"I want to emphasize that the size of the sample was so small," she began, "my opinion is far from definitive. I found no watermark on that single sheet of paper. Next, I compared it to all six of Shakespeare's known signatures, most written with a feeble hand. The down-strokes of the initial *w*s, the loopy links between the *h*s and *a*s, the badly formed   *k*s–all found in Shakespeare's signatures–are almost entirely absent from the sample. After thoughtful consideration, I can only conclude that the manuscript is a forgery of some sort. That opinion might change if I had a larger sample to work with.

"I hope you're not too disappointed, Miles?"

Disappointed was hardly the word he would have used. *Devastated* would have been more like it. Despite his misgivings about the part Theobald had played in preserving (falsifying?) the manuscript, Miles' hopes for its authenticity had been undermined by an expert he trusted, who was telling him that the new *Hamlet* was a fake.

"Are you certain?"

"As I say, barring additional material to work with, I'm afraid so."

"And there's nothing in the manuscript that might be Shakespeare's?"

"Not exactly. The script and angle of the letters are much the same as Shakespeare used. In those cases, it's difficult to say anything conclusive because the majority of Shakespeare's signatures, the only truly authenticated examples we have of his handwriting, were written in his dying days when he may have been too weak to hold a pen properly."

"I guess then there's no way...." Miles couldn't continue his futile cross-examination any longer. "I'm not certain why my daughter sent you only one page when she had the entire manuscript in her possession then. I'm going to put my friend Nick Reed, who's a lawyer, to work on this. Maybe he can get the police to let you analyze the whole of it. That might, in fact, help them with their case."

In the meantime, Miles would have to let April know Dr. Duke's discouraging news and ascertain from her just how in god's name the manuscript, his *invaluable* manuscript, had ended up in the hands of the police.

33 DINNER FOR ONE

Earlier in the day, Charles had been only too happy to get April for the caller, Miles Oliphant. The tousled, handsome actor knew her father had discovered the play the company was working on. He was not about to let the source or quality of the manuscript come between him and the young woman who had really grown to be quite something in her time away from the company. Any excuse, no matter how flimsy, to talk to her and whittle away at her defenses was more than welcome.

Surely she knew by then that she would find in Charles the perfect ally at Queen Joanna's court. He was well-informed, friendly, quick-witted, and supremely gifted at steering his way among the various courtiers, especially the female courtiers, who found him a charming companion. And more.

He thought it an especially good sign when, later that evening, he climbed the stairs to her room to ask what she'd like for supper, and she asked where the others were dining.

"They're outside where Joanna's barbecuing baby back ribs. The patio's in shade now and it's really quite delightful out with just the slightest scent of honeysuckle in the air," he said through her door in an attempt to draw her out.

"Really? Maybe I will come down then."

"You will?" Charles gulped. After all he'd heard about her aloofness, he didn't think there was a chance she'd accept his invitation. Now, he didn't know if he really wanted to share her with the others. That Stephen Ransom was such a sexual predator!

"Not to eat with them, but perhaps just have some salad and maybe a glass of wine on the front porch."

"That would be perfect. Tell you what. I'll set everything up for you so you won't even have to come into the kitchen. Salad, lightly dressed. There's a broccoli casserole...a little of that. And a nice California cab."

"You don't have to go to all that trouble. I can get it myself."

"No trouble at all," Charles called back to her. "Give me, say, five minutes to get it ready. You might dab on a bit of mosquito repellent. They're not too bad this year, I hear, but it is *that* time of night."

April thanked him and he took off down the stairs. So caught-up was he in the success of the moment, he had almost forgotten his intention to get a little recharge to help make it through dinner, but now...well, maybe he wouldn't need it.

He got everything set up for April on a little metal cocktail table at the very corner of the porch, then slipped back into the kitchen. Putting a little of this and that on his own plate, he joined the others out back under the grape arbor. Samuel Pilgrim was in the middle of regaling them with one in a seemingly endless supply of Hollywood stories.

"...that thing looked like a grenade, it acted like a grenade, and it was coming right toward me. Now, this was about our twentieth take. I was supposed to catch the muthafucker in midair and toss it back at the squad of Iraqi Republican Guard that had ambushed us. Only it was made of rubber. When I snagged it, all this yellow goo came spurting out. Someone had filled the dummy grenade with paint. It was only acrylic, but I was covered in the stuff. It would take forever to get it off my face and clothes, so we had to wrap for the day. Let me tell you, the director, Syd Powers, was furious. I still don't know who pulled that little stunt, and it's a damn good thing I don't."

Charles more stirred his food than ate it, but he wasn't nearly so reluctant with the wine, which was better than it had any right to be after only two years in the bottle. Whoever had selected it, Joanna probably, had taste, but when Avery stood at the end of the table, Charles wished he could dive into his glass and resurface only after their resident *wunderkind* finished speaking.

"I see you're drinking," Avery ambushed him.

"Just a little glass now and then," Charles said as smoothly as if the church fathers had scripted the line themselves to celebrate communion. "I can handle it."

"I hope so." But Avery's eyes drilled into him with their message of irredeemable guilt. Damn him, the rest of them anyway. Couldn't they see how vulnerable he was, how little he had in life since Paige had left him? Not wine, women, or even theater could fill the gaping void he felt now.

When he saw that Avery intended to go on, he pointed his finger to signal that he needed to go inside. He intended to take a bottle of cab, pour April another glass and see if she didn't desire just a little company.

"If you would, Charles," Avery called out behind him, "this next announcement involves you."

"Oh, shit," Charles muttered to himself.

Valerie chuckled, telling him that his comment had been overheard by some of them at least. When combined, the two words *involve* and you *cut* through all the blather of the evening like no other words could. Charles dreaded what was to come. He was going to need something stronger than cabernet sauvignon to ward off the slings and arrows Avery was about to launch at him.

"I've decided to cut the last part of scene five, fourth act, starting with line 112. It's too long. Doesn't really advance the action."

This announcement didn't bother Charles until he did some calculating and determined Avery was talking about the conclusion of the scene in which the severed heads of two Norwegian counselors were presented by the King to a crowd of blood-thirsty Danes.

"But that's my best scene," Charles protested without bothering to raise his hand.

"It may be the scene in which you have the most lines, Charles," Avery admitted, "but it's hardly your best. You have not one, but two banquet scenes and...."

"They're just so much spectacle."

"The part of the presentation scene I'm cutting is nothing more than that, spectacle *ad nauseam*. Shakespeare wrote it, I'm certain, to recapture his audience before the final act."

"What's wrong with that?"

Charles couldn't suck up his disappointment a single moment longer. He had constructed the whole of the king's character around the blood-thirsty, vengeful tyrant that Hamlet's father showed himself to be in the very part of the scene Avery intended to cut. In it, Charles could strut without prancing, bark without much bluster. In short, show himself to be the well-trained, polished actor of the old school that he was, a type all but extinct on the contemporary stage.

April was undoubtedly still sitting on the front porch, her wine glass in need of refilling. Charles would, of course, be only too happy to oblige, and in doing so prove to Avery who was the true master of the two of them. Certainly not the peacock with the bastardized French surname.

He grabbed a bottle of California red Joanna had so generously provided to lull the others into apathy, and set out across the patio and in through the kitchen doors. To hell with Avery. He was going to his room for a little boost, then back out onto the front porch for a glass or two of wine and a little *friendly* conversation with April Oliphant. It would be just the two of them against the world.

Somehow, he'd lure her to his room that evening.

Or die trying.

34 A TAWDRY LOVE TRIANGLE

A knock at the door caught April just as she was getting ready to go downstairs.

"Yes, who is it?"

"Valerie. Your father's waiting in the garden."

April's heart seized up a moment, fearing the truth of that statement. It had been foolish to think she could avoid his questions about the manuscript forever, and that meant making a double confession. That she had given the new *Hamlet* to Avery, *and* that the East Village Players were performing it with her, his thieving daughter, in the role of Ophelia. She had no time to explain it to him now. Nerves rubbed raw by the sultry, late summer air, she was nearing the point of exhaustion. They all were, yet everyone except April seemed to go on with unimaginable grace.

Then she realized Valerie couldn't possibly be talking about her real father. She could only be referring to Charles Cassidy, who was reading Polonius' part for Richard Metz who had been called to testify in Boston that day. She dreaded working with Charles again after the previous evening's debacle on the front porch. She had known, of course, the way he was with women, but somehow he had always treated her with respect before. Perhaps it was the wine, or something stronger, but this time he simply had not known where, or when to stop. She had repulsed him so bluntly she was afraid she'd driven a stake through his boundless ego, as if that were possible. Now, apparently, he was ready to rehearse as if nothing had happened.

April opened the door, and there stood her competition. In fact, Valerie Schneider couldn't possibly be younger than forty with a figure any beauty-pageant contestant half her age (and Avery?) would give anything to possess. So what if a few strands of gray streaked her hair, and her aquiline features were sharp enough to cut paper? April didn't know whether to be jealous, or downright envious, so she opted for both.

"It can't be my father."

"No, dear. Charles, subbing for Richard. The three of us are scheduled to rehearse in the great hall."

"Oh, god!" April gulped.

"Don't worry. He's harmless, really."

"We can't be talking about the same Charles Cassidy?"

"Fear not, I'll walk down with you. Avery said we should start without him. Something came up about the theater rental and Joanna needed to talk to him. He'll join us in a few minutes."

April hesitated a moment, then grabbed her script to make it look as if she wasn't trying to put Avery's lover off. Avery's *former* lover, she told herself and prayed that she was right. They had just started down the stairs, April a good four steps behind, when Valerie picked up the conversation.

"I want you to know I think it takes real courage to do what you're doing." Here, she paused and turned around. "According to Jung, all truly great artists have a touch of agoraphobia. You can't go out on stage and..."

"I wish you wouldn't use that word!"

"Word...? Oh, you mean agora....Forget I mentioned it, but I don't see why it distresses you? It's a badge of honor in some people's eyes."

"I simply don't have the illness you're talking about. Not completely, that is. I just...like my own company a little too much, that's all."

"See? There you are. I'm the same way. You have to be or what meaningful contribution could a person ever make, no matter whether an actor or a dentist?"

"That's all very nice," she told Valerie, "but it's hard to do that locked away in your room. Unless you're a genius of some sort, the only thing you contribute to is yourself, and that's so ultimately selfish. I ought to know."

"Then more people should suffer agora...what you do. The world would be a far better place without everybody trying to fix it. Most of the time, they only end up making things worse. And if you think that sounds cynical, you should hear me on...."

"Ah, there you are," Charles crooned from the bottom of the stairs. "You look so...well, beatified this morning. *Both* of you."

"Skip it, Charles," Valerie shot back, then turned to April and whispered, "he's ninety percent adorable bull shit and the other ten percent is cologne to mask the smell. Ignore everything he says but his lines."

April didn't really know how to act with Valerie at her side now, and Charles waiting for them. It was just too many people. Too fast. She began to back up the stairs one at a time until she stood perhaps five feet above them. Still her heart thudded against the walls of her chest.

"I'll be waiting for my cue just inside the kitchen door," Valerie said.

Charles understood April well enough after the previous evening's fiasco. He stepped aside while Valerie left the room. With only two of them there now, April inhaled several times, gathered herself and descended the stairs once again. From there, he led her to the far end of the room. Without even trying, she slipped into the role of the dutiful daughter, helping her ailing father assume a seat on the daybed.

Ophelia. Did you see Prince Hamlet at court this day?

Cassidy pivoted toward her is if he abruptly realized he'd stepped back in time almost eight hundred years.

Polonius. No, not as much of him as of a ghost

    Though I did see too much o'the king's disgust

    For he did treat his wife with such contempt

    I thought he was intent to do her harm.

April heard only a few more words of Charles' lament about life at King Hamlet's court. For the whole of it she was caught in the web of his effortless performance. Without a word of prompting, he had settled into character even though just reading Richard's lines. He was now both courtier and doting Father. The one time he touched her shoulder, it was as a sign of paternal affection, not with the grasping paw she had experienced the night before. It took a leap of will to remind herself she was not watching a performance, but a part of it.

Then Gertrude entered seeking Polonius' advice. Without doubt, she knew what she had done to provoke her husband, the king. In part, she sought Polonius' absolution, in part his advice.

It took April until Avery, Steve, and Joanna joined them before she began to mesh with her two fellow actors, and it felt wonderful. There she was, acting as if that were a perfectly natural way of being, far different from the impoverished life she normally lived.

All this unnerved her, but Avery insisted they keep replaying the scene. April willed herself through it again and again, driven by an adrenaline high, the product of Avery's presence there.

Some thirty lines into what she hoped were his final adjustments, she suddenly understood something she hadn't before. The youthful Shakespeare had squandered his talent on a tawdry love triangle. The king loved his wife, Gertrude, which was boring stuff really. So young Will had Claudius fall top knot over tin cups for Gertrude, the sex goddess of Denmark, and she reciprocated his interest. Friend of all, Polonius was the trusted advisor whom Shakespeare had assigned the task of harnessing the three raging libidos.

"Are you with us, April?" Avery asked when she dropped a line.

"Sorry," she apologized. "I just had one of those sudden wake-up moments."

"Then you'll be fully focused from here on. Again from the top."

His words stung worse than a swarm of African bees. She allowed her eyes to return the favor. No way to avoid her non-verbal assault, Avery took a couple steps back. April banked the flames that fired her tongue until the end of an inspired reading. Then loosed them after Gertrude left to return to the castle, and Ophelia confessed her love for Prince Hamlet to her father.

Polonius forbade his daughter to see the prince in private ever again. The potion had left Ophelia no choice but to love Hamlet, even if that meant defying her father. April knew she should, in reality, also have applied Polonius' advice to Avery LeMaster. As it happened, she

172

was as helpless as Ophelia when it came to love, the true depths of which she had not felt in years, if ever.

By the time rehearsal ended, she could not have spoken another word if she'd wanted to. Starting toward the stairs, she marveled at the minor miracle that had occurred in the great hall that morning. She had just worked together with not two, or even three, no, with six other people. The greatest part of that by far was the thrill of being caught up in something larger than herself.

"Brava," Joanna Priestly whispered hoarsely as she caught up with April immediately afterwards. "You were magnificent, April. Simply magnificent."

"Thanks," she bumbled, not knowing how else to respond. She was so drained, she couldn't find any other words. It was going to take all the energy she had left just to get ready for the next in a seemingly unending schedule of rehearsals.

35 EARLY TO BED

Joanna turned the Jacuzzi jets down to a dull purr and allowed the pulsing water to dig into her aching muscles. Citing a massive migraine when, at worst, she had a tension headache, she had handed kitchen responsibilities over to two of their understudies, Larry and Rachel, poured herself a large glass of Maker's Mark and retreated to the master bathroom. She would not have made even passable company at dinner that evening, and wanted only to drown her sorrows, and more.

The scene between Gertrude, Ophelia and Polonius, taken in while she was seated on the stairs, had shown her why Avery had held out so long for April to take the role. She *was* Ophelia, there was no other way to put it. She played the hesitant, love-stricken teenager without need of costume or scenery, utilizing every part of her body, especially that quicksilver face of hers, as if she were so utterly in love she couldn't possibly escape its sweet grasp. It was such a remarkable portrayal, Joanna would never again chide Avery about matters of casting. With Samuel Pilgrim and now April Oliphant, they were certain to get the kind of reviews, even from Shawn Kirby, the Players hadn't seen in years.

All this left Joanna with feelings of inadequacy no amount of bourbon or bath water could wash away. Yes, maybe she had helped pull the company through tough financial times, but what did that mean really? Only that she had a good head for business and a network of wealthy friends that any decent manager could patch together. At best, her accomplishment was something akin to playing the role of Ophelia's mother. Nobody knew who the woman was. Nobody cared about her. And certainly nobody remembered her.

RJ was back at college now. All she'd heard from him was a single, two-minute phone call telling her he'd arrived safely. And that was it. Both Rob and Gene were gone as well, Rob in Washington and his brother back to the city for the beginning of the new school year. She was going to miss Gene more than she'd admit. She hoped she'd see him at the opening of their *Hamlet, Part One*, as they were now calling the new play. She'd made a special point of sending him a letter with a comp ticket two days after he'd left The Gables.

She let the water drain, toweled off and began to dry her hair. When she went to take another sip of bourbon, the towel fell to her ankles. She should have picked it up immediately, but instead examined herself in the bathroom mirror. At forty-six, she'd held together fairly well. Yes, she'd developed a bit of a tummy, and cellulite had begun its inevitable creep down the backs of her thighs. But neither was so bad she couldn't work them out with a nice, long spa vacation. Her breasts would hardly pass for those of a teenager, but Rob still liked them, or he had until a couple years ago anyway. If she could change anything, really, it would be her hair which was unglamorously straight and just beginning to gray. Maybe she'd have it cut and streaked, but would Rob notice? She doubted it.

She really didn't understand when things had started to go wrong between them. Perhaps it had begun as early as his appointment to the Governor's Task Force on Prisons, and certainly by the time he had become chairman of the county Republican Party. The elephant had snuck its trunk under the tent, then taken Rob's place in bed. Joanna didn't blame the party, *her* party, she could never do that, but there was a time for politics to stop and for life to begin. And it looked as if Rob had begun a new one without her.

Hair dry now, she brushed her teeth, then slipped into her nightgown. The bedroom was a welcome change after the steamy bath. With only a moment's thought, she shut off the air conditioning and opened the windows to let in the evening breeze.

Even though it was barely eight, she got into bed, but hardly felt up to reading. She would lull herself to sleep, or try to, thinking about ways to ensure the success of their

Ur-Hamlet. She'd need to write a press release about April rejoining the company, but there timing was everything. She couldn't come right out and lie, saying that April Oliphant would be assuming the role of Desdemona since they were no longer doing *Othello.* Nor did she want to announce April's return at the same time she informed the entire world of the New York premiere of a new play by Shakespeare, then built on the buzz created by that news. After, of course, the experts weighed in with their preliminary findings on the authenticity of *Hamlet, Part One.*

Things were just getting too damned complicated.

36   A CRITICAL GUEST

"That's right, Mrs. Priestly," Lars Carlsson repeated over the office phone, "the 22,000 dollar figure includes back rent plus a deposit for the coming season. We'll be happy to open the doors once your check has been deposited in the Settlement House account, and cleared. Or, I'm afraid, we'll have to lock you out."

"Lock us out? Entirely? You can't mean that?"

"Sadly, I do."

"But I thought...."

Joanna swallowed the rest of her sentence. Carlsson had left her no choice really. It was either find another theater in very short order, an almost impossible task, or go to the bank, write a check on their joint account, and say good-bye to her husband of twenty years, and to either The Gables or their two-floor Manhattan apartment. Certainly she'd get one or the other in the divorce settlement.

"The best I can do is get you a certified check Friday. It's as good as cash."

"If you want your theater open...." Etcetera, etcetera. Carlsson might know the amount of the check he was demanding, but he knew nothing of what that would cost Joanna once Rob reviewed their September bank statement. That gave her almost a month to smooth his ruffled feathers, massage his far-too-well stroked ego in an attempt to get back in his graces. Fortunately, she still had time to ship the things she loved from The Gables to New York. If Rob wanted any of them, well...their lawyers could fight it out.

"I'll bring by the check in person."

"Just so we get to the bank before closing. You drive a tough bargain, Joanna. I must say, I like that about you. Like it very much in fact. Maybe we could go for drinks afterwards?"

Was it possible? The well-chiseled Lars Carlsson, with whom she'd been sparring for weeks, was coming on to her? It sounded seriously as if he were asking for a date...or something more? Fortunately, she didn't have time to reply. The sound of scuffling on the front porch interrupted her train of thought entirely.

"I'll be there by four," she said and hung up abruptly.

"You could be arrested as a peeping Tom, you know?" barked a familiar voice outside.

"What do you mean? I wasn't looking in the window. I was just about to knock."

Unmistakably, the first speaker was Samuel Pilgrim. She vaulted from her desk chair to the north windows. Beyond them, she saw their Hamlet wrestling with a man in a Hawaiian shirt and crisply pressed khakis. She could tell nothing about his face because of the straw hat he wore for protection against the blazing sun. Samuel twisted the intruder's arm behind his back and pushed him toward the door. In seconds, Joanna was standing at the entrance to the great room, where four or five others were rehearsing the confrontation with the Catholic priest. The front door slammed shut, interrupting Valerie in mid-sentence.

"Stop, that hurts!" the stranger protested.

"It'll hurt more if you don't shut up," Samuel said.

"Take him to my office," Joanna intervened, thinking she recognized the newcomer now. She raised her voice. "Back to work everyone."

She lead the two struggling men to her summer office, concluding on the way that their unexpected visitor was none other than Shawn Kirby. She hadn't recognized him at first because of the hat that covered his face, that and he'd put on so much weight his paunch lapped the belt cinching his pants. His face and hands had grown so pale they were almost translucent. Dark stubble cut into his pink cheeks and masked his chin.

"What the hell are you doing spying on us?" Pilgrim demanded as he shoved Kirby into a chair. "Who are you anyway?"

"Easy, Samuel. Easy," Joanna said in her most maternal voice, thinking to draw out Kirby enough to learn the reason for his unannounced visit. "Let's start this conversation all over again. It's beastly out there this afternoon. Perhaps our guest would like something to drink? Some iced tea? Cold water? A soft drink of some sort?"

"I'd take a beer, if you've got one?"

"Get him a Genesee, would you, Samuel? And ask Avery to join us while you're out there."

"Now, what's your name?" she inquired once Pilgrim left.

"You know very well who I am, Mrs. Priestly."

"Oh, I do?" she continued to play dumb.

"I'm Shawn Kirby."

"I don't believe it. It's been so long. And you look so...."

A knock at the door interrupted Joanna. It couldn't be Samuel back with beer so soon.

"I'm busy," she called in response.

"I...I need to speak to you," a female voice echoed from the hallway. It sounded like April Oliphant.

"Come in then."

"It would be better if we talked outside."

"Of course." No harm in catering to her little aversion toward people.

"This will only take a second," she told Kirby before slipping into the hallway. April stood to one side in the shadows about ten feet away. With sense enough to keep her distance, Joanna took only a step or two toward her.

"Why don't you want to come into the study?"

"You know, it's my...."

"Oh, right, your agoraphobia. Now...."

"Please, that word!"

"Give it up, okay?" Joanna couldn't help saying. She'd had enough of April playing the emotional cripple when she could act like Joan of Arc with all that fire under her serving only as further inspiration.

"Wasn't that Shawn Kirby I saw come in the front door just now?"

"Yes. Why?"

"He comes by the bookstore sometimes. I...I think he likes me."

That last sentence explained so much to Joanna, especially why Kirby had reviewed them only once since April's departure from the Players' stage.

"You don't know how important that information is, April. Did you want to tell me anything else? Has Kirby been stalking you perhaps?"

"Oh, no, nothing like that. Sometimes I think he's trying to flirt, but he just comes off sounding like an overgrown schoolboy. If there's any way I can help with him, let me know."

Joanna didn't know why, but the offer surprised her. Was their Ophelia beginning to come out of her shell?

"I will. And thanks for stopping by. That took real courage."

The poor thing looked like a fish an angler had gently set back in water as she swam down the corridor in the opposite direction. Joanna had no real sense what she was going to do with Kirby, but, according to Rob, next to golf, catch-and-release was the most civilized sport ever.

As she turned to go back into the study, she saw Samuel at the other end of the hall, three beers in his hand. And she wondered who'd declared happy hour.

"Where's Avery?" she asked.

"He's just wrapping up. He'll be...oh, there he comes now."

They waited until the preoccupied director joined them, then all three entered the study together.

"Here you go," Samuel said, handing a Genesee to Kirby once they shut the door behind them.

"Thanks. You're okay, Samuel, despite the rough treatment outside."

"Enough chit-chat," Joanna said. "I know who our visitor is."

"Who?"

"Shawn fucking Kirby, that's who. Son of a bitch!" Avery muttered, supplying the name for her. He didn't swear often, but when he did it was never with such venom as Joanna detected in his voice just then. It had taken him far less time than she to recognize the much altered looking critic.

"If you wanted to visit, you could have always called," Joanna attempted to redirect the conversation.

"That wasn't the impression I got," Kirby replied.

"Someone must have told you what we're doing. Who?"

"I'm not at liberty to divulge my sources." Kirby lifted the bottle to his lips, taking only a nervous sip.

Just as Joanna suspected, one of the company *had* let out news about their new *Hamlet*, inadvertently or on purpose. If the latter, she was fairly certain she knew who had done it. The same person she'd glimpsed in the phone booth in town a week ago.

"Someone's been feeding you false information," Samuel stepped in.

"I don't think so. You're rehearsing a play, I could see that much. I heard Hamlet's name mentioned twice while I was on the porch. And I caught a glimpse of April Oliphant. You don't mean you've actually talked her into appearing with you again? How did you do that after...well, you know?"

"Avery got to her," Joanna said cryptically.

"Her comeback, if that's what it is, is a megastory in itself," the critic continued. "She'll make a fabulous Ophelia...if she's really going to go back on stage again?"

"Who said anything about Ophelia?" Pilgrim cut in. "We're doing *Othello*."

"That's alright, Samuel," Joanna said. "Let's not play games with Mr. Kirby anymore. In fact, I think we should invite him to this evening's rehearsal since he's come all this way to see us." Both Avery and Samuel looked at her as if one of her front teeth had just fallen out. "It's going to be alright. There's a free bed in RJ's room now. Shawn can spend the night, drive back to the city in the morning. On one condition."

"No deal. I'm not writing a favorable review for the price of a beer and a night's lodging."

"If we ever got a good review from you, Kirby," Avery snarled, "I'd know what we were doing was pure crap."

"Please, Avery," Joanna intervened. "I'm not asking for a favorable review, Shawn. I want something else."

"I already know you're doing *Hamlet*. And that Oliphant's your Ophelia, if that's what you're thinking."

"You won't recognize a line that she, or anyone else speaks."

"You mean LeMaster's rewritten the entire play?"

"No, Shakespeare has. Now here's the deal. We'll give you an exclusive on a story that will be the biggest of your career, and April's only a part of it. You'll see what I mean this evening. But you've got to make certain it gets in the weekend edition. Do we have an understanding?"

"I get an exclusive?"

"You do."

"And I don't have to say anything positive?"

"Just keep an open mind."

Kirby examined his beer bottle as if it were made of fine crystal. "I'll have to check with my editor."

"Fair enough."

"I want to reiterate. I don't have to gush about what I see?"

"Not unless you feel like stepping totally out of character," Avery complained.

"Pay him no heed," Joanna said. "You can use the phone on my desk here."

They left Kirby alone in the office to call his editor. As Joanna followed Samuel and Avery out into the kitchen, she asked herself what was going to happen next in the strange sequence of events that had begun to unfold with the discovery of the *Ur-Hamlet* and, most recently, had brought the *Chronicle's* critic to her door. She wished she knew the answer to that question. Whatever it was would certainly be interesting, or she might as well start selling insurance.

37 A CONFESSION OF SORTS

April's father refused to give up. He'd left four messages the day before, so she resigned herself to the inevitable. Anybody might overhear if she used the kitchen phone. Even though she'd never seen the inside of the Priestlys' bedroom, they had to have a telephone there, and Rob was in D.C., Joanna out grocery shopping in Albany.

April knew the master bedroom from the outside only. Located in the turret on the second floor above the study, it was surrounded on three sides by windows. Opening the door, she peered in and spotted the phone on the nightstand. Abandoning caution, she entered, sat on the bed and went to pick up the receiver, but her hand fell back to her side. Perhaps having money and marrying well were not such awful goals in life, especially if they allowed her to live in light-filled rooms like the Priestlys' bedroom.

Life with Avery certainly didn't hold out much prospect of that. It had taken only one night in his sun-starved, single-window bedroom to figure that out. She'd been able to do nothing to sort through the mix of emotions she'd felt since then. Whenever she thought of him, which was pretty much all the time they weren't rehearsing, she was as confused as ever. Even if he meant all the things he whispered to her in the throes of passion, how long would those feelings last? A week? A month? Certainly no longer than a year, given the way he apparently went through women. She tried putting those bleak thoughts out of her mind. After that failed, she picked up the phone again and dialed.

"Oliphant's."

"Is that you, Dad?"

"April, thank god. I was afraid you'd never call."

"I've been busy."

"I'm sure you have, but I've got to talk to you about something. A friend of yours actually."

"A friend?"

"Yes, Sgt. Cochran. He stopped by the store Monday. And do you know what he had with him? My manuscript. Evidently some art dealer tried to sell it to a colleague of mine, Walter Dinsmoor, who reported it to the police. I don't understand how it ever got into his hands when it was supposed to be at Elizabeth Duke's?"

He didn't know how relieved she felt when she heard the news. The manuscript had been found! Perhaps that had calmed her father. He hadn't sounded nearly as angry as she had imagined when he mentioned Dr. Duke.

"I know."

"You mean you know someone attempted to sell it?"

"I know Dr. Duke didn't have it." She hesitated here, but knew she couldn't put him off any longer. "You see, I...I asked Avery LeMaster to examine it for internal evidence that it was by Shakespeare. It was stolen from him before he finished."

"How did *that* happen?"

"Someone broke in and took it from him. They don't know who. From what you're saying, though, the police have recovered it?"

"A stroke of luck actually." Her father's voice fell off. "Well, what did Professor LeMaster think? Is it by Shakespeare?"

April couldn't quite believe it. While she hadn't lied, she hadn't told her father the whole truth either. Still, he hadn't demanded to know why she had let the manuscript leave the store. Evidently he was more interested in the question of authorship than in placing blame, which wasn't like him at all.

"Yes, he's convinced it's by Shakespeare. One of his early plays, perhaps the earliest."

"He's sure of that?"

"As sure as he can be, based on internal evidence. We'll have to wait to find out what Dr. Grossman and Elizabeth Duke say for further confirmation."

"About Dr. Duke. I should tell you something."

From there her father went straight on to say that he'd received Elizabeth Duke's report. Based on it, he'd concluded the *Ur-Hamlet* was likely an 18th-century fabrication, probably by an early editor of Shakespeare's. Or perhaps someone he thought a friend, Reg Sloane, was trying to put one over on him.

By the time he hung up, April didn't know what to think except that she *knew* the play wasn't a hoax. It couldn't be, not with the quality of the writing, the depth of characterization found in it. More than anything, she couldn't grasp why an early editor of Shakespeare's, or her father's friend would have manufactured it? It just didn't make sense.

Of course, she hadn't yet told him the East Village Players were performing his *Hamlet*, and she was their Ophelia. Better to inform him in advance than to have him read about it in *The Times* that weekend.

If Dr. Duke was right and the manuscript turned out to be a forgery, it would have her father's name forever attached to it. The Great Oliphant-Shakespeare Hoax. Worse yet, April would be part of it. A very large part.

She had to explain everything to him, and soon.

38 A CALL TO LONDON

Miles had been happy there wasn't much business on his return from England, but that was changing slowly. His fellow bookmen in the city had heard the story of his mugging and subsequent amnesia, and did little things to steer business his way. Naturally, it was less desirable business. Referring a difficult customer. Calling about volumes that moved slowly. Offering unwanted items from a larger auction lot. He could have told them that he didn't really have amnesia, in fact quite the opposite, but he still couldn't afford to let anybody except Nick in on his secret.

He didn't really miss having April at the store to guide him through things. In fact, he rather liked working alone with no one to oversee his life there. He faced more than enough supervision at Nick's, and insisted on taking care of business matters himself to be free of all that. At least he could breathe in at the office and not feel he had to breathe out a certain way.

That morning, his second day alone at Oliphant's, he decided to call Reg Sloan. There were questions he needed to ask. Questions only Reg could answer. At first, he thought he had missed him, but let the phone ring longer than usual. As he was about to hang up, he heard a break in the static, then a voice come over the line.

"Sloan's," Reg half panted into the receiver.

"This is Miles. Miles Oliphant."

"Of course, Miles. I was just locking up when I heard the phone. Had to dash all the way back to the office. Excuse the heavy breathing. I should really get more exercise, I suppose. How are you getting along?"

Miles told his friend in as few words as possible, playing up his supposedly failing memory.

"Matter of fact, I've been meaning to ring you," Reg went on. "I wanted to put together one final piece of the puzzle before I did."

"Yes?" Miles said, not wanting to seem too eager.

"About a week after you left, I called out to Marston Bigot, but got little more than the usual run around. Very corporate. As you know...sorry, I guess you may not. Anyway, a big international mining conglomerate has taken over the manor there and started renovating it, all very carefully. It was Mother's friend, Loren Pritchard, who called me after one of the workers came across the cache of old papers you purchased. Evidently, it had been secreted in the attic of a wing scheduled for renovation."

"Do you know how I can get in touch with Pritchard?" Miles asked to see how forthcoming Reg was.

"Yes, he lives in a retirement community outside Plymouth. I've made inquiries, but evidently he's on holiday somewhere in the south of France now. Perfect time of year for it really. Most of the French have returned home after *les vacances*. He's got no message service, so I try calling Plymouth every few days to see if he's back yet. So far, I haven't raised him. It's probably better that you speak with him yourself anyway."

"Thanks," Miles said. "Did he mention anything to you about a manuscript in that lot of papers?"

"A manuscript?" Reg asked after the longest of pauses. "No. What kind of manuscript?"

"That's just the problem. I was hoping you might know. You see, April, my daughter, found it when she was unpacking a crate I sent with papers, that sort of thing. But it was stolen immediately afterward. I don't remember anything about it. Not finding it. Not buying it. I didn't say anything to you about it when I returned from Marston?"

"Not a word."

Miles held his breath a second before speaking again.

"I think you know more than you're letting on, Reg?"

"Why on earth would you say that?"

"Because you were the one who suggested I go to Marston House in the first place. You must have known I'd find something of interest there?"

Miles hoped he hadn't pushed Reg too far.

"If I knew something about a manuscript, why wouldn't I have wanted to look at it, perhaps buy the lot myself?"

You knew my mental state at the time and wanted to foist the *Hamlet* you'd concocted on me. Miles didn't say this, of course, only, "I don't know, Reg. That's what troubles me."

"Whatever it is, it must be valuable. Couldn't your daughter tell you anything more about it?"

"I thought you might be able to?" he replied evasively.

"Sorry. I doubt Pritchard knows anything either, or he would have said something."

Reg gave him Loren Pritchard's phone number and they spoke several more minutes before saying good-bye. Though Miles couldn't be certain, he felt that if Reg had truly had a hand in inventing the *Ur-Hamlet*, he'd have said something to give himself away, but he'd made only one misstep, the long pause while he gathered himself after Miles first mentioned the manuscript, which didn't prove anything really except that Reg was no fool. He wasn't going to implicate himself openly. But maybe Loren Pritchard would be able to offer up some crucial piece of information once Miles contacted him.

The most troubling thing in his life just then was that manuscript, which held the shape of his future. If indeed it was by Shakespeare, Miles Oliphant would be in possession of the only complete manuscript yet known in the Bard's hand, which would bring him the instant fame he was all but certain he had wanted before he was mugged. But not anymore, and he didn't know why.

Perhaps it had something to do with Teddy?

39 HUMILIATION

"I'm afraid I can issue you a cashier's check for only 4,985 dollars, Mrs. Priestly. Minus our fifteen-dollar charge, that's all that's left in your account. 5,000 dollars."

Joanna stared right through Arnie Rice, with whom she'd been doing business for six years now. She had to keep calm, maintain her dignity no matter the cost, but it was obvious to her, and undoubtedly to the Vice-President of the Oakville Bank as well, that Rob had withdrawn everything from their joint accounts, leaving only 5,000 dollars for her to live on. The belly-dragging turtle.

That told her everything. He had found a place in D.C., furnished it to his liking, no doubt installing Alicia there as well. He was also sending her another message he was too spineless to deliver in person, if only over the phone. Their marriage was over and he was leaving her only a pittance to live on until she came begging.

Much as he might relish that prospect, Joanna would never give him the satisfaction. When her lawyer, Laura Castillo, was finished with Rob, Joanna would have more than enough money to fund ten theater companies. As things stood, however, she would have nothing, short of one more promise, to offer Lars Carlsson for use of the Settlement House theater.

"I should have expected that," she said without a hint of the grief she felt in her voice. "Sorry to have troubled you, Arnie."

"No, the trouble was all mine," the disconcerted banker replied. "I mean...well, you know what I mean, Mrs. Priestly. I wish it had been someone...anyone else who told you. But I felt it was my duty."

"I only wish some other men felt as duty-bound as you."

Joanna rose, shook the banker's hand once briefly, and stepped toward the door in resolute strides that revealed none of the heartbreak she felt just then.

40 A LATE-NIGHT INTRUDER

April had tried, but couldn't get back to sleep.

As she lay there, she allowed her eyes to trace the swelling line of Avery's bicep to his shoulder, down his collarbone to his neck, then to the back of his head, all in porch light that filtered through the bedroom window. Not once while they were making love had opening-night jitters beset her. That dread event could come tomorrow, but she was safe for the moment with Avery beside her.

She didn't have to think about it much to realize she was more deeply in love than she ever had been in her life. She'd had a couple serious boyfriends in high school, more in college and afterward, but they were no more than phantom lovers compared to Avery. Everything about him made her think she was the luckiest woman alive, especially the depths of his mind. There didn't seem any directorial problem that, with thought, he couldn't solve in the most ingenious ways. Avery LeMaster might not be Sir Peter Hall, but he was just as brilliant in his own right.

She was still caught up thinking how lucky she was to have him when she heard a slight tap on the door.

"It's me, Avery. Are you there?" Before April had a chance to place the voice, the handle turned and the door opened. Instinctively, she rolled off the mattress onto the floor under the bed. From there she could see two slippered feet and legs under a nightgown against the night light in the corridor. They vanished from view when the door shut. Seconds later, the bedsprings creaked above her head.

"Wake up, Avery. It's me."

By this time, April recognized Valerie Schneider's voice. Suddenly she understood why the little minx had taken up with Charles Cassidy. All along she had been trying to make Avery jealous, and to think that, only moments before, she herself had been sitting in the very spot Valerie now occupied. She wanted to grab the two feet dangling in front of her, jerk them back and break them at the ankles. How could anyone, especially Valerie, take her place in bed just when she was thinking how much she loved Avery?

The springs creaked above her as Avery rolled over.

"Is that you, April?" he murmured.

Avery had spoken April's name, not Schneider's or anyone else's, and she felt a momentary surge of relief.

"April?" Schneider gasped. "What do you mean, *April*?"

"Oh, it's you, Valerie?"

"Do you know what you just called me, you pedophile? April, as in April Oliphant, our cute little Ophelia just out of middle school. You're screwing someone half your age, who you cast, not because her sheltered ego's perfect for the role, but to satisfy yourself with someone whose skin is so youthful she doesn't have to wear make-up. You disgust me!"

The creaking of the springs was replaced by very theatrical sobs.

"None of what you say is true, Valerie," Avery tried to calm the late-night intruder.

"Every word is, and you know it."

"It's over between you and me. It has been for months."

"It will never be over. I won't let it."

"Stop with the melodrama, Valerie. You can play the scorned lover if you want, but only in this room with me. You have been phenomenal so far, not letting our past come between you and this production. That's acting like the true professional you are. I expect to see that same behavior through the final night of the run. I know you won't disappoint me."

"Oh, won't I? Well then, consider this, Mr. Polanski. I won't be there to disappoint you on that last night because I won't even be there the first night. And I hate to say that because this is such a breakthrough play, and, despite you, a clever production. Gertrude is a complex character, unlike some cheating wives I've played before. I'm going to trash it, trash you, and...."

At this point the bedsprings above April give one final groan as Valerie vaulted from the mattress.

"You ought to be arrested for seducing a minor, or whatever the hell they call it," she shouted before slamming the door.

April wanted to melt into the floor and disappear as Avery slid off the bed and knelt beside her.

"It's safe now, April. You can come out."

He was lying. It wasn't safe, and never would be again. Just when she had persuaded herself that Avery was the love of a lifetime, Valerie appeared and shot holes all through that ill-founded theory. She was never going to come out from under that bed.

"Look, Valerie said some awful things, I know. Because you look so young, she doesn't realize you're almost twenty-five. I'm not a pedophile, a philanderer or anything of the sort. I just happen to love women, but none the way I love you. And that's the truth. Now, please come out and let's talk this through like two sensible people."

April's profile began to rise slowly from the wax of the floor. Avery had been honest about his attraction to women, his previous affairs. He had come right out and said he loved her. Not only that, but he loved her as he had no one else. Did he mean it, or was he simply using words the way he usually did, to smooth actors' ruffled egos? He sounded sincere, but how could she be sure?

"My affair with Valerie is over. It has been for months now. There is simply no place for her in my life anymore. That belongs to you. It has from the time of your Rosalind at Stony Brook. I held back, didn't say anything then because you really were too young. Not anymore. Valerie's wrong about that. You're all the woman I could want. All the woman I will ever want."

Still, she said nothing. How could she when he had just told her she was all the woman he could ever want? Was he really talking about her?

"You have to come out sometime. When you do, you can go to your room and I won't take it as a sign of anything except a need for sleep. That's all I'll say."

April couldn't possibly sleep after what she'd been through the last ten minutes, but she couldn't stay there on the floor either. The wood was hard and dust-bunnies swarmed all around. She turned on her side and began to ease out from under the box spring.

"Did you really mean all that?" she asked tentatively.

"Of course I...."

She stopped him by extending a finger to his lips.

"Think before you speak, Avery. I want the truth. I'm not going to put you through any more Valerie-type antics tonight. I'll go back to my room, and be vaguely bright-eyed tomorrow. You can tell me everything you just said to me under the bed was a lie, and I'm not going to walk out on you. This *Hamlet's* too important for me to do that. But, please, you must mean what you say."

"But I do. I'm mad for you. Have been for the last six years."

"You probably said the same thing to Valerie, and all the others?"

"I did not, and would not. I never make false promises in that regard. Never utter the L-word unless I mean it."

"And you mean it now?"

"How can I make you believe me?" April didn't really know what she wanted from him after that. He had said all the right things, which was the problem. Could she really trust anyone who had spoken them so easily? She wanted to believe him, she really did, but if she were ever going to pull back, this was the time to do it, or risk losing her heart forever.

"I'm going to my room," she said. "Let's see how we feel about this tomorrow."

"I understand."

"I really think you do."

She was the one who was lying then. Still, she stood tall when she walked past Avery, successfully resisting the impulse for a passionate kiss as she left the room.

She did not, however, leave her doubts behind.

41 THE ACCUSED

Charles' head was throbbing and his mouth dry. His heart was beating so fast it felt as if he should go straight down to the kitchen and dial 911. Or had he just awakened from a nightmare he couldn't remember? He looked over at his alarm. It was 5:37. In the morning! He'd been in bed less than two hours, yet he was so completely awake there was no sense even thinking about getting back to sleep. What had he done to himself the night before?

He remembered Valerie coming to his room, or was it April? No, definitely Valerie. Their sweet new Ophelia was still unmoved by his many charms. Not by those of their hapless director, however, Charles was all but certain. Evidently, she had a selective form of agoraphobia, fearing not all people, just most. But why would she let down her defenses for someone as unworldly as Avery when Charles himself was there? The female of the species was indeed a mystery. If the opposite were the case, he'd have cashed it in long ago. He still thought his chances with her were better than fifty-fifty.

Anyway, Valerie had come by to talk. And was she ever in a state! Something to do with Avery. They'd done a line or two to calm her down. But what after that? Had she fled in tears? He couldn't remember. He paused a moment. Nothing like a little booster to clear the cobwebs that had cut off blood to his brain. He was just about to slice and dice when he thought about the challenges of the coming eighteen-hour day. A good, strong hit of caffeine was, by far, the better option, and so he stored the remnants of their little party in the lacquer vial at the back of the dresser drawer, slipped on his bathrobe and grabbed his script.

In the kitchen, he flipped the switch on the coffee maker to make a full pot, and opened the refrigerator. Sugar in its purest form, that's what his system needed.

Joanna had diced some melon for breakfast, and there was a new jar of strawberry jam. He piled as much as he could on a single slice of toast and consumed the melon straight from the Tupperware container, leaving a few pieces on the bottom for the others. Coffee done, he mixed it with a splash of cream and loads of sugar, and carried it to the barn, where he could go through his lines by himself. He switched on the light and shut the door behind him. By the time he dropped onto the folding chair that would serve as his throne, caffeine and sugar had replaced the torpor left over from the previous evening.

He was determined to be so good Avery would restore the scene he'd cut to allow him to show his character at his haughty, bloodthirsty best. He put aside both script and coffee cup and raised his chin imperially.

King. Do come, good queen, and let us say farewell
To those who came to celebrate with us.

He extended his left hand for Gertrude to take, only to find she was no longer seated beside him.

See how she talks alone with Claudius,
Who in my stead did occupy my throne
But not my lady, too? Is that the truth?
A brother must not too brotherly be
Else what belongs to one belongs to all.

Here, Charles had just started in the direction of the invisible couple when he heard someone applaud his effort from just inside the barn door. Because of the shadows there he couldn't tell who it was until she spoke.

"Bravo, Charles. Bravo!"

Charles didn't know why, but he felt a sudden jolt, not unlike fear, stiffen his spine. He stood there, in pajamas and robe, his senses on high alert.

"You're up early, Joanna."

"In case you hadn't noticed, I'm an early riser. It seems you're up early this morning, too?"

"I want to be at my best for everyone. As you know, the others arrive today."

"That's commendable of you. Here, I brought some more of the coffee you made. I figured you might be able to use it."

Charles decided not to ask what she meant by that, because it was fairly obvious. Had he and Valerie caused a scene the night before? Had their high spirits permeated the entire house well after the excruciating first run-through of the entire play? Or worse?

Joanna lifted a thermos to his cup and poured a mixture with just enough cream to coat the froth on top.

"I added some sugar, too."

"Uh, thanks, Joanna. All contributions greatly accepted."

"I take it that includes the breakfast compote?"

"Compote?"

"The fruit and melon I had diced. When I got the cream for your coffee, I noticed the bowl was almost empty."

"That?" Without the caffeine surging through his brain, Charles knew he himself would have been as defenseless as melon under Joanna's knife. But his mind was working faster than usual now, and he had the distinct feeling this was just the warm-up. "Well, I was going to cut more once I finished here. The others won't be up for another hour at least."

"There is no more, Charles."

"Then I'll just drive to town and get some."

"The Round-The-Clock doesn't sell melon."

"There's always some farmer's field this time of year."

"Poor, poor, Charles." She regarded him as a doctor would a dying patient. "Look, I hate to interrupt your laudable morning labors, but this won't take long, if you don't mind?"

Charles did mind, but Joanna had already picked up a folding chair and started toward his canvas throne. Obviously she expected him to follow. He could have easily ducked out the barn door, but got the feeling whatever was festering in Joanna's brain would only get worse the longer he put her off. It didn't take much to guess what she wanted to talk about.

"That time I saw you in the phone booth in town last week?"

"Me?"

"Don't play the innocent with me, Charles. I don't have much patience on this, of all days. I want to know who you were calling?"

"I don't know anything about...."

"You're far too good an actor to waste your talent imitating yourself. Remember the promise everyone made. No trips to town. No calls except from the phone here at the house. Now, I want to know precisely who you were calling?"

"Those are really silly rules, Joanna. We're all adults here. You have no business telling us where we can and can't go. Who we can talk to. You don't have to treat us like children."

"Then you shouldn't have agreed."

"As I recall, I protested."

"But still you went along. Now, you don't have to stay on with the Players. Nobody does, because we won't be a company beyond this season if we don't fill the house every night. And more. That's what I'm trying to do, Charles. Everyone else is, too. Everyone except you. We made a deal—no town, no calls outside the house—and you're the only one who thinks he's above the law. Now, who did you call?"

"People are sneaking out all the time, you just don't know about it."

"The only person I've seen is you, Charles. I want the truth."

Somewhere in the distance, a rooster crowed. Charles was content to let that stand as his response.

"If you won't say anything, then I will. I know who you were calling. Shawn Kirby."

"Kirby? You've got to be joking. That wasn't me."

Charles was genuinely offended. Joanna had introduced Kirby effusively at dinner two nights before, and no one was more shocked at his presence there than Charles.

"Then you spoke to someone who knew someone who knew Kirby?"

Charles took another guilty gulp of coffee. Strange, but he didn't remember seeing Joanna or her car on the one day he had slipped into town the previous week. He'd made only two calls. One to his dealer. The other to his agent. Perhaps he'd mentioned something to Mort very casually, and, of course, he was connected to everyone in the business. There were so many other ways Kirby could have found out about the Players' new *Hamlet*. Still, Charles couldn't bring himself to an admission of guilt on either of the charges Joanna had leveled against him.

"Maybe?"

"For god's sake, get it together, Charles. Loose lips sink ships."

"This isn't war, Joanna. It's theater."

"Better start treating it like war then, or we won't have a theater left to defend. I want a full apology from you to the entire group before the day is over. No further consorting with Valerie. And hands off our new Ophelia. As you say, this is theater, not a bordello."

With that, Joanna stood, turned a crisp 120 degrees and strode toward the barn door, thermos at her side. There was nothing Charles could do to right his wrong except, perhaps, call Mort, ask him who he'd told about their retreat at Oakville. But that was already so much milk out of the cow's udder. If Charles had only decided to pull the covers back over his head and get a couple more hours sleep that morning, none of this would have happened. But then Joanna would have caught up with him sometime.

The day had not stepped off to a particularly promising start. The only question was, how much worse would things get? He was going to need something far stronger than caffeine to help him make it through.

42 THE FINAL ACT

Not until April was walking back in from the mailbox did she realize how big a coward she'd become. Actually, she had known that ever since she'd quit, literally walked out on everyone in the middle of *Menagerie*. This time, though, any spine she had left had collapsed into a pile of limp vertebrae. She hadn't even had the courage to face her father's anger in person, or as close as she could come over the phone.

So she'd written him a letter confessing everything. It was April, his own daughter, who had foolishly called Avery LeMaster, let him take the manuscript with him to Oakville where it had been stolen. If that weren't enough, she'd offered only the mildest resistance when her former professor had told her he wanted to stage the *Ur-Hamlet*. Then she'd let him cajole her into stepping into the role of Ophelia. There would be two tickets waiting for her father and Nick opening night. Would they please come see her? All as if the letter she'd written was more an invitation than a confession.

By the time she got to the barn, she tried her best not to look around to see exactly how many in the cast were seated there. Absent Valerie, all the seats were taken by the rest of the players and the entire crew up from the city now. This was the first time she would be together with all of them since she left the Players, something of a milestone in itself.

Avery looked almost as bad as she felt. His eyes, usually flash points he used to ramp up the group, wandered off into the darkness of the rafters above and stayed there. His jeans were rumpled. His hair hung in limp strands that he'd brushed back behind his ears because he'd lost his cap. His mind was completely elsewhere. He didn't say a thing about her tardiness, which she feared others would take as favoritism. As he stood there in front of them, he was trying to explain why Valerie had quit.

"I must apologize to everyone, especially those of you who have just joined us," he said, back against a wooden center post, foot propped on the seat of a folding chair. "Valerie has been angry at me ever since our break-up, and that anger came to something of a head last night. She won't be returning, so Rachel will be going on in her place.

"Now, this next part is important. Craig, since you're not in the opening scene, will you go get Charles so we can start?"

That at least partially explained why Avery hadn't blown up at her when she'd slinked in late. He was waiting until Charles got there to tear into both of them.

Craig nodded in acknowledgment and left by the side door.

"Not that I would expect any less," Avery continued, "but each and every one of us must be in first-rate form opening night. Most in the audience will have read Shawn Kirby's preview in this weekend's *Chronicle*. Some will be waiting to extract their pound of our mutual flesh, and as much blood as they can draw from the first scene on. That's warning enough."

April was about to raise her hand and ask Avery to say something about the manuscript. She hadn't told him all of Dr. Duke's preliminary findings, just enough to warn him that the handwriting was suspect. For some unknown reason, he hadn't made an announcement to the entire group. Perhaps he didn't want to undermine their efforts that morning.

Then someone to her left gasped in shock.

"It's Valerie!" Dale Farley offered a moment later.

"Yes, it is," the wayward actor announced herself without a hint of melodrama in her voice. No tears or breast beating either. "I thought you would already be well into act one by now?"

"We've been delayed by a couple of rather longish announcements," Avery said diplomatically, "one of which had to do with you. I informed the company you had decided to leave us and Rachel would go on in your place."

"She won't have to, I'm back and ready to work."

"That's not an opt...." Avery let his eyes, burning through Valerie by this time, finish his sentence for him. They followed her to a chair in which she sat without the director saying another word. Either angry or dumbstruck, he used the ensuing silence to choose his next words carefully, drumming his fingers all the while on his raised knee.

"Is that alright, Rachel?" he asked the blonde in the second row.

"No complaints. She's got the role down."

"Thanks for being so understanding," he told her. "Alright, then, Valerie's back, prepared to accept things as they stand and to work as hard as she always has, I'm certain. Now, we'll largely have to imagine the sets that will greet us at the first tech on Friday. Picture the heavy, gray stones of a great hall, trestle table to my immediate left. Lights will be up, the mood festive. Ophelia, if you'll move your chair beside your brother's, we'll begin."

As April picked up her chair to move it, she, and perhaps Avery, could see through the open door behind them. Craig, whom she'd never thought could move so fast, was sprinting across the lawn from the main house, hand over his chest as if the exertion were too much.

"It's Charles," he called out even before he reached the barn door. "I can't seem to wake him."

Samuel Pilgrim rose and took off just as he did in his movies, like a 235-pound sprinter, streaking past Craig.

"I can't stand around here doing nothing," Avery said, and followed after Samuel, running until he caught up with Joanna. He slowed to a hurried jog beside her, talking to her at the same time.

"What am I doing?" Valerie asked herself in front of everyone. "I've got to go up there."

April would have been right there with the others as they followed behind, but this was the same Charles who had twice tried to force himself on her. Charles whom she pegged as an alcoholic, or worse. Good-time Charlie who never shied away from a joke at others' expense. Fighting her instincts to hold back from the crowd of over twenty-five now, she struck the improvised saw-horse table with her fist and hurried after them. By the time she got to the entrance to the great hall, Joanna and Avery had already reached the top of the stairs. She didn't exactly catch up, content to cling to the railing while everyone else huddled immediately outside the door to Charles' room.

"It's his heart!" Valerie called out. "Sam's doing CPR. Someone call 911. Get an ambulance out here. NOW."

"I'm on it," Avery said.

"Does he have a pulse?" Joanna wanted to know.

"Yes, a whisper of one," Samuel replied. "Probably an overdose. I've seen it before."

"Overdose?" Valerie whined. "How do you know?"

"Get real, Valerie," Joanna said. "You've been sleeping with Charles, how long, and he never brought out a razor when you were in his room?"

As these events played out, April told herself that Charles would be alright. He was too vital a spirit not to. She forgot entirely about the way he had treated her almost since the first day she rejoined the company. Instead, his other qualities, for which he would be remembered by so many, flashed across the marquee of her mind. Charles Cassidy, the Great Actor. The cunning, comical Iago who had all eyes in the house riveted on him and him alone. The incomparable Jamie Tyrone, who was Charles, himself, writ large. So much about the man was ultimately memorable that she wondered why people had to have personal lives at all? Why couldn't everybody, herself included, be actors all the time and not have worry about the troublesome things in life like money? Family? Fame? Drugs?

Then it would all depend on who wrote the script of a person's life, wouldn't it? Definitely Eugene O'Neill for Charles' life. Shakespeare for Avery's. For April herself? Wendy Wasserstein probably, but why would any self-respecting playwright want to take on a subject so much smaller than life?

It was time for April to change that.

43 A PLACE IN THE COUNTRY

The large Victorian beyond the hedge was somehow just a little too picturesque, too overgabled for Miles, who wanted to turn around and speed back to the city where people lived in normal buildings with flat facades, flat roofs, flat walls, no turrets or porches. The sign at the head of the driveway told him he was about to enter a property called The Gables, appropriately enough, owned by Robert and Joanna Priestly. There was something about the place vaguely reminiscent of the Museum of Natural History just down the street from Nick's.

He parked his rental car in the drive and mounted the stairs to the seemingly endless porch. The door was open, perhaps to catch the gentle breeze from the north. The enticing aroma of something, a vegetable soup or stew maybe, drifted through the screen. He rang twice and waited. When no one answered, he opened the inner door, took one step inside, and announced his presence.

"Hello? Is anyone home?" he called.

The sound of hammering footsteps answered his summons. Without introduction, he knew he was about to meet the woman Nick had said would cut off his balls without a knife immediately after he'd finished talking with her on the phone. Involuntarily, Miles put his right hand in the pocket of his blazer, and moved it over the fly of his summer-weight khakis.

"Do you normally enter peoples' houses without an invitation?" a metallic voice cut through the air.

"I apologize profusely," Miles replied at his silken best. "I took the liberty of opening the screen door because I need to speak with my daughter, April Oliphant. I'm Miles Oliphant, her father. I take it you're Joanna Priestly about whom April has told me so much?"

The footsteps, produced rather surprisingly only by running shoes, stopped and Miles found himself looking at a statuesque brunette. Her handsome face, if not immediately welcoming, projected a look that changed rapidly from open hostility to benign tolerance.

"Pleased to meet you, Mr. Oliphant." Here, she extended her hand and shook his with a strength that took him aback. Amazingly, her tone of voice had modulated from caged lioness to lap cat in the course of a single sentence. "You've made introductions unnecessary. I hope the things April's told you about me aren't too awful?"

"To the contrary, she has only praise for you as both a wonderful hostess and a producer *par excellence.*

"Please come in. Everyone else is out in the barn. They're putting the finishing touches on *Othello*, our opening play of the season."

To Miles, just then, Joanna Priestly seemed both welcoming and, at the same time, unimaginably sad. The military bearing with which she had approached him was that of a commanding general. But her face? A map of sorrow of which he hadn't seen the like since shaving that morning.

"*Othello*, you say?"

"You thought otherwise?"

"I didn't think actually. My knowledge of theater, once extensive I'm told, has taken a bit of a hit recently. The result of a small bump on the head. Doctors say my recovery is coming along quite well."

"At least you know *Othello's* a play," she affirmed. "That's something anyway."

"It would be something far greater if I knew who wrote it and when."

"That, I assume, Mr. Oliphant, is the result of the amnesia April told us about?"

"It is. Please call me Miles."

"And I'm Joanna. *Othello* is one of the great tragedies of all time. It was written by William Shakespeare."

"Yes, I do know Shakespeare. He wrote *Hamlet*?"

"So you knew that he wrote *Hamlet*, but not *Othello*?"

Miles noticed Mrs. Priestly's voice had grown cautious. He couldn't press his luck much further.

"That's what I've been told. I have no idea what it's about, though. A small town in the Midwest perhaps?"

A throaty laugh made Miles respond in kind until he remembered that, above all, he must remain in character or give himself away, and that would be disaster.

"That's very funny, Miles. You may have lost your memory, but not your sense of humor. I can't tell you how good it feels to laugh again after the last few days. Perhaps after my divorce comes through I'll commission someone like Lee Blessing or August Wilson to take up your idea. Would you like to sit down? I've made a chili for the cast when they break for dinner. Perhaps you'd care for some yourself?"

"Thanks, that's very generous of you. But I'd really like to speak with my daughter. Would you mind if I went out to the barn to see her? Don't worry, I promise not to interrupt anything."

"Not that you would be interrupting at all, but why don't I get her for you? I'll snatch her away first break they take."

"Whatever you say."

"Come with me, I'll show you the kitchen."

She led him down the corridor and through a cavernous two-story living room with a series of painted cardboard panels, perhaps part of a set, stacked against one wall.

"Help yourself to the chili. Bowls are on the counter. Cornbread on the cutting board under the tea towel. There're soft drinks and beer in the fridge."

"A soft drink will be fine. Anything you have."

"You're sure I can't get you something stronger?"

"Positive."

She handed him a Diet Coke. "Anything else?"

"No thanks."

"I'll be back in no time."

Miles sat on one of the barstools at the kitchen counter. Not really hungry, he watched Joanna as she crossed the patio in the direction of the red barn, whose gambrel roof he could see in the distance. Quite obviously, she didn't want him witnessing the rehearsal under way there.

He couldn't help thinking about his hostess, who seemed, on first meeting, so many different things at once.

Nick's first impression, left by a brief phone call, was undoubtedly correct. Joanna Priestly was a ball-cutter without a blade. From the aroma of her chili which pervaded the ample house, he could tell she was also a good cook. And a first-rate producer, at least according to April. More than anything, though, she was a walking advertisement for a mortuary of dreams, and he wondered if the divorce she'd just mentioned didn't account, at least to some degree, for the pain that showed on her face, but not in her precision-made voice.

There was just enough of the atmospheric haze of nightfall in the view out the French windows to one side of the kitchen to make Miles think of the south of France where Loren Pritchard had gone on vacation. If only he could join Pritchard there and ask him a few simple questions about the Boyle papers. Perhaps, too, he could prevail on the vacationing Brit to provide another bill of sale and enough necessary information about the provenance of the manuscript to satisfy any doubts that carping academics or skeptical journalists might come up with. If not, then Miles' vague suspicions about the man who had sold him the manuscript would certainly bear further investigation.

It looked as if none of this, however, were going to happen before the Players' opening. And that had prompted his trip to The Gables. He needed to stop any premature performance of his play, and the association of his name with it if, indeed, it turned out to be a fabrication, either by Lewis Theobald or of more recent origin.

This latter possibility had seemed even more likely when, two nights before, he got April's mailed confession, informing him the East Village Players were staging the *Ur-Hamlet*. What if there had been no manuscript in the crate of papers he'd sent back from England? What if, after opening it, his own daughter had decided to write out the long-lost play herself?

After all, she had ample motivation. The counterfeit manuscript would bring her closer to the persistent director who'd been dropping by the store for the past year. And a new play by Shakespeare would provide just the vehicle she needed to launch her comeback.

There was certainly enough old paper to be found in the flyleaves of books in the store, formulas for 16th-century inks in the public library around the corner for April to put to use in such an ill-advised project. As Miles himself had discovered, they had a facsimile copy of *Sir Thomas More*, in part by Shakespeare, on their own shelves. April could have familiarized herself with his hand from it, then copied out the manuscript while Miles was laid up in the hospital.

That idea had got him thinking. Perhaps he'd been concentrating on the past for too long? Perhaps neither Theobald nor Boyle, individually or together, had produced the manuscript? Perhaps, if the play turned out to be a forgery, he might think about those, alive right then, who would benefit most from the appearance of a new and very different *Hamlet*?

Certainly April fit that description. At least she had motive enough. Then there was Reg Sloane. Perhaps his friend was no more than a counterfeiter in tweed? And he couldn't eliminate Loren Pritchard, who clearly had the time and the all-important geographical proximity to Marston House to cook up a forged *Ur-Hamlet*.

He was trying to sort through these different possibilities when he saw April mount the patio steps and cross toward the kitchen. When she pulled back the doors, he held out his arms. But she hesitated.

"It's alright, April," he said.

"Is it really?"

44 LEGAL INTERFERENCE

April had felt her knees weaken when Joanna pulled her aside and told her that her father was waiting in the kitchen. She didn't know how he'd found out where she was staying. Intentionally, she'd left her return address off the letter she'd sent him, but there was the postmark. It wouldn't have been so hard to find the Priestly place really. All he'd have to do was ask around town.

As she cautiously climbed the hill toward the rear of the house, Joanna's parting words came back to her. "Whatever you do, don't tell your father we're performing his *Hamlet*." April should have replied that she had already told him, but, of course, she didn't say anything of the sort. If she couldn't muster the courage to make a simple confession like that, how would she ever work up nerve enough to go out on stage again?

With the exception of a reddish scar on her father's forehead, and a patch of greenish blue around his left eye, he looked exactly the same.

"It will go away," he said rather seriously when she told him that. "Even the scar will in time. I don't tire quite so easily and I'm taking longer and longer walks."

"That's great."

Here, Miles frowned briefly. "I'm afraid Mrs. Priestly is coming back."

April followed his gaze over her shoulder. He was right, Joanna was climbing the slight rise that led up from the barn. Naturally, she would claim she was just getting dinner ready for everyone, but April suspected she would be spying at the same time, checking to make certain their new Ophelia didn't give away the ugly secret that they were performing her father's recently discovered *Hamlet*. The others would be along soon too, hungry and more than ready for a break.

"Is there somewhere else we can go?" he asked.

"Follow me."

Cautiously, April took her father by the hand and led him up the stairs. Except Avery, she'd never touched anyone for that long in years. Only when they reached her room did she let go, then locked the door behind them. She pulled the rocking chair over for him and lowered herself to the edge of the bed, almost directly in front of him.

"Look, I appreciate all the things you've done for me, April," he began before she had chance to say anything. "Even though parts of my memory are still blank, you don't have to keep looking after me from a distance."

"Looking after you?" she repeated in genuine amazement. "I walked out on you just when you needed...."

"I'm talking about Teddy," he cut in abruptly. "You're doing everything you can to keep me from finding out what happened to him."

"That's because I want you to get well. Worrying about the past won't help restore your memory."

"Worrying about the past?"

"You know what I mean."

"No, I don't."

But the momentary retraction of the irises of his eyes told her that, if he wasn't lying, the memory of that horrible night was coming back.

"I...I didn't try to kill...?"

Here, April simply nodded at his unfinished question. Evidently, that was all she needed to do to send his mind shrinking rapidly inside itself. He slumped back in his chair. Mouth motionless, eyes closed, his head sank slowly to his chest.

"That letter I sent you," she picked up after a long silence. "It wasn't the bravest thing I've done in my life. I'm sorry."

His eyes opened quickly, now ablaze with anger.

"You should have told me *much* earlier."

"You're right, but the unexpected arrival of that manuscript set off a whole chain of events I couldn't stop. Other things got in the way after that. I didn't really have control over any of them."

"You didn't have to give it to your old professor," he snapped. "That was utterly irresponsible."

"You're right again. It was. But at the time he seemed the perfect person to call. After that, I didn't know what happened to it until...well, until you told me Sgt. Cochran had it. You don't know how relieved I was."

"I still don't understand how you could have done something like that!"

April lowered her head and spoke a single, barely audible word in the face of that accusation.

"Love."

"What did you say?"

"Nothing....No, that isn't true. I said the word *love*. Because I was, I still am in love, desperately the way only a twenty-four-year-old can be. What else can I say? I'm guilty? I'm sorry? Punish me however you want, I deserve it."

As she spoke, the anger that she first saw in his eyes now reddened his entire face. He slipped his hand under the lapel of his blazer. At first, she thought her admission had brought on a heart attack, but he simply left his hand there a moment, motionless. When he pulled it out again, there was an envelope in it. He handed it to her, looking straight at her as he did. His silence was too much. She wished he'd just blow up at her and get it over with.

The embossed return address on the outside of the envelope, which read JUSTICE ROCHELLE WALTERS MANHATTAN SUPREME COURT, caught her off-guard. April opened it to find a temporary, *ex-parte* injunction, which prohibited the East Village Players from presenting *Hamlet, King of Denmarke*, or any other drama on the same subject taken from the manuscript owned by Mr. Miles Oliphant.

In dismay, April shrank back on the bed, then crumpled into the comforter. She didn't have to read any further to comprehend the meaning of the document. Her father had actually gone to a judge and won a court order prohibiting any performances of the new *Hamlet*. She knew what she had done with the manuscript was wrong, and that she was a coward for not telling her father sooner. He was a good man. An honest man in an era when good, honest men were an endangered species, but this was going too far.

"Did...did you really have to get an injunction?"

"I had no other choice. You open in a week."

"What do you mean, no other choice? You could have talked to me. To Joanna. Anything but this!"

"Remember how hard it was to reach you, and then you refused to return my calls or hung up."

Only then did April understand. "It was Nick, wasn't it?"

"What do you mean?"

"He's the one behind the injunction. I like Nick, Dad, I really do, but just because he's a lawyer doesn't mean *you* have to think like one yourself."

April could see she'd stung him when that hadn't been her intention. She just wanted him to put that horrid injunction back in the pocket it had come from and forget all about it.

"If this *Hamlet* turns out to be a forgery," he said, "and my name and yours get attached to it, think of the harm that could do. I can't risk that. Neither can you. And certainly not just because you've fallen in love."

As her father muttered this, April thought she heard footsteps on the stairs. Only one person could be making them. She had to make herself understood, and quickly.

"This is my one big chance, Father. Please, reconsider. You don't know what an effort it's taken for me to get this far. Just yesterday, I spent the entire morning in the barn with everybody. Everybody! I was fine, as long as I was acting. Please, don't make me give that up."

"The injunction in your hand gives you no choice."

"You're serious about it then?"

"It's my reputation we're talking about," he snarled so loudly anyone in the hall could overhear.

"It's my career...my *life* that I'm talking about."

As she spoke, she tore the document in two, then again before her father, seething now, grabbed her hands to make her stop.

"Give me that. I'll tape the pieces together and present it to Joanna myself. All along, I thought you were reasonable. I know better now."

As the two struggled and pieces of paper drifted to the floor, someone knocked on the door.

"Dinner's served, you two," Joanna called to them as April wrenched herself free from her father's grip. "It's just homemade chili, but I'd be delighted if your father would join us. Such a thoroughly charming gentleman. Afterwards, we'll all go to the barn and he can watch acts four and five, and see for himself how truly wondrous his daughter is."

April couldn't believe Joanna had called her father *charming* at the same time he was fighting with her over his heartless injunction. Still, she opened the door as he stooped to gather pieces of torn paper from the floor.

"You mean he can...he's actually invited to see our *Othello*?"

"Come, come, April. It's been three weeks since we've rehearsed *Othello*. I'm talking about our brilliant new *Hamlet*, of course."

In the time since April left the barn, Joanna had somehow intuited the situation. She'd realized that Miles knew almost everything, and that he was determined to stop them from presenting *Hamlet, Part One*. Now she intended to coax and cajole him as if he were a board member or a prospective donor. There was only one problem with that strategy. She didn't know her father the way April knew him, nor did she know about Judge Walters' injunction.

"Alright," she said, "I suppose we'll come down?"

She didn't know if she was speaking for herself alone, or if her father would join them. For dinner maybe. Certainly not for the last two acts of the *Hamlet* he was determined to stop before it ever opened.

45 A PLAY NAMED *OPHELIA*

Tears, big bauble tears, gathered on Joanna's lower lids, then, after a few moments, brimmed over and slid down her cheeks. It wasn't Samuel Pilgrim who was making her cry. No, that privilege went to Miles' daughter, who, in Ophelia's shore-side speech, had just dissuaded Hamlet, after murdering Father Daemon, from taking his own life by walking out into the waters of the Oresund and drowning himself.

The only times Joanna ever cried were in the theater, and that hadn't happened since she'd seen Derek Jacobi in *Breaking the Code* two years earlier. In rehearsal that evening, however, April's portrayal of a girl in love convinced Joanna there was indeed still love to be found in the world. In response, she'd had to hang her head and let her hair cover her face to keep the rest of the company from seeing her in tears.

As the play drew to a close with the appearance of the ghost of Hamlet's father on the battlements of the castle, Joanna leaned over and, clapping loudly, whispered to Miles, who sat beside her only after she had walked him to the barn with Samuel, his arm around the elder Oliphant's shoulder so tightly he had no possible means of escape.

"Wasn't your daughter sublime? Shakespeare should have called the play *Ophelia*, not *King Hamlet*. She was just brilliant!"

"Mrs. Priestly? If you have a moment?"

Before Joanna could look around to see who had interrupted her, she knew his identity from the pervasive odor of musk that crept up on her from behind. Detective Crowley. Talk about a chilling comedown from the emotional high of the beach scene! Still she knew she had to speak with the man. She feared Crowley would want to keep them all there at The Gables while he continued to investigate Charles' death. But then Joanna's husband was

Robert Priestly, the newly elected Congressman from the Twentieth District. That, and their property taxes could have funded the entire police department, and Crowley knew it.

"Oh, Detective Crowley, I didn't realize you were here," she exclaimed. "This is Miles Oliphant, whose daughter you just saw as our Ophelia."

"I took the liberty of a sneak preview," the detective admitted. "I'm not much of a theater-goer myself, but that Samuel Pilgrim is really something, isn't he?"

"He certainly is."

"And your daughter, Mr. Oliphant. I mean, WOW!"

"Wow is a bit of an understatement," Joanna said. "I'll comp you any night you and Mrs. Crowley want to come into the city for a show."

"I'd take you up on that in an instant if ethics rules allowed."

"Ethics?" Joanna gulped.

"I'm afraid so." Here the officer coughed quietly. "I have some news. Perhaps we could talk in private?"

"You don't mind, do you, Miles?" she asked, placing a hand tenderly on his shoulder before she and Lieutenant Crowley stepped toward the door. Joanna didn't really want to leave her guest before she'd had a chance to work him, really work him, but she had no other choice. The detective's news could only be bad, just how bad she had no real idea.

"Yes, what is it?" she asked once she and Crowley had reached the leeward side of the barn and stood beneath a mature red oak just beyond the cone of light cast by the lone bulb above the entrance.

"I'm afraid we found more cocaine." He paused here to give her time to reflect.

"Where?"

"Triple-bagged, inside a roll of toilet paper at the bottom of a twelve-pack, east-wing bathroom. The guy–assuming that's all it was, one guy–was good, let me tell you."

"That was Charles alright," Joanna couldn't help saying, "so good, I guess he was bad to himself sometimes."

"Very bad," the detective agreed. "I'll bet there was a good quarter kilo there, more or less. He resealed the plastic of the toilet-paper package so well we'd have never found the coke if we hadn't had sniffer dogs. I'm afraid we're going to have to ask everyone to stay here a bit longer while we search the rest of the house."

"The place is huge!" Joanna exclaimed, not quite comprehending the enormity of Crowley's proposition yet. "And we leave for Manhattan day after tomorrow. All of us. The show opens next Wednesday."

"We'll finish soon as we can, even if I have to bring in every swinging dick...every swinging detective in the county. If we find any more, however, it could mean detaining somebody or bodies."

"I see."

But Joanna didn't really. First Hope had broken her ankle then Charles had died. And now this. Joanna could only imagine who Crowley might detain. In all likelihood Valerie Schneider. She had been Charles' accomplice in almost everything the past month.

"Thank you for taking it so well."

"I'm not taking it well at all. Do what you must. But do it as fast as you can."

"I will, Mrs. Priestly. We owe you that much. We'll be done ASAP, if not sooner."

"Both Rob and I thank you, detective."

Joanna took a few extra seconds as she watched Crowley, bowlegged as a pair of parentheses, walk back through the light uphill toward the house. She couldn't believe anyone, not even Valerie, would repeat Charles' stupidity. And it was that. Just plain stupidity. Now, it might keep them all prisoners at The Gables even longer.

Of course, she'd been grieving when she had broken the news of Charles' death to his wife, Paige, who'd taken it like a icebreaker that had plowed through one too many glacier fields. In the end, she had agreed to tell no one but their children, though word was bound to leak, especially after Joanna had persuaded Erskine Strathmore, a veteran actor and former company member, to replace Charles as King Hamlet. With all the announcements she was going to have to make at the opening, she might as well have a minor role in the play whether Avery liked it or not. And he wouldn't.

The tepid applause of perhaps five hands clapping interrupted her interior monologue. Evidently the cast, or what remained of them, appreciated something Avery had said in critique. Waiting a few seconds to regain her composure, Joanna started back toward the barn, about to go inside when April came slipping through the doorway.

"There you are!" she said. "I've been trying...."

"You were brilliant," Joanna cut in. "I was thinking as I watched you in that last scene, I hadn't seen a performance like that in years."

That stopped April, who looked at Joanna through eyes that blinked slowly in disbelief.

"Really? You mean, you think I was okay?"

"Okay? You were magnificent!"

"I can't believe you're saying that. I'm...I'm so completely flattered. I don't know how to...." She hesitated and looked down. "What I'm about to tell you isn't going to sound like much thanks after that."

"Then don't say it. Let's go back inside."

She started toward the door, but April caught her by the forearm and pulled her back under the same tree where she had been standing with Detective Crowley only moments earlier.

"Alright, what is it? Don't tell me. Your father's leaving unpersuaded?"

"He is?" April said as if Joanna were the one with the bad news.

"No...no. It's just that so many awful things have happened already, I don't...." Joanna stopped there, a swell of emotion rising so rapidly that it caught her unexpectedly and she turned away. For support, she leaned against the barn.

"Well, I'm afraid this isn't going to make things any better, but I've *got* to tell you. I've been waiting for two days, but there just hasn't been a good time. First, you went into Albany, then Charles' death, and all the police. I thought Avery might have said something?"

"God, just tell me, April. I'm sturdy as this oak we're standing under."

"It's about the manuscript. Father heard from the handwriting analyst, and she...well, she thinks it's a forgery."

Joanna simply stood there, unable to speak. Such crushing news, all contained in the course of a single, brutal sentence. Usually she took things in stride, but this was too much. Not even the boards of the barn could support her under the weight of April's news. She flattened her back against the old wood, but even that was not enough. Slowly she began to sink to the ground, failing to register the splinters that dug through her clean, white blouse. April's hand shot out to help her, but it was too late. She came to rest, buttocks on dirt grown hard in the absence of summer rain.

"Why did you wait so long to tell me?" Joanna finally stammered.

"I just went through that. With everything that's happened, I didn't have a chance. I told Avery, but...well, I guess I sugar-coated it in the hope that we could get Dr. Duke to examine the rest of...."

"Dr. Duke, huh? Who is the woman, anyway? Some hotshot academic with Ph.D.s in Shakespearean tragedy and forensic chemistry?"

Joanna had begun her response in a low, breathless moan, but when she heard herself, she realized just how badly the news had hit her. But she was not going to cave in to despair. She struggled to pull herself off the ground, only to feel the pain of several slivers in the vicinity of her shoulder blades.

"No degree in Shakespeare, I'm certain," April came back, "but she is a doctor. I'm just not sure what she's a doctor of. She says...."

"Ballistics probably. She certainly knows how to shoot people down. In this case a company of twenty-seven people."

"If you'll just give me a chance?" April paused here until Joanna half nodded her agreement. "Dr. Duke says that the sample she had, no more than sixty words, is small. When she analyzes the entire manuscript, she might change her mind."

Joanna did not know if April was saying that to ease the pain, or if there really was at least some limited hope contained in her words.

"Do you think this so-called doctor might do that?"

"She told my father she might, and I'm pretty sure she meant it. Who knows when she'll get around to the entire thing."

"I'll talk to your father, see if there's anything he can do to get her to move on it."

"I don't think that's a good idea. Not after everything he's been through this evening."

"You're probably right."

"What if it turns out that Dr. Duke's right?" April asked. "We can't still go on in that case, can we?"

"We can't? Do you realize just how fabulous you are in the shore scene?"

"I don't know...maybe?"

"Would you want me to cancel the entire show? Close down the East Village Players as a result? That would mean no one outside this company, except Shawn Kirby and now your father, would ever see your magnificent Ophelia."

April's head fell toward her chest as she considered the proposition. "I guess not."

"Well then, keep this to yourself until I decide how to handle it. I can't believe the play we're about to bring to New York is a forgery, but then we must be cautious. Now, shall we go back inside?"

Without waiting for the messenger who had just broken the worst possible news, Joanna headed toward the barn where she intended to chat up Miles Oliphant once again. The opening was just days away. She was determined to go forward with the project whether it was by Shakespeare, or by someone else foolish enough to attempt to take up the Bard's pen.

The first thing she had to do was call Shawn Kirby, get him to revise his article ever so slightly to say that the East Village Players' *Hamlet, Part One* was *probably* by Shakespeare, pending authentication. Then change the posters and all other printed material to reflect that same spirit of caution. Such honesty might depress ticket sales created by Kirby's article, but the ensuing controversy about authorship would, just perhaps, keep the Players' season opener in the headlines well beyond the time the last reviews came out.

And the price was definitely right.

46 ONE GOOD WORD

April pulled her luggage from under the bed. Both pieces were locked. By the time she'd finally found the key, anger was tearing at her insides. She yanked out the dresser drawers and dumped them wholesale, one on top of the other, into the larger suitcase. Grabbing blouses from the closet, she bunched them together without thought of folding them. The one dress she'd brought with her went on top and she slammed the lid shut, closed the latches with hems sticking out. Even though it was pitch black outside now, she crushed her sunhat down on her head without thinking to collect her things in the bathroom.

Avery the Hun had driven her to The Gables, so she had no idea how far it was to town, or when the next train would be coming. It didn't matter, she'd find her way even if it meant dragging her suitcases, or abandoning them by the side of the road. She could never move back in with her father, not after their fight the day before. She couldn't go to Avery's either, not after what he'd just done. Maybe, if her friend Shelly had really moved in with her boyfriend, she could use her place for a few days.

She hadn't been more than a hundred lines into her opening scene with Hamlet when it had happened all over again. On this occasion she ran from the improvised stage in the barn. Last time, she'd realized her second week into *Menagerie* that she couldn't continue the charade, not even after Shawn Kirby had crowned her "the Laura of our generation." Her mother's soliloquy had done it, telling, as it did, the entire audience about her daughter's breakdown in business school. How, in fear, Laura had thrown up and been carried to the bathroom. She never went back to that classroom again. Never, in cowardice, told her mother she'd quit school, the same way April hadn't told her father about the manuscript.

She had been foolish to think she could ever leave the safe confines of his apartment, leave Manhattan. Foolish to think she could act again. It hadn't been so hard to rehearse with only a few of them in the great hall downstairs, or out in the barn. With everyone else there now, she realized just how impossible it would be to step out in front of a real audience.

April didn't just burn her bridges behind her, she constructed them out of wood and dynamite before she ever crossed them. That way she could watch the glorious fire go up the moment she reached the other side and lit the fuse. There was only one problem with that. The flames lasted such a brief time, a short scene in an evolving, lifelong drama.

Just as she was lifting her suitcases from the bed she heard footsteps in the hallway outside. She checked to make certain the door was locked. Moments later, someone knocked, so gently it couldn't possibly be Joanna, who had undoubtedly dispatched Avery, the obvious peacemaker, in her place. No matter how long he knocked, how much he praised her, she wasn't going to give in to him. How could she after the way he'd upbraided her in front of everyone?

"Please open the door, April. I know you're there."

The voice wasn't Avery's at all. Nor was it Joanna's. In their place, the two cowards had sent Valerie Schneider, the worst possible person. Avery had to know that. He'd done it intentionally, on top of everything else.

"I know how you feel," Valerie began. "Avery can be a real asshole sometimes. He just doesn't know when to keep his mouth shut. If I were you, I'd have walked too, and I told him so. Now, please come back down and join us so we can all get a few hours sleep tonight."

Sleep April wanted to yell. Who could sleep after everything that had just happened. She'd gone on briefly after Avery's insult, but then it had all come home. He was just using her. Using her in every way. To sell a few more tickets. To pump himself up in front of the entire company. Worst of all, to have his way with almost every night.

"You've shown so much courage until now," Valerie went on when April said nothing in reply. "Believe me, I

222

know what it has cost you to venture out in public again. Please don't pull back. Not now. Not when you need us almost as much as we need you. Just tell Avery to fuck off. And get on with life."

Oh, but wouldn't Valerie just love that? She'd swoop down on Avery the moment April walked out the front door, never to return. All she wanted the woman outside her door to do was leave her alone. Give her one single minute, two at most, so she could slip out the front door and not have to say good-bye to anyone. Especially not to Avery.

"Look, I was the one who told him not to come up here now. If you want, I'll go down and get him. Just give me the word."

Valerie shouldn't have said that, she really shouldn't have, because there was one word April was very good at giving. She had been her entire life.

"NOOOOOOO!"

47 JOANNA PLAYS TOSCA

In her bedroom, formerly *their* bedroom, Joanna contemplated what had gone wrong out in the barn during the run-through with full cast and understudies. April had been doing so well until the entire company got there. She'd turned from wall flower to sun flower, finally to become almost sunny herself. Then Avery had taken it upon himself to unload on her in front of everyone, and she'd stormed off. They couldn't afford to lose her now, not with Shawn Kirby ready to trumpet her return to the stage. She'd get over it. She had to, for her own sake. For everyone's. All they had to do was get her past opening night and she'd be fine.

Joanna's thoughts turned to the move back to the city, if and when Detective Crowley gave them permission to leave. Her first order of business would be a distasteful visit to Lars Carlsson's office. She would take with her the cashier's check for $4,000 made out to the Eldridge Street Settlement House, which she'd had Arnie Rice draft for her in Oakville that afternoon. It represented less than twenty percent of the amount Carlsson was demanding, but she would also bring with her copies of their last year's tax returns, plus property tax statements showing the worth of their residences in Oakville and Manhattan.

If that wasn't enough, she intended to wear the modestly revealing black cocktail dress that she had just put on to rehearse the little act she would perform for their good looking, if stone-hearted landlord. Freshly washed hair coaxed into a double bun, she would apply just enough make up to remind Carlsson that he had mentioned something about going for cocktails after she stopped by with her check for the theater rental.

Yes, Joanna would do almost anything he asked of her at that meeting. What other choice did she have? She did not intend to tell one person of the devil's bargain she would make with Lars Carlsson on her first full day back in the city. No one in the company would know about it. Nor would Rob. And certainly not his brother Gene. No one!

She'd actually gotten the idea from an opera she'd seen in college. But she wasn't going to sell herself for a tenor, as Tosca had, though Carlsson did remind her a little of Placido Domingo, which would make her task that much more bearable. She would indeed be selling herself for art, an idea she had actually fallen in love with by the time she finished packing for the trip. She just prayed Rob hadn't changed the locks on their Fifth-Avenue apartment. What would she do then?

In front of the mirror, she practiced slithering out of her dress. On her fourth, more accomplished attempt, the phone rang. She had no idea who might be calling at that hour, but anything was better than rehearsing a striptease that had so little heart in it.

"Yes?" Joanna said, sitting on the edge of the bed in just her panties and bra, dress around her ankles.

"Hi, Joanna. Hope you don't mind a spur-of-the-moment call. I just wanted to see how you were doing?"

The voice sounded like Rob's at first, but then she realized it was his brother Gene. She hadn't heard from him at all since he'd returned to the city. It was a good thing he didn't know how she was dressed just then. She thought about telling him, but then remembered whose brother he was.

"You must be coming back to the city soon?"

"Tomorrow, I hope. Why do you ask?"

"I just had an idea, that's all. Something of a lightning bolt, actually."

"Sounds promising." She could always hope, couldn't she? "What was it?"

"It rained here in the city today."

Had he called just to give her a weather report? An old one at that.

"We got a couple brief showers here, too."

"Anyway, there was a leak in the ceiling of my classroom, so I went up on the roof to investigate. Have you straightened things out with the Settlement House yet?"

"I will tomorrow, and I have to say I'm not looking forward to it. Why?"

"What time will you be going there?"

"Four."

"Can you stop by school first? Your appointment can't be more than twenty blocks from there."

That was an interesting proposition, but why wouldn't Gene come right out and tell her why he wanted to see her? P.S. 39 wasn't the most romantic place in the city to meet.

"Won't you be teaching?"

"Classes are over at three-ten. I'll meet you at the front door."

"What is this about?"

"I'll tell you then. Say three-fifteen on the front steps."

"See you there, mystery man. I might even have a little surprise for you, too," she said, thinking of the dress she would be wearing to educate Lars Carlsson on the finer points of landlord-tenant relations.

Joanna had no idea what Gene had been thinking about when he made that invitation. They'd probably just go for coffee, and he'd tell her that he had talked to his brother, who wanted him to break the bad news about filing for divorce. At least she could vent to Gene and he'd understand.

And what was all that about rain and the school roof? Perhaps her brother-in-law was slightly quirkier than she had imagined, and that idea appealed to her. A great deal in fact.

48 FANNING THE FLAMES

As he had many times before, Miles found himself dressed as a janitor, sweating in a high-school boiler room. A small stack of books lay at his feet. The school principal, who stood to one side, ordered him to burn them. When Miles the janitor protested, the stocky man in polyester told him he had ten seconds to start the process or lose his job. By the time the countdown reached two, he bent over, picked up a single book and threw it into the furnace. Soon he was pitching in three and four at a time. Fierce flames consumed the books, giving off the wretched, sulfurous smell of burning paper and glue. But he could never get to the bottom of the pile because the principal kept adding more books until Miles realized he'd be burning every book in the library, in the entire school before his gruesome dream was over.

Then he sat up in bed fully awake, thinking he smelled smoke, real smoke this time. Pulling on his robe, he staggered out into the hallway. The noxious smell originated in the stairwell, he was certain. That could mean only one thing. Something was burning downstairs.

He sprinted toward the apartment door, threw it open and descended the stairs three at a time. But there wasn't a hint of fire anywhere in the store below. Miles knew he would never get back to sleep, so he slumped into the chair in front of his desk and tried to make sense of the most recent version of his book-burning nightmare. Maybe it had come from sleeping at home for the first night in months? Nick had had a fit when Miles told him about the injunction, so he'd decided to spend the night at home alone. Then, too, it could have been the curry in his Indian take-out that had sparked his fiery dream.

Whatever the cause, a warning lay behind it. Something was threatening to destroy Miles' stock, his home, everything he owned really! And with it his life. Or was it even more horrendous than that? His dream foreshadowed an even greater conflagration? Manhattan burning? The country going up in flames? Armageddon?

Right there, Miles decided to make a list of the different possibilities. That way he could cross out the most outlandish and draw connecting lines to those that might be related. He unlocked the top drawer, pulled blank paper from one of the slotted trays, and started to jot down different ideas as they came to him. By the time he finished the second sheet, he was exhausted, almost ready for bed again.

In the process of switching off the desk light, he looked down at the supply of stationery he had pulled from the drawer. Two sheets of paper stood out from the rest. They were deckle-edged and slightly larger. Holding them to the light in hasty succession, he could see they were coarse and opaque, but there was no visible watermark. Immediately, he realized both sheets were less perfect, and much older really than the ones on which he had just written out his dream list. He had no idea what they were doing there unless...unless he had put them there himself! But why? Slowly, and far more painfully than in the imaginary fire of his dream, he choked on the answer. Was it possible that he himself, Miles Oliphant, had used paper like that to forge the manuscript before going to London? Then, in the confusion of early Alzheimer's, he had forgotten entirely about inventing the story of the *Ur-Hamlet* and writing it out in Shakespeare's hand, based on the sample found in *Sir Thomas More*? After that, could he have taken it to England with him and planted it in the crate he'd shipped back from Marston Bigot?

The entire proposition was so contrived, so devious Miles didn't think he could have possibly executed it. Had he been that hungry for fame? For financial gain? If he had, that was then. He knew for certain he didn't feel that way anymore, not after his mugging. Or was all of it–first pointing the guilty finger at Theobald, then Reg and April, and now at himself–the product of one great, smoke-filled dream that obscured the all-too-precious truth. Whatever that was?

He got up from his desk and switched off the desk light. If only it were that easy to put out the fires still raging in his mind.

49 A ROOFTOP VIEW

"Well, what do you think?"

Gene's hand swept slowly out 180 degrees in front of them as they stood there on the old tongue-and-groove gym floor atop the school roof. The arc described by that gesture took in an expansive terra-cotta building to the west, the city skyline to the north and the stunning drop off toward the East River to their right, all of it visible from under a steel dome that covered the former outdoor rooftop gym above P.S. 39. A chain-link fence ran inside the decorative, wrought-iron railing that supported the metal dome, with various fans, vents and chimney stacks jutting from the roof behind them.

"What am I supposed to think?" Joanna replied.

"You could do your *Hamlet* here, at least until you found another place."

Had Joanna heard correctly? That's what Gene's surprise had been all about? He was offering her the school roof for a theater? How could she not help but fall in love with the place on a brilliant, late-summer afternoon with a clear blue sky, handsome views, the billowing metal dome overhead? It was as provocative a venue as there was in the city, but it would be impossible to get it ready in just six days, to say nothing of informing ticket holders for the first few nights of the change in location.

"You said the roof leaked?"

"Don't worry. My classroom's at the other end of the building. They need to make some repairs to the old metal roof, that's all. It was built in 1915, right at the height of the drive to provide fresh-air playgrounds for booming populations of immigrant kids in lower Manhattan. There was a time when we used to hold early-spring practice for the baseball team up here, pitching try-outs in particular. I should have thought of it while I was in Oakville, but I haven't been up here in years."

"It's a glorious space, Gene. And I mean it, I really do. If we had more time, more advance notice, it would work beautifully. It was sweet of you to think of me, but I'm going to have to go with the Settlement House. And you have no idea what that's going to cost me."

"I've already talked to my boss, Ron Saunders. You won't have to pay the school a lead penny."

"I don't mean money. This is going to cost me personally. Besides, with all the logistical hurdles we'd have to jump and everything, I'm afraid this just wouldn't work."

"Why not?"

She could tell she had hurt his feelings. "The sight lines for one thing."

"I thought about that yesterday. We could use the band and choir risers."

"And there's the lighting."

"Heather Owens, our drama teacher, owes me. They're going to have to install lights up here for the fall production of *Barefoot in the Park* anyway. The school auditorium's being remodeled. It was supposed to be finished by Labor Day, but it's way behind schedule. It was Heather who gave me the idea actually."

Joanna wondered if there wasn't something between Gene and the school's drama teacher? She hoped not, but then Gene was a man, and men had their needs. The two Priestly boys weren't immune from that, witness Rob, the most needy of all.

"And the noise?"

"It's not really all that bad in this part of the city at night. I came back up here before I called you. It's a thrilling space, Joanna. Admit it."

She could not deny that. The mere thought of extending the audience's summer out-of-doors appealed to her, even in the face of their comfortable, indoor quarters at the Settlement House. But the difficulties involved in changing venues were almost insurmountable. The actors could certainly overcome them, but she just couldn't put them, and the crew in particular, through the move. They deserved better, especially after she'd changed productions half-way through rehearsals.

At least Gene's offer told her he was thinking about her. Even if his invitation seemed purely professional, there had to be another motive behind it. To show her appreciation, she gave him a generous hug as they said good-bye on the entrance stairs.

Now it was on to meet with Lars Carlsson and hope that he was in a generous mood. If not, she knew what she would have to do to win him to their cause.

50 BLACK INK

"I'm wondering if you can help me?" Miles asked the young librarian with long, rather straight dark hair that curled up on the yoke of her stripped blouse. With just a little makeup, she could have been an L.L. Bean model, he thought, even though neither Bean women nor the clothes they wore had any real appeal for him.

"Yes, what are you trying to find?"

Miles looked over his shoulder at Nick, who sat awkwardly at one of the heavy library tables in the high-ceilinged catalog room, light cutting in through transom windows above the handsome, built-in bookshelves that made up the walls below. Nick was not even pretending to look at the large black volume of photocopied catalog cards on the desk in front of him, meant to make him look like just another researcher.

He'd been peevish ever since Miles had finally told him how April had torn up the injunction at The Gables, and he'd failed to deliver another to Joanna, largely as a result of seeing his daughter in rehearsal. Now, Nick didn't trust him to take care of anything himself, an attitude Miles found too lawyerly for words.

For a moment, he was distracted by a pair of passing Japanese tourists. The woman snapped a photo of the elegant long, wooden information desk as her companion adjusted a black plastic apparatus in his front pocket. From the attached headphones that momentarily blared a reggae beat, Miles guessed he was overhearing a Walkman. Like April's computer with the entries for their monthly catalog on it, and Sgt. Cochran's email, Miles was now experiencing yet another aspect of the contemporary world that seemed utterly alien to him. Or was he once again playing the role of Mr. Stuck-in-Mud, for which Nick claimed he was so perfectly suited?

"I'm sorry, sir," the librarian prompted him, "but how can I help you?"

"I'm interested in inks," he said absently, head still turned in the direction of his self-appointed guardian.

"Then you'd begin along that wall over there." Here she pointed directly over Nick's head. "Look on the spines of the tall, black catalogue books alphabetically for *ink*."

"I'm sorry," Miles apologized. "I meant to say, if I had come here in the past looking for books on ink and how it was made in the sixteenth century, is there any way I could find a record of the volumes I consulted just for...for bibliographic purposes?"

"I'm afraid not. You see, call slips for ordinary research materials are discarded once an item has been returned."

Miles had come to another dead end. "Sorry to have troubled you."

"No trouble at all."

He retreated to the desk where Nick sat and dragged him out into the foyer where they could talk more freely. They sat on one of the marble benches under the paneled ceiling, with darkened murals on the walls around them.

"They don't keep any records of patrons who use general research materials."

"That's another of your hair-brained ideas down, Miles. The police haven't found your fingerprints on the manuscript, and...."

"Not yet anyway."

"Don't cut me off," Nick said so that everyone in the vaulted room, down the halls and flanking stairs, could hear. "No fingerprints. You never came home with ink on your...."

"Not that you saw, anyway."

Nick scowled at this additional interruption.

"No fingerprints. No ink-stained hands, at least that I ever saw you with. No record of any books taken out on ink-making. Judging from the absence of evidence, any *sane* person would conclude he didn't forge that manuscript."

"None of the things you mention is conclusive."

"Of course not, because it's impossible to prove a negative. But when enough negatives pile up, Miles, any reasonable man would conclude that he's just plain wrong to think he could have created that play himself when his mind was like Swiss cheese with new holes in it every day. And then somehow you copied it out in such a way that you've still got the experts puzzled? Give it up."

"Maybe. We'll see what Loren Pritchard says."

"Oh, right. Loren Pritchard. What if he doesn't remember the manuscript? Will you finally quit chasing the Great Ghost of Shakespeare so our lives can get back to normal?"

Miles nodded his agreement. What else could he do with Nick upping the ante each time he spoke? Even if Loren Pritchard didn't remember the *Hamlet*, what would that mean when Miles knew, in the very core of his being, that he himself had forged it, even though he still had no real proof of that.

51 LAST-MINUTE DETAILS

It took Joanna less than ten minutes to get from Gene's school to the Settlement House where Lars Carlsson had agreed to meet her. The whole of the cab ride, she ran through the motions of the little act she intended to put on for Carlsson. First her scarf would come off, then her dress and slip until she would be standing semi-naked before the financier.

But as she opened her purse to pay the cabdriver, she thought about Gene's offer, about Gene himself, and then let her feelings take over. It was true, she was a woman of the theater. She knew better than almost anyone that the fucking show must go on, but she could not go on and fuck the show's worst enemy, a money grubbing fund manager who had so little regard for the arts he was prepared to lock out his longtime tenants.

She stared down at the money in her hand, then stuffed it back in her purse and instructed the driver to turn around and drop her off where he had picked her up, in front of Gene's school. Self sacrifice was one thing, self hatred something else entirely. And that's what she would have done, hated herself months afterward for an act of prostitution that no amount of high mindedness about the importance of theater could ever absolve.

But Gene had already left for the day.

Immediately after Joanna got home, she called Lars Carlsson and apologized for missing her appointment. She did not rant, did not tell him what she thought of him, just informed him that he'd have to find a new tenant for the coming year. Next, she called Gene, who was home by then, and told him in the sweetest voice she could muster that she accepted his offer, which would mean rehearsals next morning at ten, and he promised to recruit every student he could scare up that weekend to move sets, risers, lights, folding chairs, everything they needed.

Next on her list was Avery, then Joanna called every last member of the company, cast and crew. She told them of the change of venue in terms so glowing she began to choke up each time she recounted the splendors of their new domed, outdoor theater. In most cases, she just left messages, but when she got real people—like Craig Sommers and Michael Ridley, their gaffer—in whose voices she detected some hesitation, she simply let them know the company really had no other choice. It was either adapt or adieu. And neither voiced an abiding desire to take a sudden vacation to France.

In the time that remained before opening night, everyone worked tirelessly. With promises of participating in a once-in-a-lifetime experience, Gene's students had everything they needed for rehearsal waiting for them on the school roof on Saturday morning. Cute Heather Owens, the drama teacher, turned her people over to Michael to help with the lights—anchoring the booms, climbing like monkeys and hanging the teaser and light bridge from the undersides of the metal roof. Together, they resized the sets slightly to fit the north corner looking out over the East River, then strung an improvised proscenium curtain that resembled a quilt of sixties' patchwork shirts. It was so awful it was almost perfect.

Joanna went to at least part of every rehearsal, primarily to see how Erskine Strathmore was fitting in as Hamlet's father. The remainder of the day and much of the night, she and her tiny staff were tending to a host of last-minute details that accompanied the change of venues: new tickets and press releases, radio and newspaper announcements, shuttle service between the Settlement House and P.S. 39, late advertising, costume adjustments for new cast members, then a broken toilet in the fourth floor women's room that now doubled as a dressing room, last-minute inclusions in the all-important press kits. And the tawdry list went on and on.

She spent far more time on the telephone than she should have, but there was no choice after Shawn Kirby's article on their completely new *Hamlet* appeared. As she predicted, box office sales spiked from that moment on. Joanna had known all along the new play would be just the thing they needed, no matter whether by Shakespeare, Thomas Kyd, or Tom Stoppard.

It was all a matter of damage control when it came to questions about authenticity, to which she responded as honestly as possible, attempting to spin a tale that would encourage prospective audience members to purchase tickets. She told no outright lies, which was almost impossible after the death of Charles Cassidy, given the fact that either you were alive. Or you weren't. And, knowing Charles, he was enjoying the afterlife even more, and causing just as much havoc in his new permanent home, wherever that was.

She had new posters and playbills printed that accurately stated what they were doing, and where: *Hamlet, Part One* by Shakespeare? in the new Skyline Theater at P.S. 39. She scheduled two vans to shuttle those who hadn't heard they were no longer performing at the Settlement House. And she moved the curtain back to 8:30 to accommodate late arrivals.

At the first dress rehearsal, she thought the production fell somewhere between austere and boldly modern, too gloomy really for Joanna's tastes, which ran to something more colorful, but the New York night sky just ate up their lights. The modular sets of interchangeable exterior-interior castle walls were a few degrees too ominous, but they did set an effective mood for the play. With a simple change in furnishings, the battlements could become the great hall, or, with a moveable set of stairs, a turret or dungeon. Whatever the critics might say, the sets were both simple and economical, and that much, at least, pleased her.

All she...all any of them could really do now was wait.

52 MY OWN TRUE SON

For opening night, Joanna chose a sleek, black Victor Costa that was just a stitch or two too tight but, hell! how many times was she going to introduce a new play by William Shakespeare? And to all of New York really? Lips plastered in a perpetual smile, she visited cast members in their adapted, single-sex bath and dressing rooms to buck them up. In all the years she'd performed this ritual, she had never sensed so much mutual nervous energy, heightened, naturally, by her own. Richard Metz and Erskine Strathmore were jostling one another as they attempted to make themselves up in the lone mirror in the men's room. Samuel, back against a narrow strip of cinderblock wall, was doing toe lifts, the reason for which only God knew.

Next door, she found Valerie in the foyer of the woman's room, murmuring a repeated prayer to St. Jude, the patron saint of lost causes. When Joanna peered inside, she saw only Olivia Jennings, their Marguerite. April was nowhere around, nor had Olivia or Valerie seen her at any time that evening. For that matter, neither had Joanna. So she alerted Rachel Bohmer, her understudy.

Joanna couldn't help wondering if April hadn't let opening-night anxieties overwhelm her. She tried calling her at her father's, but got no answer. In fact, Joanna didn't even know if she was staying there after the argument the two had had at The Gables. Didn't even know if they were speaking. There was still time for April, for both of them, to get there. Perhaps they were just caught in traffic?

She went outside to look for their wayward Ophelia, and found instead a balmy September breeze that sent the first leaves of autumn scuttling down the sidewalk. Standing there, looking up and down the street, she contemplated everything that could go wrong that evening. The noise of passing jets drowning important lines. Insecurely anchored lights that might come clattering down. Pigeons worming through the chain-link fence. Wind whipping around the sets, even though Jerry Grantland had assured her they could survive a category-two hurricane.

And then there was April. Where was that girl?

As members of the audience began to show up, Joanna stationed herself beside one of the new posters, ready to respond to questions that were certain to come from those few who arrived, still expecting to see *Othello*. Her stock answer was simple. That evening, they were going to be among the fortunate few to witness history in the rewriting. She also had a brief, rehearsed speech to offer in the face of one other inevitable question.

"I didn't know there was a *Hamlet, Part One*?"

"Until a month ago, no one else did either," she planned to explain. "Your playbills have today's date stamped on the cover. Save them to tell your grandchildren about the evening you saw the other *Hamlet*, the first new play by Shakespeare mounted in almost three centuries."

Of all the people she spoke with, only two, both men, voiced open disappointment. When she opened her purse and offered to return their money on the spot, both accepted, one with the observation that she should pay his cab fare too, and she immediately gave him twenty dollars more. Chagrined, he returned the bill and the ticket money, and shrank in among passersby on the sidewalk.

As 8:15 approached and went, Joanna still hadn't spotted April. There were other doors to the school, of course, but she didn't think they were open. She had already seen and greeted four of the critics she had gone to such lengths to lure to the rooftop theater that evening. Martine Vorhees of the *Village Voice*, and Shawn Kirby were yet to make their appearances.

"Hey, Joanna. Sorry, we're late."

Without looking, she knew it was Gene calling to her from behind. She stopped breathing a moment, fearing that the *we* he was talking about included the young, attractive Heather Owens, not a good omen for the evening. She turned to see that indeed the drama teacher was at his side, along with another man, who, dressed in a black sport coat and jeans, reminded her a little of Avery. With any luck, he would turn out to be Heather's boyfriend. Maybe even her husband.

"Hi, you two," she said at her enthusiastic best. "Who's your friend?"

"This is Derek Graham. He teaches twelfth-grade English here. And don't worry, I didn't tell him a thing about...you know what."

"You don't have to keep it secret anymore, Gene," Joanna said, pointing to the poster on the column behind her. "Hamlet's cat clawed its way out of the bag this weekend. Didn't you read Shawn Kirby's article in the *Chronicle*?"

Gene shook his head. "No time."

"Well, I did," Derek observed, his thin lips drawn into a scowl. "At first, I thought he was writing about a Charles Ludlam spoof. I can't imagine a prequel to *Hamlet*."

Dropping her usual rehearsed explanation, Joanna gave Gene and Heather's colleague a thirty-second synopsis of events leading to that evening's premiere. She didn't have time for a longer explanation because it was almost 8:35 and still no sign of April.

She offered a hurried good-bye that was far cheerier than she felt, checked briefly with the box office, then took the back stairs to the roof. She emerged to find the atmosphere in their jury-rigged amphitheater supercharged, the audience obviously anxious to see what Shawn Kirby's preview was all about. Undoubtedly some of the more recent ticket purchasers had come just to be able to say they had witnessed an opening-night fiasco.

Joanna efficiently glad-handed those with seats on the side aisle until she reached the curtain. Behind it, actors were in their places. She turned her head up toward the metal roof in relief. Dressed in a loose fitting gown with embroidered over-jacket, April stood by the metal railing in a different world, eyes staring motionlessly ahead even when responding in broken sentences to other actors' encouraging remarks. Somehow, she had escaped

Joanna's attention and come in one of the side doors perhaps.

Just inside the curtain, she turned toward them all, bowed to thank them silently for their hard work, then clasped her hands above her head in a silent sign of victory. Steve Benedict handed her the mike and the lights came down. The din of talkers didn't begin to fade until a few in the front rows started clapping after she stepped out from behind the curtain and the spotlight found her.

For an unsettling moment, Joanna didn't see the need to offer any introductory remarks. Everyone was certainly aware by then that they weren't doing *Othello* anymore. And she had known that Erskine would be replacing Charles well enough in advance to include his name in the playbill. What's more, Joanna simply hated to address audiences before a performance.

From her vantage point, she could see a few empty seats in the audience. Perhaps once word had spread that they would be doing *Hamlet, Part One*, a small number of their more conservative subscribers had stayed home. The Players could ill afford to alienate them since they were among their wealthiest patrons. Good reviews, or an offer to honor their tickets at future performances, which she hoped to add, might lure them back.

"Welcome...." She paused here waiting for pin-drop silence. "Welcome to the new Skyline Theater. There are so many who deserve our thanks this evening–especially teachers and administrators of P.S. 39: Heather Owens, Ron Saunders and Gene Priestly–for making this the East Village Players' home for our first production of the season."

Here, Joanna started the applause, then had to wait minutes it seemed until it died down.

"This evening is at once a very sad, yet joyous occasion. As you've perhaps noticed in your programs, Erskine Strathmore is taking the role of King Hamlet, previously to have been played by Charles Cassidy. I...I am sorry to tell you that Charles...died recently."

She lowered the mike because she was strangely overcome there in front of the audience. She didn't bring it back up until their expressions of dismay had subsided, and she herself had partially recovered.

"As all of you know, Charles was one of the...of the founding members of the East Village Players. Among the roles in which you will remember him, he was an incomparable Vershinin in *Three Sisters*, Cullen in *The Doctor's Dilemma*, Shylock in *Merchant of Venice*. He started his career with the company as Iago in *Othello*, a role he was originally scheduled to reprise for you this evening, had circumstances not intervened.

"We dedicate this performance to Charles. May he...may he blaze an even more glorious path in heaven than the very fiery one he lived on earth, and on the Players' and...and many other stages during his time in this world. A moment of silence, please, for Charles Cassidy."

Joanna needed that time to tamp down her own emotions which, at several points in her memorial remarks, threatened to choke her words. Only when she could breathe normally again did she bring her head back up. Before she could speak, however, a pigeon swooped toward her from the metal dome. Involuntarily, she ducked, then told herself not to worry. How many pigeons had they all survived in the barn at The Gables?

She lifted the microphone again.

"By this point, all of you know that the play we are about to perform for you tonight is not *Othello*, but *Hamlet, Part One*, so-called because the action in it precedes that in the *Hamlet* everyone knows. The play was only recently discovered in England and came to us by rather fortuitous means. You will be the first audience to see it performed in four hundred years."

As she spoke, she searched the risers for Miles Oliphant. He had to be present, if only to see that she had not betrayed either his trust in her, or her word to him. But, if he were out there, she couldn't find him. Once again, she had miscalculated and prayed that Miles' absence didn't portend anything more ominous.

"The East Village Players are now pleased to present this, the world premiere minus England, of *Hamlet, Part One*. It is Shakespeare's shortest play, only a hundred minutes in length, so there will be no intermission. I know you'll enjoy it."

To far greater applause than that which had greeted her, Joanna stepped back behind the curtain, handed the mike to Steve and exhaled deeply. In the time it took her to recover from her opening remarks, she realized she couldn't possibly assume her normal seat in back beside Avery. His occasional, furious scribbling of notes would drive her to do the unthinkable, take out her nail file and skewer his right hand, the one he wrote with, to his thigh. Instead she slipped out from backstage and sat in an empty seat on the far side aisle.

In the course of the evening, she came to see that her decision to have the cast rehearse at The Gables that summer was something short of disaster. The principals seemed lost on stage. Erskine was not yet fully in synch with the others. And, for whatever foolish reason, April slowed her lines to a lava-flow pace with an audience in the house. There were countless other minor disasters that evening—police or ambulance sirens blaring, dropped lines and miscues, costumes askew, feet seemingly nailed to the floor, lighting cues lost.

At times, it was all Joanna could do to keep from rushing for the exit, down the stairs, and out onto the sidewalk to seek anonymity in the crowds on nearby Canal Street. She might easily have done that had it not been for those stalwart actors performing against the backdrop of city lights, the glow of dusk beyond and a lone star rising over Queens.

Then, toward the end, Samuel, dressed in jerkin and doublet, had followed his mother and the new king, his uncle, up the tower steps to an apartment that overlooked the Oresund, where Hamlet overheard muffled, amorous sounds that appalled him. Retreating to the main floor of the stage, he had then more strutted than delivered his finest soliloquy in the play, decrying the opportunistic character of his Uncle Claudius in bedding his own, still grieving mother.

With two straight-backed chairs placed where the stairs had stood, the tower became an audience room in a matter of seconds. One of the chairs, that served as thrones, stood empty. Gertrude sat in the other with Hamlet towering at her side while two guards brought Claudius in chains before the royal mother and son.

Gertrude. But he is still your uncle, soon our king
    And he hath sworn affection toward me.
    Pay the captain of the guard no heed.
Hamlet. Do you return his loathsome feelings, too
    Those you held but days ago for my dear father?
    Do come, for everything depends on this.
[Pause]
    You are silent dearest mother. Take him
    To the scaffold, guards. Bring me his severed head.
Gertrude. Not that. He is your father's brother.
Hamlet. And more than that to you, our country's queen?
Gertrude. So only in that it preserves our state.
Hamlet. Am I to know that truly in my heart?
Gertrude. I swear an oath it is the truth, my son.
Hamlet. I would have thought it troth to Claudius
    But if it be the truth as you proclaim
    To save the state, then must himself be saved.
    It suits me not to be the king so young
    And see my uncle soon dispatched in guilt
    So let him go, but not to worser deeds
    Than I do think him destined for at court.
Exeunt guards
Claudius. With all my soul I thank you, noble sire
    For you are worthy of your father's name.
    I will in time prove all accusers false
    Or then may you bestow on me that fate
    That you have saved me from this day.
Gertrude. Here I do see fair justice blend with reason.
    You are my own true son and savior both.
Exeunt Gertrude and Claudius
Hamlet. Is that the fair report of truth I've heard
    Or but a counterfeit in honor's clothes?
    I know it not, and do not want to know.

These last three lines were lost on Joanna, not because Samuel underplayed them. Something far worse happened. The engine and churning blades of a newsroom helicopter drowned them out completely. Their Hamlet did as Avery had coached them. He stood there motionless and silent, his eyes not blinking once while Joanna swore under her breath at the WNBC news chopper that violated their sacred airspace. Only after Pilgrim's resonant voice could be heard again did he repeat his introductory lines and continue.

Hamlet. Is that the fair report of truth I've heard
    Or but a counterfeit in honor's clothes?
    I know it not, and do not want to know.
    But must, for on it hangs my right to rule
    Which I do not desire at my young age,
    Though it be mine in name if not in fact.
    Nor does it suit for now my ill-formed youth
    Which I will always be if left to learn
    Those things of which I would know even more
    For they are broad and deep as oceans wide
    And endless as its curving sands and shores.
    For if my uncle be as guiltless as is said
    Then I will be a student evermore
    And will go knock at sweet Ophelia's door
    But if my uncle guilty be, then I
    Am both a judge and executioner
    Two crafts I would know nothing of, but ones
    That I must master if to rule henceforth.

                   Exit

Now Joanna saw that Samuel, nearly twice Hamlet's true age, had not come along in the role nearly as much as she had hoped. Just days before, she was certain he was going to prove wrong everyone who claimed she'd asked him to play Othello just because he was a box-office draw.

At least Samuel and April had somehow worked things out between them. As late as the second dress, April was even more standoffish with her Hamlet than with anyone else on stage. But there, before her own eyes that evening, the couple finally gelled, especially in the shore scene at the end. And it was April who had brought them closer, whether teasing or taunting Hamlet, only fractions of an inch from him, when before it seemed the entire stage stood between the two. The effect really had been quite something to witness.

Once again, Joanna pulled the corners of her mouth upright as the lights came up and the audience applauded politely. Shawn Kirby and Tad Applegate were among the first to leave, neither bothering to consult or congratulate her, which only confirmed her own opinion of the evening. *Hamlet, Part One* was a semi-disaster. Of course, the production would improve with time, but this had been their first best chance at winning over doubters, chief among them the critics, whose speedy departure signaled their opinions only too well.

If the performance had gone better, perhaps it wouldn't have mattered that they did not yet have irrefutable physical proof of Shakespeare's authorship of the play. The critics would naturally do what they did best and blow their own horns so loud they made themselves deaf. When they examined the transcript Avery had prepared for them, however, they would see, as he had, the hand of a youthful, headstrong Shakespeare at work.

Just as she was about to go backstage for an obligatory round of congratulations, someone tapped her on the shoulder. She turned to see RJ.

"It was wonderful," he told her, giving her a very welcome hug.

"You're just saying that. It was awful."

"No, it wasn't. I loved it. Honest."

"It was a Packard in a Toyota world. And one that tried to run on flat tires."

"You're way too critical, mom."

"And you're far too accepting."

"Then I'd rather be me."

"I would, too. We've got the same genes. I can't understand how you came out as wonderfully as you did. I thought you were back at Wittenberg? How did you get here?"

"I flew. Dad paid for my ticket."

"Your father paid for your...your...?"

Joanna couldn't finish, didn't even want to, in fact. Fortunately she was spared having to say anything further when Gene and Heather came up to them, their friend Derek nowhere in sight.

"Hey, RJ," Gene said, high-fiving his nephew. "I didn't know you'd be here. This is Heather Owens, the world's greatest drama teacher. RJ's awesome. His youth outreach won his father's election for him, no doubt about it."

"Don't remind me," Joanna muttered, tempted to walk away from the jovial threesome.

"You ever play Ophelia?" RJ asked Heather the Divine.

"The kid's got a thing for Ophelias," Gene explained.

"I wouldn't even think of it after what I saw tonight. April Oliphant's first time on stage in years right here at P.S. 39! I can't tell you how excited my students are. And, Mrs. Priestly, I mean, my god, what you pulled off tonight!" Here Heather unexpectedly wrapped her arms around the surprised Joanna. "It should go down in the Guinness Book of Records."

"Better than that," Gene said. "We're going to name the new theater after her. The Joanna Priestly Skyline Theater."

"Substitute Jenkins for Priestly," Joanna said. "That's my maiden name," she explained to Heather.

They spoke for another minute or two before Joanna invited all three of them to the cast party at O'Flaherty's, then went backstage and, false smile still tugging at her lips, offered praise all around. Not one person, cast or crew, tried to refute her; all seemed genuinely happy. What children, she thought. They hadn't seen the effect of the whole, as she had.

That particular evening, she didn't have the luxury of retreating to the confines of her office to compose herself before the cast party, which she dreaded. Matt Tyler was there, continuing work on the press kit. They had run off fifty complete scripts for distribution to anyone with questions about the source of the play. Interns had already overnighted six to leading *Hamlet* scholars in the U.S. and Great Britain the day before. Better to be preemptive, get the text and Avery's take on it out there as if they had nothing to fear from academics. That, she figured, was the best way to blunt the reaction that was certain to come. Yes, she had taken a gamble, but if producers like her weren't willing to take the occasional chance, theater might as well be put on an assembly line to churn out countless cloned productions that often could not be told apart.

The yo-yo went up and it went down, Joanna concluded as she left for the opening-night celebration. This time, however, the string had broken, and the spinning disk had gone crashing through the roof and down four stories of P.S. 39 below, taking the East Village Players with it.

53 A BALCONY SEAT

Joanna Priestly was something of a marvel, she truly was. From her place at a balcony table at O'Flaherty's, April had looked down, watching her off and on for well over ten minutes. The tireless promoter had shaken hands or embraced virtually every well-dressed man and woman who had come to the cast party, many of them among the Players' most generous supporters.

And then there was Gene Priestly. When he wasn't at Joanna's side, he was looking her way with eyes so wide April could see it all the way up there in the balcony. His colleague Heather was off in the corner with a man-in-black she didn't know.

At one point, she glimpsed a woman in a pinstriped pants suit with flaring shoulder pads, who had to be Martine Vorhees of the *Village Voice*, talking with Joanna. Within moments, the two of them slipped off to one of the back booths. The only part of the reporter's body she could see, her hands, poked out beyond the table, palms out a couple times to ward off others who approached, also wanting face-time with the Players' producer. April would have given the most expensive book in her father's store to know what the two women were discussing.

Seconds after Martine left the booth and got caught up in the crowd, Joanna emerged and took Avery in tow. That lasted only minutes before he branched out for a refill of champagne, and a large man in a double-breasted blazer caught up with him. From there on it was wall-to-wall smiles and congratulations, all of which Avery accepted with amazing grace. Perhaps he wasn't the best-looking man there, but he alone stood out in the spotlight of April's mind, despite his occasional lapses. It had been difficult, but she had forgiven him after their little flare up that last night at The Gables. It would happen again, she knew, if he

250

ever directed her in the future, and that was something she would have to think about. No matter, she still longed to be at his side, not doing what he and Joanna were doing that night certainly, although she might be up to that in another year or two.

April, herself, had been able to endure her own well-wishers only so long. They had been so lavish in their praise she initially thought they must have been talking about someone else, yet she knew too well she had been the only Ophelia on that stage. In her own mind, hers had not been a particularly compelling performance, but then she was far too self-critical. Who wouldn't have been with parents like hers?

In a way, she was glad her father hadn't come to see her that evening. He was still far too angry at her. That, and her technique was rusty. Her lines were rushed, her timing off by whole minutes it seemed, but she would improve, she knew that. She could have blamed it all on Erskine Strathmore if she had wanted. After all, she had never worked with him before, but it wasn't really his fault. She was never at her best opening night.

Acting was such a complete sport, involving the whole of a person, body and soul, and she wasn't quite at that level yet. Still, for her, theater was far more immediate and much less frightening than everyday life. Only when the final curtain descended was it time to be on-guard again. Life on stage was...well, staged. By comparison, real life was far too real, and therefore a more threatening proposition. She would take the theater any time. Evidently, most who had congratulated her in the mosh pit below agreed.

Of all the people who should have rescued her (Avery!) from the great clamor, Samuel Pilgrim had graciously given himself to the cause again, as if she had done anything to deserve it. Somehow he had finally silenced her mother's voice urging caution, and made Ophelia into the flame-drawn moth Shakespeare had intended. She didn't know how he had managed it, but he had. It felt so good to truly connect with someone on stage, and then he'd done it again there at O'Flaherty's. The evening had been less, and yet so very much more than she had expected.

That was until Valerie, who'd drunk about a barrel too much wine, started in on her and Avery. After that brief debacle, April had retreated to the balcony that had been roped off and darkened for the celebration. It had been forever since she'd been in a crowded bar. While O'Flaherty's was nicer than most, all the good cheer and especially the camaraderie wearied her well before it should have.

Having stayed longer that she intended, she pulled on her cardigan and started down the stairs. This time of evening, she didn't really think she'd have much trouble getting a cab.

"There you are," she heard someone call out behind her. "I was afraid I'd missed you."

It was her brother Lawrence. Somehow he'd wrangled an invitation to the party. Instinctively, she quickened her pace.

"It's me, April. Wait up. Please!" He had come all that way, perhaps even given a large donation to the company to be invited to the opening-night celebration. He'd catch up with her on the street anyway, so she turned toward him.

"Thanks for coming," she said coldly.

"I wouldn't have had it any other way."

"How did you know? I mean, about the opening? The party? I didn't realize you kept up on theater?"

"I don't actually. Father thought I'd like to know, his way of returning a favor, I suppose."

"A favor?"

"The passport."

It would have been just like their father to call Lawrence with news of her appearance with the East Village Players, even though he hadn't come himself. Perhaps he had exploited his new acquaintanceship with Joanna to make certain Lawrence got invited to the reception. She imagined Father and Son growing closer as a result, then dismissed the idea. It simply wouldn't be possible after everything Lawrence had done.

"You were magnificent up there, April. I couldn't believe that was the little girl Mom and Dad had so much trouble coaxing onto the stage for the Christmas pageant at school."

"You just said you don't keep up with theater. How would you know if I was good or bad?"

"You forget, politics is ultimate theater. Let me tell you, you weren't just good. You were the best person there, by far."

"That wouldn't be brotherly pride speaking by any chance?"

"Maybe, but take my word for it, you were so natural as that Ophelia girl it seemed like you weren't even acting. Or trying to. I just wish...."

April could tell Lawrence had stopped as he was about to say something important.

"You wish...?"

"Look, I've got an early meeting tomorrow at Borough Hall. I see you're on your way home. Maybe we could share a cab?"

April didn't know how to tell her brother she wasn't really going home. Nor did she particularly feel like being trapped with him in the back of a cab, but then they wouldn't be going far together.

She marveled that, even though two other people were hailing cabs on the same side of Canal Street, the first one along swerved away from them and pulled up right in front of Lawrence Oliphant. What was the magic attractant, she wondered? He was no taller than the others, nor did he whistle, or even wave his hand. It simply went up in the air, and a cab pulled up in front of him.

Inside they traveled the first block or two in silence. Then he started to speak.

"Look, I know you hold Teddy's death against me, and I don't blame you. Not a day goes by...."

"I don't want to talk about it. Please!" she pleaded, already hugging the door on her side of the taxi.

"But I do. I have to because who knows when I'll get to talk to you again, and I've got something I have to say. Not a day goes by when I don't see Teddy's mangl...his body, sometimes when I least expect it. I'll be putting on my shoes. At Gristede's. In a meeting. On the handball court. I know that doesn't make things any easier for you. There was something special between you two. Something not many other brothers and sisters have."

April needed to get out, but it was late at night and the taxi kept hurtling along the empty streets.

"Stop the cab!" she yelled so loud the driver had to hear her through the pitted plastic panel that separated the front and back seats.

"You sure?" he called back to them. "We're not there yet."

"Go ahead and pull over at the corner," her brother said in resignation, then turned away from her. "I tried calling, but your phone had been disconnected. I only found out where you were staying months later when I called Dad and you picked up."

By this time the cab had stopped. April thrust open the door, bolted out into the middle of the intersection and started running, she didn't know where.

"It's your silence that's killing me, April," she heard Lawrence call out behind her. "Killing everybody. I don't know how much longer...."

Out of shouting range and almost out of breath, she just kept running. Running until her sides began to ache. Her pace faltered and she bent over in pain. The one in her stomach would go away soon enough. The one at the very center of her being, however, would live as long as she did. All her brother's empty words were not going to alleviate it, and she didn't want them to. Teddy was too special for that. If ever she became a truly great actor, it would be because of him, and the absence, the great, gaping void his death had left in her life. Out of that she could shape any character the greatest of playwrights had created. Even Shakespeare.

54 EATING HER WORDS

Disoriented, April wandered the streets of the West Village trying to regain her bearings. When she did, she found that she was just blocks away from Avery's. Still, she approached his building with caution, expecting her brother, who'd heard her give the driver the address, to be waiting outside, but she found the street deserted and felt a little cheated. If he had truly wanted her forgiveness, he would have been there to plead with her again.

She let herself in with keys Avery had given her earlier, went straight to the refrigerator, took out the ice, and poured herself a glass of Scotch, perhaps not the best thing to do after her most tumultuous evening in recent memory. She had been too hard on Lawrence after he had gone to all the trouble of coming to see her that evening, and to attempt an apology when no apology would ever be enough.

The alcohol helped nudge her toward a more indulgent view of her performance that evening. The one she'd given on stage, not the far more pathetic one at O'Flaherty's and afterwards. Perhaps it hadn't been as bad as she'd initially thought. From the second act on, it had been pure joy to portray the infatuated Ophelia, and she wondered if she hadn't just projected her feelings for Avery on stage, or was it the other way around? Ophelia's love for Hamlet had heightened hers for Avery? It didn't matter. Maybe someday she'd believe all the autograph seekers and well-wishers who saw something in her performance that ingrained psychological blinders prevented her from seeing in herself.

She was about to take a seat on the couch when she heard the lock turn in the door. Quickly, she bolted the last of her Scotch to help forget everything. Her squabble with Avery at Joanna's. The intervening nights she'd spent at Shelly's, unable to stay at her father's because of the guilt he made her feel over the theft of the manuscript. Unable to come to Avery's for obvious reasons. Then, too, there had been the cab ride with Lawrence.

"You actually came. What a pleasant surprise," Avery said cheerfully, attempting at the same time to kiss her, but she pulled away. "I thought you'd gone to Shelly's because the party turned out to be too much for you?"

"The party and other things. We've got to talk."

"Okay, but you've had the advantage of a drink," he said, and started toward the kitchen. "I'm going to fix myself one, too. Care for a refill?"

"I'm fine, thanks. Just needed something to take the edge off, that's all."

"I counted four critics there tonight, all local," he called to her from the kitchen. "Joanna said she saw Tad Applegate of the *L.A. Times* as well. And she was certain there were others from out-of-town she didn't recognize."

"Are you going to wait up for the reviews?"

"Unless you've got something better to propose, and I hope you do. It's almost three."

April was thinking how to respond to his invitation when the buzzer sounded.

"Don't answer that," he called to her.

"It's me, Valerie," a slurred voice echoed from the call box. "Let me in."

April couldn't help wondering if Valerie hadn't come to Avery's after rehearsal every night since they'd returned to the city. It would have been just like her.

She heard the tinkle of ice in a glass as Avery hurried back into the living room. Steeling herself for the inevitable, she pressed the button. Better to let the skeletons in now than keep them out in the cold, threatening to rattle around and spoil the future, however long that lasted.

"Are you crazy?" he demanded. "She'll spoil our evening."

"Assuming there is one. I thought the thing between you and her was over?"

"It is, but Valerie's a Roman candle. Who knows where she'll land when she explodes."

"In your apartment, evidently."

After April undid the locks, Avery took her in his arms. Despite the objections roiling in her mind, she didn't resist. Nor did she kiss him with any passion until the door creaked open beside them. Then she refused to let him go.

"I get the message," Valerie said haltingly. "Is that why you let me in?"

"He didn't," April told her. "I did."

"Little Miss Muppet," Valerie hissed as she walked past them and dropped onto an arm of the couch, "eating her words and, hey, what do I care?"

"She gets like this when she's had too much to drink," Avery whispered to her, then turned toward Valerie.

"What do you want, Val?"

"From the looks of things, I'm not going to get what I want tonight. And if I can't, I'm going public with my story."

"What story?" Avery said, breaking from April and standing threateningly in front of his former girlfriend.

"About you and the manuscript. How you miraculously found it, then tri...tricked the company into believing it was real."

"That's not true."

"Maybe not, but you'll have a hell'uva time proving it."

"Listen to me, Valerie, and listen carefully," Avery said as April tried to pull him away from her. "You're drunk. You don't know what you're saying. If you go telling people that, especially the critics, you're going to bring the house down on everybody's head, your own included."

"Then I hope they give me a gr...great funeral afterwards. Just like Charles. I miss him, I really do. He was just like you, Avi, except the opposite. Treated me just as b...badly, but at least he was fun to be with. Fun as in funny, not so drop-dead serious as another East Villager whose name I won't mention 'cause we both know who I'm talking about, don't we, April?"

"Let me handle this, will you, sweetheart?" April intervened.

"Oh, 'sweetheart' is he now?" Valerie babbled. "His heart's about as sweet as coal, and just as hard."

April tugged Avery's arm and asked, "do you have some extra sheets and a blanket?"

"Extra sheets? What are you talking about? She's not going to spend the night."

"Just tell me where they are."

"This is definitely not a good idea, April."

"Better to tame the she-tiger before you set her free," she whispered in reply.

He folded his arms over his chest and cocked his head just slightly. "Bottom drawer of my dresser in the bedroom."

April retrieved the sheets and grabbed the top blanket from the bed. When she walked back into the living room, Valerie was pummeling Avery's shoulder with her fists, and crying at the same time. He held his palms up toward the ceiling as if to indicate he had no idea what to expect next. While he tried to calm Valerie, April started to make up a bed on the couch.

"You're in no shape to go home by yourself, Valerie," she said. "You might as well stay here."

"Where are *you* going to stay? Not in his...his bed?"

"If it'll make you feel any better, I'll leave."

"Nothing will make me feel better. Not after Charles' death. I'm going to go home and drink myself to sleep. Don't worry. I'll be alright. There're always cabs, this time of night."

"I really think you should stay," April came back.

Valerie shook her head violently. "Not with you and him fucking behind my back. No way I'm staying here at *Avery's*."

She pronounced his name with chilling hatred, then started toward the door.

"I'm not planning on doing any such thing, in front of or behind *anyone's* back," April told her. "Now, you're sure you won't stay?"

"Positive."

"And you're not going to talk to the press?" Avery demanded as she turned the door handle.

"You can't stop me from talking. No one can."

55 FACT CHECKING

The wooden slats of the bench in Bryant Park were punishingly hard, and the pigeons flocking around his feet, fed by the man at the other end, even harder to take. Miles could have easily left, but he was rooted there in that welcome patch of sunlight at his end. He just didn't have the strength or the will to move, not until his meeting with Sgt. Cochran at eleven-thirty, a meeting he feared more than he was willing to acknowledge, though Cochran had said nothing about finding his fingerprints on the manuscript.

In spite of Joanna's insistence that those in the opening-night audience who knew him would think he was there only to see his daughter perform, Miles had refused to attend because he might be spotted by some reporter who'd start asking questions about the source of the play, and soon discover the trail that led inevitably from the stage of the East Village Players all the way back to Marston House. And behind it all was the hand of Miles Oliphant. Yes, literally his own hand since it had been responsible for writing out the play. Any association between him and the new *Hamlet* would destroy his reputation, or what remained of it. He saw all that now with a mind so clear he could look right through himself. Everything was so transparent he might just as well evaporate right there in that little pool of sunshine.

Miles had wanted nothing to do with April, and especially the play in which she was performing. But Nick had read the reviews, all of them, and shouted out every word of praise lavished on her. The critics alone persuaded him to go two evenings later when he scored a ticket from a scalper. He was so completely captivated that, after days of badgering, he finally talked Miles into going with him on comp tickets given to them by Joanna Priestly with the promise she wouldn't say a thing to April about his presence at the rear of that evening's audience.

About twenty minutes into that performance, Miles let down his defenses just enough to sense how much his daughter had matured as an actor during her absence from the stage. She'd read a great deal while working at the store, it was true, but she could have never learned the brilliance he witnessed that evening from books alone. He did not know what was responsible for the change unless it was her withdrawal from people, the very people who now helped her peer into and almost through their souls.

The next day Miles had searched his office, from the bottom of each and every file drawer to shadowy corner nooks, but found nothing more than a small rounded piece of quill from a pen (or was it part of a clipped toenail?), wedged at the bottom of the wastebasket beside his desk. It and those two sheets of paper he'd pulled from his stationery drawer were proof that he, not Shakespeare or Theobald or April, had put word to foolscap in the *Ur-Hamlet* that he had just seen at P.S. 39.

In those two objects he perceived that the former Miles Oliphant, hungry for money and fame, had tried to channel Shakespeare's words, working late at night, quill pen in hand filling sheets of flyleaves he'd trimmed to size. The quills must have been difficult to cut at first, Shakespeare's tiny looping secretary hand impossible to duplicate, and yet both had, with time, come to him as if his fingers possessed a latent memory of writing that way in another, former life.

That same day, Shawn Kirby had started phoning the store. The first time he did, Miles made the mistake of answering. Somehow the guttersnipe had managed to dredge up some things Miles himself didn't know. *The Chronicle's* critic had talked to Joanna Priestly, who he claimed had told him everything from Miles' trip to England to Avery LeMaster's examination of the *Ur-Hamlet.* He'd also mentioned the manor at Marston Bigot where Miles had first found the play. But Joanna didn't know that. Only Reg Sloane and now Miles himself had that information. Maybe the persistent reporter had talked to April, even to Sgt. Cochran, but if he had he hadn't mentioned a thing about them.

After that initial conversation, Miles used his message machine to screen calls. Then Kirby had shown up at the front door. Thank god for the security monitor. Miles had closed up immediately after the reporter left and walked around the corner to Bryant Park to think.

Joanna Priestly had left a message earlier that morning, pleading with him to attend a press briefing she had scheduled the next day, or at least to allow her to release any version of the story he approved that told about his discovery of the *Ur-Hamlet*. She also admitted she had talked to Kirby, but had not mentioned Miles' name once in those discussions. If that was true, and he thought it was, Joanna had done what she could to protect him.

Still he had no intention of appearing with her the next morning. Kirby's dog-nosed fact checking left him no other choice.

56 EMOTIONAL COURAGE

Eighty-six. That was the number of reporters who showed up for Joanna's press conference, held, appropriately enough, in the rooftop theater at P.S. 39. Attendees represented media from all parts of the world—Great Britain, of course, but also Australia, Canada, France, Germany, India, Japan, New Zealand, Russia, South Africa, South Korea, even Zimbabwe. She hadn't run off enough additional press kits with copies of the findings of Elizabeth Duke and Hans Grossman, plus reviews from twelve different newspapers including *The Times, The San Francisco Chronicle, The London Daily News, Die Zeit,* and *Asahu Shimbun.* So she'd sent Matt out to Kinko's earlier to make extra copies.

Shawn Kirby's generally positive review had appeared Thursday morning after the opening. Rather amazingly, he had liked their production, almost half his review devoted to the return of April Oliphant, whom he thought even more luminous than she had been before her self-imposed exile from the New York stage. Perhaps his fondness for her colored the remainder of his comments. He even had something positive to say about Samuel Pilgrim, whose performance he called "bold and often moving." He liked the sets and lighting less (*Bravo!* Mr. Kirby), but saved some of his strongest criticism, as he usually did, for Avery LeMaster's direction.

Kirby really went on the attack, however, in the accompanying sidebar which laid out the flawed history of the play's manuscript, as Joanna had related it to him, minus any mention of Miles Oliphant. Many of the circumstances of its discovery were unknown, and its provenance shrouded in mystery. All of it seemed too implausible to Kirby, more the product of a modern wannabe than William Shakespeare. Even though Kirby didn't mention Valerie Schneider by name, Joanna couldn't help but think she had been the source of much of his misinformation.

While she would have liked to have Samuel Pilgrim up there on stage with her to charm the audience, she had decided to spare her actors. Because of soaring demand for tickets, they had added four performances a week—two matinees, Tuesday night, and a late-night on Saturdays. All, cast and crew alike, were running on nothing more than foul-smelling fumes. Joanna had only Avery beside her, both of them seated in folding chairs, the stage behind them set for the opening scene, Prince Hamlet's return from Wittenberg, all against a view of the Manhattan skyline. That morning the heat of the long summer had finally broken, turned cool, in fact, for the first time since early August.

Joanna trembled at the thought of the coming winter, especially on the heels of the luxury of warm summer nights spent among friends at The Gables. And, yes, they were friends, even dear, departed Charles Cassidy. Strange how the distance of a few weeks turned sour memories just slightly bitter, and then, after a little more time, bittersweet. Rob aside, that was the way the last month of summer now struck her, a slight bitterness to accent the overall pleasant taste that glazed the memory of those sainted days.

Avery had been the obvious choice to take the rooftop stage beside her. Until that morning, Joanna had been holding out hope that Miles Oliphant would join them, but he hadn't shown, for reasons only he understood. Finally, when she saw Matt burst through the stairwell doors panting, she stood and gestured for him to hand out the freshly printed material he'd just picked up.

"If those of you who don't already have press kits will please raise your hands, my miracle worker, Matt Tyler, will hand you one straight from Kinko's.

"In your packets you will find a transcript of *Hamlet, Part One*, which the East Village Players have been pleased to present to sold-out audiences for going on two weeks now. There is also an analysis of the early Shakespearian drama by the Players' own Avery LeMaster, here on my left, plus reviews, and the reports of Dr. Elizabeth Duke, a handwriting expert, and another by Dr. Hans Grossman, a forensic chemist.

"A synopsis appears at the front of each expert's assessment, conclusions at the end. If you will read them, you'll quickly learn that nothing in either field is conclusive, more the case with handwriting analysis than with chemistry. After carefully examining the entire manuscript, Dr. Duke has concluded that it was indeed written by William Shakespeare. The script found in it matches that used by Shakespeare, based on the only universally acknowledged examples of his handwriting that have survived, six signatures, though Dr. Duke also consulted his last will and testament, and his contribution to the play, *Sir Thomas More*. The twelve pages of her report lay out the reasons for these conclusions."

As Joanna spoke, several in the audience raised their hands. A few, she couldn't tell how many, actually called out to her.

"If you'll hold your questions for another minute or two," she chirped, "I'll be happy to address them after I've concluded my remarks. Dr. Hans Grossman's findings are less open to question than Dr. Duke's. He examined both the paper and the ink used in the manuscript of our new *Hamlet*. In almost every case he found that the document dates to the late sixteenth century, thus it comes from Shakespeare's time. That is not to say it is by the Bard for certain, just that it is not a more modern fabrication. We do not have proof positive from either two scientists that our *Hamlet* is unquestionably by Shakespeare, but, added to Dr. LeMaster's analysis of the internal evidence found in the drama itself, I'd say we feel confident that the East Village Players are now presenting a new, very early work by William Shakespeare. Naturally, it will take far more time, years in fact, before the authentication process is concluded. We urge you all to judge for yourselves by attending a future performance. Matt will be in the back after we wrap up things here. He'll be happy to provide each of you with complimentary tickets."

Joanna had spun the reports as only a great spinster could. By now, it seemed the hands of half her audience were hovering above their heads. Many who held them aloft also jumped to their feet. She knew the names of just seven or eight of the press corps, critics all, in attendance. Only one of them, Shawn Kirby, had a question for her. After his libelous sidebar questioning the play's provenance, he was the last person she intended to call on.

"The woman in white, second row, side," she said pointing in that direction.

"Marcy Sommerfield of *The Guardian*." Joanna recognized the voice. She was one of the reporters who'd shouted questions before. "In relating Dr. Duke's findings, you stated that she said she had found similarities between the handwriting in the recently discovered manuscript and that of Shakespeare. But didn't Dr. Duke also offer an earlier report in which she came to the opposite conclusion?"

"Yes!" Joanna heard someone in the press corps mutter triumphantly, and she could have sworn it was Kirby.

"Indeed, Dr. Duke did send us an earlier, preliminary finding, based on a sample that represented less than one percent of the manuscript. The report you have in your hands now is based on the entire document, and in it Dr. Duke spares no detail in explaining her change of mind. It all has to do with parallels between the formation of certain letters in Shakespeare's known signatures that are also found in the manuscript. To my way of thinking, it is exciting and conclusive work. Now, are there any follow-up questions on Dr. Duke's report?" A few hands went down. "Yes, the gentleman in the baseball cap in back."

"Isn't there some disagreement about Shakespeare's role in drafting *Sir Thomas More*?"

"Indeed there is. That's why Dr. Duke used only Shakespeare's signatures in reaching her conclusions. Still on the handwriting, now. Yes, the woman behind Ms. Sommerfield."

When Shawn Kirby's right hand came down, Joanna offered silent thanks only to see his other take its place.

"Tamara Jenkins, *Newsweek*. Have you placed too much emphasis on handwriting analysis? I mean, isn't it a kind of woo-woo science?" As she concluded her sentence, her hand rippled the air in front of her like a surfer tacking through a sequence of rolling waves.

"Woo-woo?" Joanna asked. "Or Voodoo?"

This drew a few laughs from the audience, precisely the response Joanna had hoped for.

"Actually both," the slightly ruffled *Newsweek* correspondent responded.

"I wouldn't go quite that far. Handwriting analysis, or graphology, has come a long way in the past century, and, as the brief biography attached to the report will show, Dr. Duke is respected world-wide in her profession. There is a list of contacts appended to her findings. You can call any one of them to check the validity of that assertion.

"I will agree that, of the two, handwriting analysis and forensic chemistry, the former is less verifiable. That is why we also sent the manuscript to Dr. Grossman for analysis. His results are even more compelling."

"With one, very major exception," responded an older gentleman whom she couldn't quite make out in the shadows at the rear. "I see here that he found alum as a binder in the paper, and, according to Grossman himself, that did not occur in paper-making until twenty years after Shakespeare's death."

The question left Joanna without a good answer. She had certainly read that part of the report, but tended to ignore it in light of the rest of the evidence which showed no trace of modern chemicals in either the paper or the ink used in the manuscript. Here, Avery came to her rescue.

"I called Dr. Grossman myself when I read that," he said, standing up. "He, too, was surprised when he discovered alum, given that all other chemical tests pointed to paper made during or before Shakespeare's time. In the end, he admitted that perhaps the papermaker, whoever he was, could have been a generation ahead of his time. And that he experimented with another type of size and excluded gelatin from the paper used by Shakespeare."

That was precisely the reason Joanna had wanted Avery up there on stage with her. He read everything with great care, even scientific reports, it would appear. Now only Shawn Kirby's hand remained raised. She had no choice but to call on him. For that, she used her most practiced, cheerful voice.

"I see nothing sufficient here," he said, waving portions of his press packet in the air, "to explain events leading to the rather amazing discovery of the manuscript in England. Can you tell us how that came about?"

Joanna knew the question would come up. She knew also that she had no satisfactory answer for it.

"The owner of the manuscript, who, by the way, gave us permission to use it in our current production, does not want his name disclosed, in the main, I think, in preparation for its sale."

"If I might interrupt...?" a voice echoed from the rear of the auditorium. "I'm Miles Oliphant, the person Mrs. Priestly just mentioned."

April's father started up the center aisle. He had been standing behind the risers to the rear, which explained why Joanna hadn't seen him. After his repeated refusals to be associated with the manuscript, she couldn't believe he had come, and didn't know whether to be grateful or to fear his unexpected appearance.

"I must ask your patience, Mr. Kirby," Miles continued, "if I cannot provide all the information you rightly feel you deserve. You see, my good friend, Reginald Sloane, first made me aware of certain eighteenth-century letters and miscellanea, offered for sale at Marston House, the former estate of Charles Boyle, Fourth Earl of Orrery. There, I was shown papers that had been discovered in a trunk in the attic. I purchased them from the estate and had them shipped back to New York. I must admit that, at the time, I did not see the manuscript in question, which, I gather, was buried among those papers. It had nothing, really, to distinguish it from similar items in the trunk. It's very unassuming in appearance, I must tell you."

"A follow up, please," Kirby continued. "Is that not a very unusual way for papers like that to be sold, to an individual rather than at auction?"

"No, there is nothing extraordinary about it. I have come by papers in any number of ways—at auction certainly, but also rooting around in old carriage houses, even in dust bins there, in old wine cellars, in the shops of colleagues, at country sales, in church presbyteries, at old hunting lodges, even in the chinking of a former loo."

This drew a round of gentle laughter.

"What I'm getting at is this," Kirby persisted. "Would it not have been possible for your friend, Mr. Sloane, or anyone at Marston House really, either on their own or mutually, to have taken advantage of you? That is, to have created a hoax that you bought into a little too easily?"

Miles drew himself up dramatically and came forward several more steps.

"I don't know about you, Mr. Kirby, and perhaps it's a good thing I don't, but let me tell you one of the greatest truths I've learned in life. Friends, true friends, are hard enough to come by, and Reg Sloane is the best of friends. I've known him twenty-three years. He is both considerate and loyal. He would never, repeat *never* do such a thing as you have proposed. I must admit to you that I did not meet the individual from whom I purchased those papers until my last trip to England, but anyone Reg would recommend is completely trustworthy, I can assure you.

"Now, for the second part of your question. Am I too easily taken in? Perhaps I am. I can recall several times in my life when I bought too high, sold too low. Yes, I was taken in on those occasions, and naturally I regret it, but I have a feeling they made me a better businessman, a better person. In my own life, I find that I have been taken in on more than one occasion. Fortunately so, I might add. When I get down, truly down, it's others who come along and pick me up. My partner, Nicholas Reed, flew all the way to London, brought me back to the States, and has nursed me every day since. He has been my therapist, my cook, my financial bedrock, my lover. Yes, he has taken me in in every way, and I'm thankful for it. There should be millions of Nicks in this world, there to take in...take in innocent victims like me. I hope you have a Nick in your life, too, Mr. Kirby?"

In response, the *Chronicle's* critic shook his head once and sat back down.

Joanna couldn't believe the emotional courage Miles had displayed just then. Afterwards, he braced himself on the back of a chair in the aisle, but throughout his little speech his voice and determination remained unwavering.

The questions kept coming until Joanna finally had to call an end to the affair. Three or four reporters came up to her as others were leaving, but none with queries she couldn't readily parry. The line for comp tickets that passed by Matt told her the press conference hadn't turned out to be the disaster she had expected. Her best support had come, not from Avery or the two PhDs whose analyses she'd passed out at the beginning of the event. No, they came from an unexpected source, Miles Oliphant, who possessed a wellspring of humanity that was as deep as it was genuine.

If only he weren't gay, and undoubtedly a Democrat.

57 LEAVING HOME

Miles pushed back from his desk. After the press conference that morning, he couldn't help reflecting on his conversation, two days earlier, with Loren Pritchard, who'd returned from the south of France and was settling back into life in Plymouth.

As it turned out, Reg's old family friend remembered the American bookman well. The papers Miles had purchased were an odd lot really, all belonging to the Boyle family, and dating to the early eighteenth century. They had been discovered in a trunk, tucked away in a remote corner of the attic. There was no record of them because, to Pritchard's eye, someone had sought to preserve those letters, perhaps for the sake of sentiment, away from prying eyes. He recalled no lengthy manuscripts among them, but couldn't eliminate the possibility because the whole thing was so completely outside his realm of expertise.

Miles had brought up the subject of the Shakespeare as casually as he could, but Pritchard could remember nothing like that in the collection. Admittedly, he had not gone through it carefully, just called Reginald Sloane, a respected London bookseller, about it. The few records Pritchard had found at Marston House informed him only that the bound volumes in the library there and many of the family papers had been sold at auction early in the century.

In advance of the news conference, Miles had gone through the letters again. Perhaps Theobald's and Boyle's had been a Platonic relationship, though he doubted that from the rhetoric found on those pages. At least that would have explained why the cache had been hidden away for well over two centuries in an attic corner. He could imagine Boyle sneaking up there late at night to read and reread Theobald's letters to him, and indulge himself in what might have been if they'd lived in another, more tolerant era.

Had that reporter from *The Chronicle* been onto something, Miles had asked himself repeatedly since that awful gathering of crows earlier in the day? Could Reg have tricked him into buying a correspondence between two leading, eighteenth-century British intellectuals that had been entirely contrived to make him believe he'd discovered a lost manuscript by Shakespeare?

No, it just wasn't possible. Months would have been required for Reg and Pritchard together to fabricate the letters, collect the old journals that made up the Boyle archive. And besides, there was no motive. Miles believed deeply that he'd told those reporters at P.S. 39 the truth that morning. Why would Reg want to sabotage something as valuable as their friendship?

Not only that but, according to Sgt. Cochran, not a single of Miles' fingerprints had been found anywhere on the entire manuscript. That should have all but eliminated any real possibility that he himself had been responsible for copying out the *Ur-Hamlet,* though he still wasn't convinced of his innocence.

Later, he thought he could see Nick levitate just a little off his seat at the dining-room table when he told him of the detective's news, but then maybe his mind was playing tricks on him. In fact, maybe it had been ever since that fateful night when he went crashing to the sidewalk in London. The growing clarity he'd grown accustomed to since waking in that hospital room was perhaps an illusion, the product of a mind shaken and stirred so much that it had muddied good gin, and he'd been groping through the resulting hangover ever since.

His thoughts were interrupted by the sound of footsteps on the stairs. Moments later, April poked her head in the door. Right then, he promised himself never, *never* to tell her there was a time, though brief, when he had suspected her, too, of forging the *Ur-Hamlet*.

"Are you busy?" she called to him in the office.

"Only if you think of busy as cross-examining myself for what must be the tenth time after that news conference this morning. Come on back."

Through the window above his desk, he could see her set down a box of kitchen utensils. When she walked through the office door, she gave him a hug, a big one.

"Joanna said you were great when she called."

"It'd be just like her to say something like that."

"I'm sure it's true."

As April spoke, she let go of her father and leaned against the desk immediately beside him. Usually she kept greater distance. She wasn't looking at him, but rather at the photo of Teddy he'd found tucked away in a drawer upstairs and had propped to the side of his blotter.

"Then you know about Teddy?" she asked.

"I know he's dead."

"I'm sorry, Dad. I hoped more than anything you wouldn't find out because it was so devastating. So unjust. I didn't want it to derail your recovery. It happened on Lawrence's thirty-second birthday. Teddy had rented a charter boat to go...."

"To go fishing off Gravesend," Miles cut in. "I know. According to the charter captain, they drank beer all afternoon then drove back through Bay Ridge for the surprise party. You, I, some old friends and a few of Lawrence's political cronies were waiting at his apartment to surprise him.

"Teddy never got there. Lawrence sideswiped a semi on Ocean Parkway and veered into a power pole. Teddy died instantly. Lawrence walked away from the accident. If, that is, he was capable of walking. They arrested him with a blood alcohol of point-eighteen, and convicted him of manslaughter, but he never served so much as a full day behind bars. All because of his connections. You quit *Menagerie* right after that."

"For someone with amnesia, you put things together pretty well."

"Let's just say maybe the doctors got my diagnosis wrong. It wasn't amnesia at all, but that blow to the head, the coma afterwards certainly helped clear away some of the mental cobwebs that plagued me before then."

From the way she looked at him, he could tell she was surprised. And a little suspicious, but she shook it off.

"It's all my fault for keeping Teddy's death from you," she confessed. "Ever since that day, I've blamed Lawrence. There was no way I could go out on stage after that, not ever again in my life. At least that's what I thought then. That's why I walked out on *Menagerie*. How could I possibly continue to recreate a character from a world that was so cruel? Lawrence had killed the only man I ever truly loved...until I met Avery. He has Teddy's nose and chin, that sparkle in his eye. No wonder the attraction."

Not certain what to say, Miles averted his eyes. They came to rest on the box of kitchen things April had set down just inside the front door.

"You don't have to move out, you know? I'm not angry any more, not *that* angry, anyway."

"You have every right to be. What I did, giving that manuscript to Avery, was foolish."

"But you did it for the right reason."

"I did?"

"Yes, because you were in love."

"Still, it was a stupid thing to do."

"At least you weren't so stupid you didn't realize love doesn't come along that often. You needed something, or rather some*one* to force you out of the isolated world you'd build up around yourself. And I only made it worse. I helped you, buying groceries, paying bills. All that."

"You shouldn't blame yourself. You just did what all parents do, tried to protect your child."

"But it had the opposite effect, allowing you to cut yourself off from everyone. Thank god Avery came along. You had this manuscript you knew would interest him, and you used it. How could I blame you for reaching out and trying to grab the one thing that could help free you from yourself?"

"Then you're not still...mad at me?" she asked.

He took her in his arms and she offered no resistance.

"I forgave you the first night I saw your Ophelia, and the true vulnerability you brought to that role. I could tell then that you'd conquered your demons, and with them your fear of audiences, of critics, of your own father. If I was angry before, I was angry at myself for being so angry all my life. Not anymore." Miles continued to hold her. "You don't have to move out all at once, you know? Avery and I can share you. You could spend a night or two at his place, then come home."

"But you're at Nick's all the time now."

"I'd come back the nights you were here."

"That's silly. Most of your things are there now. Besides, Nick is going to be far better company than I until this run with the Players ends, and it looks as if it's going to go on for some time. No, you should definitely stay at Nick's."

"You're sure?"

"What? About the move? Never less sure of anything in my life, except maybe acting. But I've got to do it."

"You don't have to do anything. Especially move in with a man."

"You don't seem the worse for it."

"No...no, I suppose not. I'm just not sure Avery deserves you. You could have any man in town who saw you in *Hamlet, Part One*, you know. Well, any *straight* man."

"That's not true and you know it."

He turned toward her, took her by the chin to make certain she was looking at him. Again, she did nothing to put him off.

"I just worry, the way he is with women. I don't want you getting hurt."

"This is an experiment, Dad. I'm taking things a month at a time. I can always move out if I have to. And I'm not giving up my day job. Not yet at any rate. You'll see me when I walk in every morning. If I'm happy, you'll know it. If not...."

"I'll know it even sooner."

April started toward the door. Instead of saying goodbye, she turned around and propped a hand against the jamb.

"Do you still plan to sell the manuscript at auction?"

"How can I, not knowing for certain Shakespeare wrote it?" Here, he was about to add that he still considered himself the prime suspect in that regard, but he knew that would only start an argument. "But maybe, once it's fully authenticated."

"Won't you miss your great discovery?"

"It's given me my fifteen minutes, plus a few more. And time, even if it's only a quarter hour, is a very precious thing. If nothing else I've learned that much these last six weeks. And that I've got a lovely, very talented daughter."

"Stop, please." April bit her trembling lower lip. "Look, I've got to go. I'll be here at ten tomorrow morning."

She came over, kissed him quickly on the cheek, then picked up her box of kitchen items and disappeared through the front door and onto the sidewalks of New York, that urban horror she no longer seemed to dread anymore.

ACKNOWLEDGMENTS

First, I'd like to acknowledge just a few of those who are, in large part, responsible for my early love of Shakespeare. When I was in high school, Lawrence Dowell taught *Macbeth* as though, himself, driven by the three witches. He also taught me to write by more than once winging an eraser at me in feigned(?) disgust at my mistakes. Professor Herbert N. Dillard, who was affectionately known as "Dodo" because he knew so much, offered two important introductions, one to *Othello*, the other to Vanessa Redgrave, who took two eighteen-year-old American boys out to dinner after her incomparable Rosalind in *As You Like It* at Stratford-upon-Avon, and who ended that evening giving each a memorable parting kiss.

I am also deeply indebted to all those who, through their thoughtful comments, helped me think and rethink *The Shakespeare Manuscript*, and especially to Paul Cohen, antiquarian and master of the handball court, who gave unfailing encouragement when I most needed it. David Ostwald, great teacher and director, made comments that were freely given and also spot-on. Without David this book would have never taken its present shape. Michael Paller, dramaturge without equal, took on this novel with the same guiding hand he would take on a theater script. A.C.T. San Francisco is richer for his work there, as am I for his suggestions.

There's no way I can give thanks enough to all my students over the years who have furthered my love of both art and theater, as I hope I have furthered theirs. I'm deeply indebted to one of them, Craig Coss, who designed the cover and website for this book, and who stirred my thoughts when it came to matters of publication. Thanks also to the ever-patient Zachary Stewart-Glazer. Without his technical assistance our website would be little more than another of the author's unrealized dreams.

Kara Adams, though she appears last here, is first in my heart. Kara has helped me at every step along the way in writing *The Shakespeare Manuscript*. Her love of theater, so freely shared all these years, inspired this book as she has inspired me in every sense, first as friend, now as wife.

POP--AZN 328